Wyatt Earp V

Alaska Bush Guardian

To Rosa

by Ron Walden

Alaskan True to Life Crime Writer

Best Wishes from Ron Walden

PUBLICATION CONSULTANTS
We Believe In The Power Of Authors

PO Box 221974 Anchorage, Alaska 99522-1974
books@publicationconsultants.com—www.publicationconsultants.com

ISBN Number: 978-1-59433-789-5
eBook ISBN Number: 978-1-59433-790-1

Manufactured in the United States of America

Acknowledgements

I thank Lydia Hayes for her diligence in searching out possible errors in this story. Her hard work keeps me and my stories honest and believable.

I also thank Dan Decker for allowing me to use his poem, *Bush Guardians*, as an introduction to my book. This work was first published in the Fraternal Order of Alaska State Troopers publication, The Banner. This poem describes well the duties of a VPSO, Village Public Safety Officer. These officers walk a thin line in the remote villages of Alaska keeping the peace and safety for areas with no permanent trooper presence. My hat is off to these brave and underpaid watchmen of bush Alaska.

Introduction
Bush Guardians: A Tribute to all VPSOs
Trooper Dan Decker

Wait, take time and listen,
I have a story to share.
Of brave men and women.
"Bush Guardians," people who care.

We call them "VSPOs,"
a strange name to some.
For people of Rural Alaska,
A name most people welcome.

They serve and protect,
their people, their land.
In spirit and body,
alone often they stand.

Against all the odds,
they struggle to fight.
The wrongs and injustice,
during day, during night.

A job often thankless,
without praise or reward.
They march into battle,
without shield, without sword.

Understand now these letters,
"VPSO," proud letters indeed.
Our brave men and women,
Bush Guardians," that we need.

Chapter One

Gold rush news from Nome, Alaska caught the attention of the famous lawman Wyatt Earp and his common-law wife Josephine Marcus (sometimes Josie and sometimes Sadie). Wyatt had ventured into many of the gold strikes in the past few years—Tombstone, California, Idaho and others. Now living in California and down on his luck he yearned for another place to make a new start, one in which his old skills would be useful. In the fall of 1898 they boarded a steam ship bound for Alaska. After arriving, they stayed the winter in Rampart where Wyatt sold beer and cigars for the Northern Commercial Company.

The two made it to Nome in the summer of 1899 to live in a one room cabin out on the "spit" of the beach. Josie became well known in the town, now numbering 20,000 residents. She volunteered her time supporting school activities aiding the poor and underprivileged as well as raising money for local charities.

Wyatt tried to get appointed to the position of town marshal, but the position was given to another local man. Wyatt knew money was to be made by digging it out of miners' pockets and not out of the sands along the Nome beach. He struck up an acquaintance with a man by the name of Charlie Hoxie and in partnership they bought the Dexter Hotel and Saloon for eighty-thousand dollars. Spending time with the customers in the saloon, gambling, and drinking soon began to wear on the Earp relationships.

Wyatt took up company with a nineteen-year old prostitute by the name of Lucinda Onarock and began to drink more and gamble recklessly. He lost most of the money he had accumulated while in Nome and began to have disagreements with both Sadie and Charlie Hoxie.

"Wyatt, you have to stop your drinking and gambling. You never use your head when you drink. Charlie says you make crazy bets when you're drinking. It has to stop, Wyatt."

It was late afternoon and Wyatt was pretty drunk already. "Mind your own business, woman. I've always taken care of you, haven't I?" He staggered into a small table, spilling a pot of tea and breaking the teapot.

"We had been doing well until you started drinking too much again. It has to stop, Wyatt. At this rate we'll be broke again in three months. Then what? We can't just get on a train and go to one of your brothers' homes. What you're doing is going to ruin us." Sadie was crying. "I've heard about that little tart you have been seeing at the hotel. I won't have it, Wyatt. That has to stop, too. If you don't stop drinking and running with that whore in town I'm going to get on the next boat out of here and go back home. I mean it, Wyatt. It has to stop right now."

"Mind your place, Josie. I don't take orders from you or from Charlie Hoxie. I'll see whom I like and drink as much as I like. I plan to stay until the boom becomes a bust and then we'll leave, not before," Wyatt was shouting. Josie was sobbing even harder. "Clean up this mess. I'm going to the saloon," Wyatt shouted as he staggered out the front door of the cabin to make his way to the Dexter Hotel and Saloon. There he would spend the rest of the day in a room with Lucy Onarock. Lucy would soothe his temper and keep his drinks fresh.

During the afternoon, while Wyatt slept, Lucy tended to other customers in other rooms. She loved Wyatt Earp deeply. She had never been outside Nome but thought that someday he would take her away and they would live happily ever after. It was several weeks later she realized she was pregnant. Despite her professional activities she was certain the child was Wyatt's. Lucy never told her lover, Wyatt, about the pregnancy and planned to keep the secret as long as possible.

As summer wore on the business at the Dexter Hotel and Saloon began to fall off. The population in the city had dwindled to less than ten thousand and the gold taken from the beach sands was becoming rare. The men who followed the gold rush from one field to another were now either gone or planning to leave. In the late summer of 1901 the Earps were nearly broke. Wyatt's health was failing and Josie spent more time with him. In early fall Charlie Hoxie offered to buy Wyatt's interest in the hotel and saloon. The offer came at the perfect time. Josie begged her husband to sell his interest and the two of them could return to California where they would be close to family.

Wyatt's illness had caused him to slow his drinking nearly to a stop. His interest in Lucy had now become infrequent, pleasing Josie very much. It was late fall when Wyatt Earp and Josephine Marcus Earp boarded the steamship Roanoke to sail back to Seattle and on to San Francisco. The remaining distance to Los Angeles was overland, mostly by horse-drawn buggy. It was a mixed homecoming for the two. Family welcomed them home, assuming they had been a success in Alaska. The joy was diluted when Wyatt learned his brother, Warren, had been killed while serving as the town marshal in Tombstone, Arizona. The couple lived out their days quietly in a small cottage in California.

In Nome, the very pregnant Lucinda Onarock was about to give birth. In the care of a mid-wife she suffered a painful birthing process. Not affording a doctor or hospital, she could only endure the long and painful delivery in a small cabin on Front Street. In labor for four days she was weakened and ill when her son, Wyatt Earp Junior, came into the world. Lucinda vowed her son would live up to the greatness of his father. He would go to school and learn to read and write and speak the American language the way his father had done.

Lucy, with a child in tow, could never go back to work in her previous profession, but took a job cleaning the hotel and saloon. She also worked for local business folks cleaning stores and offices. It was a backbreaking job, given the streets of Nome were a mire of mud most of the year. Few people walked across the muddy streets, but those who did entered businesses with very muddy boots, leaving muddy tracks wherever they stepped.

Wyatt Junior attended Nome public school and was a good student. He studied hard with prodding from his mother. She was unable to help him with his studies because she had never learned to read or write. A local storekeeper, Wesley Rostov, took an interest in the boy and taught him how to shoot and trap. When he was a little older he showed the boy how to pan for gold on the beach, but also taught him about "gold fever."

"A gold miner always says he is one foot from a million dollars, but usually he is a million feet from one dollar. Be careful of the blindness of gold fever, my boy." He repeated the message many times during the boy's youth.

Wesley Rostov, manager of the Northern Commercial Company store in Nome, kept the boy busy until he finished high school. Rostov also owned a small freight hauling company delivering mining machinery to the dredges forty miles from Nome on the only road out of town. He hired Wyatt Junior, knowing his honesty and work ethic were good. He also knew the boy's mother was falling into bad health and it would be up to him to take care of her. He needed a good job and a decent paycheck.

Lucy's health continued to decline and when she could no longer continue to work Wyatt hired a young Native girl, Greta Swan, to care for his mother while he worked. When she realized her remaining days were short, Lucy called the two young people to her bedside.

"I can see the two of you care deeply for each other. It is my wish that the two of you should marry and have a family. I am leaving this cabin to you, Wyatt. It is small, but large enough to accommodate a small family. My only request is that you and each succeeding generation name your first male child Wyatt Earp. Your son will be named Wyatt Earp III. Always love them and always keep the Wyatt Earp name alive. I loved your father very much—and he loved me. He never knew about you, but I know he would have loved you, too."

Wyatt Junior was sobbing as was Greta, "Don't talk like that Mother. I don't want you to leave us."

"We don't choose the time we enter this world and we have no choice about when we leave it. I have done the best I could to care for you and to love you. I know that isn't much, but it was all I had to give. When I pass I wish to be buried in the Nome Cemetery with a small stone engraved with my name, Lucinda Onarock Earp. Promise me you will do this for me."

"Of course, Mother," said Wyatt before turning to Greta.

"Greta, if you'll have me, I think it would be right for us to marry while Mother can still be here to witness it. Will you marry me and have my son, the next Wyatt Earp?"

There were tears in Greta's eyes, "Oh, yes! I think it is a grand idea."

Lucy lay in her bed watching the two. "Well, don't just stand there, kiss her and seal the deal. This may be the second happiest moment in my life. I love you both. Now go find a judge to come down here to the cabin and get this job done."

Wyatt went to the store to see his boss, Wesley Rostov, and ask if he would be the witness at the wedding. Rostov agreed and sent him into the store to get a new suit for the occasion. He also ordered some flowers from a local florist. Rostov admired the young man for his dedication to caring for his ailing mother as well as his work ethic at the trucking company. A check for a week's wages would be his wedding gift to the couple.

Wyatt contacted the local magistrate and set an evening time for the wedding before returning to the store for a fitting of his new suit.

Wyatt and Greta greeted Judge Barstow and Mr. Rostov when they arrived. Greta accepted the flowers. She had no family in attendance. The small wedding party gathered in the cabin in front of Lucy's bed where the judge performed the wedding. Everyone kissed the bride and shook the hand of the groom. Lucy called the newlyweds to her bedside to congratulate them.

"I'm tired now," she told them. "I'm so happy for you. I love you both; I'm going to sleep now." She never awoke but died a happy and satisfied mother.

Thus began the new family of the Alaska Earp clan. It would be a rich one. Wyatt and Greta had four children. The second was a boy, born in 1905. He was christened Wyatt Earp III. All four children went to school in Nome and went on to become prominent citizens in the community. The eldest girl even became a teacher in the Nome school system. Young Wyatt Earp III became a teamster like his father. Rostov eventually sold the trucking company to a larger trucking company from Fairbanks. Wyatt Junior became the Nome terminal manager, a position later filled by Wyatt III when his father passed away in 1939.

Wyatt III met and married a beautiful girl from Teller, Alaska. Her name was Dorothy Spooner, daughter of the manager at the gold dredge. Her father was wealthy and thought his daughter should find someone more suited to her station, but she would not relent. They were married in 1941 just prior to Wyatt entering the Alaska Scouts as part of the U.S. Army. The Scouts distinguished themselves while battling the Japanese army on the only U.S. soil occupied by a foreign military force in nearly two hundred years.

At the end of World War II, he returned to Nome and resumed his duties with the trucking company. Dorothy blessed him with two sons, the first Wyatt Earp IV and a younger son, Seth, named for Dorothy's father.

Wyatt Earp IV was the first Earp to enter a trade school to become a marine engineer. This led him to a lifelong career as a seaman and commercial fisherman in Bristol Bay, the largest salmon fishing area in the entire world. Wyatt IV was also the first Earp to become wealthy. His commercial fishing yielded him over his career a vast fortune, owning many fishing vessels and an interest in a cannery in Naknek, Alaska. Wyatt IV married late in life and had only one son. Wyatt Earp V was the first Earp to go off to college. His father chose the school, University of Idaho, which had an excellent law school. It was his father's hope the newest Earp would become a successful lawyer.

Wyatt V didn't care for school very much. He later admitted it was because he was homesick all the time and had nothing in common with others in the legal field. He liked law but didn't like the time involved in a law degree and passing the bar. Upon receiving his Criminal Justice Degree he decided he had one more thing to learn before returning to Alaska.

In Spokane, Washington he signed up for a local flight school. He loved flying and went on to acquire Commercial and Instrument ratings. It was now time to return to Alaska. With money borrowed from his father he purchased a new Cessna 206. After a few days of instruction in the new plane he headed for Fairbanks, excited to be returning to Alaska at last.

Back in Alaska, Wyatt Earp V made application for a position on the Fairbanks Police Department. This was the beginning of a lifelong career in law enforcement and returning the Wyatt Earp name to those enforcing laws in the "Last Frontier," Alaska.

Chapter Two

Wyatt Earp V presented an impressive portfolio of credentials when applying for a position with the Fairbanks Police Department: Alaska Native, Bachelor's Degree in Criminal Justice, family history in law enforcement, low time pilot, pilot instrument rating, and owner of a Cessna plane. In addition, he wanted to be in law enforcement; it wasn't just a paycheck he was looking for, it was a rare career these days.

The interview panel selected him on the first round and scheduled him to attend the next Fairbanks area police academy providing his background check didn't show any flaws. He passed the background check and it was noted that his father was an influential commercial fisherman in Bristol Bay. Wyatt was accepted to the position of patrolman recruit, pending completion of the academy. Three months later he reported to the duty commander in Fairbanks and was assigned to an FTO, Field Training Officer. One of the duties of the police academy is to make the recruit familiar with Alaska laws and the Alaska Criminal Code. Fresh from college he was a good student and all but memorized the law books. He graduated top man in a class of 36.

Ted Sparta, the Field Training Officer, was a twenty-four-year veteran of the force, a street-wise, crusty old cop, who had spent his entire career with the Fairbanks Police Department. He was originally from Montana and had come to Alaska to work on the oil pipeline, but found he was not cut out to be away from his family for extended periods of time. He was young with a pretty wife and a small daughter. Like Wyatt, Ted had applied for a position with the Fairbanks Police Department, was accepted and had been with the one department his entire career. He was now a sergeant and enjoyed working the streets with new officers.

Sergeant Sparta and Wyatt Earp V became friends almost immediately. He was fascinated by the family history of his new partner. As he drove the new officer around the city to familiarize him with the streets and alleyways, the two men traded stories, Wyatt about his family history and Ted about life on the streets of Fairbanks. Ted pointed out the likely danger spots as they drove around the city but for the first few days avoided taking calls involving confrontation. Within weeks the two were doing regular patrol, stopping speeders and arresting shoplifters. Each day the tasks became more complicated and dangerous as Wyatt's learning curve accelerated.

"You'll be on your own starting next week," explained Ted. "I have arranged for you to be on day shift for a month or until you feel comfortable driving around the city. You will get your own patrol car on Monday. I'll be on duty during the day shift and you can get me on the radio if you have questions or need advice. Do you think you're ready?"

"I think so," replied Wyatt. "You've been a good teacher. How do you think I'm doing?"

"You are going to be just fine. You learn quickly and use good judgement. I think you will be a good cop. It appears to me you have a lot of your daddy's genes." Ted was grinning as he spoke, "Take the wheel partner. You're driving today."

The following Monday Wyatt took possession of his own patrol vehicle. It was a shiny new four wheel drive SUV with all the bells and whistles for police use: Radio, siren, red and blue lights, spotlights and computer. Wyatt loaded his shotgun into the front seat rack and placed his investigation kit in the trunk beside his cold weather gear. He was issued a unit number which was to be used as his radio call number. It took most of the morning to get the vehicle ready for duty during which time Ted came by the garage to see how he was making out.

Once Wyatt had signed for the patrol car he was given a patrol area mostly in downtown Fairbanks. It was a busy sector with big box stores and heavy street traffic. The day was half over when he began his first day on patrol. He felt comfortable with his new patrol area since Ted had taken him through the downtown area many times. His first official call was an unconscious homeless man lying on the sidewalk near the Fred Meyer store. The old man was obviously passed out from alcohol. Wyatt called for an ambulance to have the EMTs check him out.

The EMT answering the call examined the drunk. The medic turned to Wyatt. "He's a regular. We'll call a detox unit and take him to a sleep-off center. The nights are getting colder and he is going to be a problem this winter. I'm Dave Lovell, by the way," he said as he stuck his hand out for a shake. "You're one of the new guys with PD, aren't you?"

Wyatt took his hand and shook it, "Yup, my first day on the job. Wyatt Earp is my name. Before you ask, yes, we are related. I'm Wyatt Earp V."

"Good to meet you Wyatt. I expect we will meet again and often if you are working downtown. See ya 'round." The detox unit arrived and Dave went to assist with loading the victim aboard.

There were notes to be made and records to be kept. Wyatt had begun to learn the routine while riding with Ted Sparta and reported to dispatch he was back on the road and a detox unit had taken the man to the sleep-off center. This type of event filled his days—drunks, shoplifters, speeders, an occasional bar fight or domestic violence call. By the end of the fourth week he was ready to move to night shift.

His first night included a squad meeting where he met several of the regular patrol officers. He was introduced to the night shift at the meeting. The entire shift was briefed as to warrants to be served, suspected drug deals, be on the lookout (BOLO) for stolen cars, known criminals, etc. The patrol sergeant informed Wyatt he would be riding with the new officer for his first shift.

In his own patrol car, with the sergeant in the right front seat, Wyatt inspected the vehicle making sure all the equipment was in place, the lights working and the gas tank full. "Any particular area you want to look at tonight, Sarge?" asked the new patrolman.

"As a matter of fact, there is. Are you familiar with the area and side roads out past the University?" he asked.

"Not really, I've been assigned to the downtown sector for my first month," replied Wyatt.

"OK, let's go out past the college and I'll show you the territory, you know, the city limits and our jurisdictional limits. There are some tough areas out there and I should show you where the dangerous neighborhoods are located. I want you to be aware it is no shame to call for backup at any time. We deal with some very hostile individuals out here, especially in the areas we're about to visit. Some of these locations are remote, so it's important you let your dispatcher know exactly where you are at any given time. We can't help you if we can't find you. The city isn't as wild and crazy as it was during the pipeline days when construction hands came off the pipeline and wanted to drink up their paychecks here in Fairbanks; but there are still dangerous people around. Don't get me wrong, I'm not telling you to be afraid, but I am telling you to be aware of your surroundings at all times. I've read your file and have had good reports on you. I don't expect you to have any trouble. I am proud to have you on my shift. Use good judgement and keep your paperwork caught up and we'll get along just fine."

"This is more than just a job for me, Sarge. After five generations I want to put the Earp name back in law enforcement. I want this to be my career and I'm willing to work hard to make it a success. I expect I'll make some mistakes along the way, but I'll try to keep them to a minimum."

"Take the next right." Knowles held on as Wyatt turned onto a side street. "I want you to be comfortable in your job, Wyatt. I make it a point to back up my men. Remember we're here to protect and serve the public. As long as you use that as a guideline when making decisions, you will do just fine." Pete Knowles was known to be a good supervisor and the other men on the shift respected him. "Slow down now and start checking out the homes along this street. A lot of bad folks live on this side of town."

Area after area they drove around Fairbanks, never having to answer a radio call as long as the sergeant was in the car. This was the beginning of a twenty-year career that took Wyatt from rookie to veteran, patrolman to investigator, investigator to drug team chief and from drug team chief to Assistant Chief of Police for the City of Fairbanks. In his police career he had been wounded by gunfire once and stabbed twice. He had been in numerous car chases and crashes without suffering serious injury. His career in Fairbanks had spanned twenty-two years in which he had garnered many commendations, been the butt of many jokes and pranks, and received many awards from business organizations for his community spirit and service.

During his career he had made many friends among the agencies he had worked with including the Alaska State Troopers, Drug Enforcement Administration (DEA), U.S. Customs, and the Canadian Mounties. Wyatt had never married claiming he didn't have time for a family. He enjoyed dating and parties, but never drank alcohol. Police, in general, use a great deal of profanity when out of public view. Wyatt never cursed and was never known to lose his temper.

It was now time for him to retire, but without hobbies he didn't know what to do with his time in retirement. One afternoon, a week before his last day as Assistant Chief and member of the Fairbanks Police Department, an Alaska State Trooper captain came to see him in the office. Wyatt had known the trooper for several years and the two had become friends.

Wyatt's secretary tapped on his office door, poked her head inside and said, "Captain Griffin wants to see you, sir. Do you have time?"

"I always have time for Griff," replied the Assistant Chief.

Captain Griffin entered the office and stepped to the front of the desk to shake hands with Wyatt. "I got an invitation to your retirement party. I just wanted to come by and shake hands with you before they send you off to some retirement home where you can spend your remaining days playing bingo, sipping tea and gossiping about the lady down the hall."

"I may not have time to see you after all," quipped Earp. Both men laughed.

"Seriously, though, Wyatt, what are your plans for the future? Are you going out to Bristol Bay and become a commercial fisherman like your dad?"

"You know, Griff, I have been thinking about that. You know I don't have many hobbies, just my airplane and flying. I've never taken time for any. Now I'm going to have all the time in the world and don't know what to do. I'm too young to just quit. I was thinking I could be useful as a VPSO (Village Public Safety Officer), somewhere on the Alaska Peninsula."

"Are you serious?" gasped Captain Griffin. "You want to move back to the Peninsula after all these years?"

"I think so. I have the airplane and can go anywhere out there. My dad still has his home in Naknek. Mom passed away a long time ago and I want to spend some time with him before it's too late. Being a VPSO would let me live out in the bush and give me time to fly to town and visit my dad."

"As you know I supervise all the VPSOs from Dillingham to Adak. If you really want the job I have an opening in Iliamna. Henry Jenks is there now, but has turned in his time. He took a security job on the North Slope. The pay is better and he has a girlfriend who just moved to Anchorage. Do you think you would be interested?" asked the Captain.

"I would like to take a month off when I retire to spend some time with Dad, but, yes, Iliamna would be perfect. I haven't been there in many years, but the hunting and fishing is great and I know a lot of the residents. If you can work it out, I'll take the job. Thanks, Griff."

Chapter Three

Wyatt was enjoying the late fall season while visiting his father in Naknek on Bristol Bay, a small town made up of mostly commercial fishermen. The population is predominantly Alaska Native. Wyatt grew up here and felt at home when he returned. Commercial fishing season had ended giving Wyatt's father time to visit with the son he had not seen in more than a year. Wyatt's father owned business interests in the Seattle area, and they planned to travel together to the northwestern state of Washington. His father owned a small home in a northern suburb where the two spent most of their time reminiscing about his early years. The two of them had chosen different careers, but their personalities had remained identical; they were more like brothers than father and son. Wyatt V's mother had passed from cancer when he was a boy leaving the father to mold the boy's character. It seemed he had done a fine job.

A week after arriving in Seattle Wyatt received a phone call from Captain Griffin. "Howdy, Wyatt. Are you tired of retirement yet?"

"I'm beginning to like it," Wyatt laughed. "What's up, Griff?"

"Are you still interested in a VPSO position?" asked the captain.

"What post?"

"You can have Iliamna, if you're still in the mood. You will have to attend an orientation class for a week to learn the duties and responsibilities of a VPSO. You won't have to attend the police academy portion of the class because of your background. I told the colonel you were interested and he became excited. He said he knew you and was happy to hear you wanted the job." This wasn't a recruiting speech, but he, too, was anxious to have Wyatt join the ranks. "Are you still interested?"

"Yes, providing I can have a couple of more weeks before I report. I'm in Seattle with my father and we're not scheduled to return until the first of the month. Will that be soon enough?"

Captain Griffin was pleased. "I'll schedule you to the VPSO orientation class for the first of November. When you return you might want to go out to Iliamna to find a place to live. It should be relatively close to the airport because you will be responding to all the villages in the area. It's a large area, but you have the experience to handle it. That's why I wanted you for this post. Welcome aboard, Officer Earp."

Upon his return to Naknek to visit with his father, Wyatt made arrangements to fly his Cessna to Iliamna. His father volunteered to go along for the ride and to visit with old friends in Iliamna and Newhalen. The flight up the Kvichak River was like a travelogue on National Geographic Channel. Flying low they were able to spot schools of salmon making their way up the river. There were many, many brown bears along the streams and rivers fattening for the winter months ahead. Small herds of caribou dotted the tundra and bull moose, in full rut now and ready for mating, were herding their cows and defending their harems. Fall months are spectacular in the North Country. The leaves were mostly gone now, but those that remained were bright fall colors. The distance from Naknek Airport to Iliamna Airport is about 90 miles, a flight of about 45 minutes, but side trips turned the flight into just over an hour.

It was a warm fall day with the sun shining in Iliamna. The temperature was near 50 degrees with little wind which is nearly constant and sometimes violent as it comes off Lake Iliamna. Iliamna means "mother of the wind" and the huge lake lives up to the name. Nearly 100 miles in length, the main body of the lake ranges from fifteen to twenty miles wide. It is the largest lake in Alaska and one of the largest in the United States. Its surface area is over 1,000 square miles.

The resident population of the town of Iliamna is around 110 but grows during tourist and hunting seasons. The community is close knit with no roads connecting it with the outside world. There is a boat portage on the east end of the lake and a short road linking the lake to a landing called Williamsport on Iliamna Bay in Cook Inlet east of the mountains.

There is also a short road from the town of Iliamna to the head of the Newhalen River at the outlet of Lake Clark. It is used more in the winter by snowmachines than by car or truck in the summer.

While Wyatt V tied down his Cessna his father walked to the hangar of the local flying service. Through the open door of the hangar the pilot and owner saw Wyatt IV walking toward them. The two men had been friends for many years.

"Wyatt Earp, you old dog," said Tom Dempsey, owner of Lake Air Service. "What brings you this far up stream.? I know you don't like air that doesn't smell of salt." Now close, he held out a hand to greet his old friend.

"Nice to see you, Tom," said the elder Earp, taking the offered hand. "I came up here with my son. He's planning on moving here to live. He's Wyatt Earp the fifth. You'll like him."

"Well, come on over to the hangar and we'll have some coffee. Maggie is in the office and she'll be glad to see you, too. How have you been?"

"You don't get much company out here do you, Tom?" joked the senior Earp. "I'll pass on the coffee, but I would like to say hello to Maggie. I hope she's well. She was a big help and a good friend when Ma passed."

"You go on into the office and say hello to Maggie. I'll wait here for your boy."

"He's going to want to talk with you. He's looking for a place to live. Maybe you can help him find a place to rent or buy."

As the father walked toward the office the son walked from his Cessna to the hangar to greet Tom Dempsey. The two men shook hands and embraced as old friends do.

"Your dad said you were looking for a place to live here in town. What brings you to Iliamna, Wyatt?" inquired Tom.

"Yes, I am. I would like to buy a small place of my own, but if I can't find one I'll rent something and buy a lot; perhaps build a cabin here next summer," informed Wyatt V. "I'm taking the position of VPSO for this area. I have to go to a class in Anchorage the first of November, but it's only for a week. I might be interested in some hangar space for the 206 if you have any or know of something. I will probably be flying the state super cub most of the time and I don't like leaving my plane outside especially in the winter. I recall the wind sometimes blows around here."

"Your dad went into the office to see Maggie. Let's go inside and we can talk about it. I can make room for your plane in my hangar, that's not a problem, but I don't know of any places for sale right now. The guy building the new lodge down by the lake rented every space in town for his carpenters, so there isn't much available." Tom talked while they walked. "I have some space in my hangar with a shower and small kitchen next to the office. If you don't find anything I'll let you live there for the winter. I'll need it next summer, though, to keep my pilots available. I wouldn't charge you anything this winter. It would be good to have a watchman in the hangar anyway."

"If I can't find any place of my own I just might take you up on the offer. I'd like to build my own place if I can find a suitable lot. Keep an ear open and let me know if anything comes up."

The two men had crossed the inside of the hangar and entered the office area. Maggie and Wyatt's father were drinking coffee at her desk when they entered.

"You two still gossiping?" asked Tom as they entered.

"I have been telling Wyatt how terrible you are," said Maggie.

Tom was about to re-join the banter when his cell phone beeped. He said "Hello," then listened for a long time before commenting. His answer was short. I'll be right there," he said and ended the call.

"Trouble?" asked young Earp.

"Yes. One of the Weaver family was getting winter wood and cut his leg badly. His dad said he cut it off, but I doubt that." He turned to his wife, "Maggie, call a medevac from Anchorage. I should be back by the time they get here." He turned to the younger Earp, "I have to go to Pedro Bay. I could use some help on the flight back. Do you feel like riding along?"

"Sure, Tom, I haven't been to Pedro Bay in a lot of years. Do we need any medical equipment for the trip?"

"Not according to the father. He says they have a tourniquet on his leg and it has stopped the bleeding. We should only have to get him back here to meet the medevac flight. The boy is 22 years old and is conscious, but weak from blood loss. We'll take the Caravan. It has plenty of room for a stretcher. Let's go." Tom waved to his wife and left the office with Wyatt following.

Pedro Bay is a small community of three families on the shore of a large bay on the east end of Lake Iliamna. It has a decent landing strip capable of handling the Cessna 208 they would be flying. Conversation became all business once the two men reached the inside of the hangar. The Cessna Caravan was parked on the ramp in front of the hangar. Tom started the turbine engine and received clearance for takeoff. He advised flight service of his mission and return time. The Caravan performs extremely well and the departure route was along the shoreline of the big lake. In minutes he was on the radio reporting his intention to land at Pedro Bay. Upon approach they could see a group of people on the upper end of the runway with someone on a stretcher beside a pickup truck. Tom taxied his plane to a parking spot near the group and shut down the engine. Wyatt had climbed from the right seat to the back and opened the large passenger/cargo door once the engine stopped.

Tom was the first out of the airplane with Wyatt close behind. "How is he?" asked Tom.

Nick Weaver, the father of the injured young man, said, "He's pretty bad, Tom. He lost a lot of blood. He needs to get to the hospital as quick as he can. He needs more blood."

"I had Maggie call the medevac jet from Anchorage. It should be in Iliamna by the time I get back to the office. Do you want to ride to town with me?"

Nick thought a moment, "No, not now. Get him on the jet and come back. Ma and I will be ready to go when you get here. I think you should fly us right into Anchorage and drop us off."

"Will do," said Tom. "Help us get the stretcher tied down and we're out of here. I'll be back in about an hour."

The stretcher was loaded into the back of the Cessna. Specially made straps held the litter to the floor to protect the patient. Wyatt closed the door while Tom moved to the pilot seat and started the engine. Wyatt examined the patient to find he was unconscious, probably from loss of blood. He sat next to the patient during the short flight back to Iliamna. As they approached to land they noted the aircraft ahead of them, the medevac Learjet, that was just landing. Tom taxied, positioned his plane so the doors of both planes would be facing one another, and stopped the engine. Wyatt, again, opened the door to see three medics standing there waiting to assist in the transfer of the patient.

Tom spoke to the medevac pilot briefly while the others loaded the Weaver boy into the back of the small jet. The transfer took less than five minutes. Tom and Wyatt stood on the ramp next to the Cessna watching the little jet take off with the injured man aboard.

"I have to go back to Pedro Bay and pick up Nick and his wife for a flight to Anchorage. I hope you find a place here in Iliamna and move in quickly. I need the help." Tom then gave Wyatt a short wave of his hand and boarded the Caravan, closing the door from the inside.

Wyatt watched him taxi to the runway and take off toward Pedro Bay. He walked back inside the office to find his father and Maggie still sitting at her desk.

"Did you have time to find a place to live?" asked Wyatt's father.

"No, but Tom offered me a place to stay for the winter. I'll check again before time to move in, but his offer may be the best for me. It would give me time to find a suitable lot to build my own cabin."

"I'll help you build, son, but I can only work until fishing season starts."

"Tom and I will love having you here, Wyatt. When do you think you will be moving?" asked Maggie.

"Sometime after the middle of November, Maggie. I have to attend an orientation class before they give me my VPSO badge. I don't want to be a problem for you, but I do need a place to live for the winter. Tom said I could leave my Cessna in the hangar, too. That is going to be a real plus. We have to get back to Naknek, but I'll see you soon."

They said goodbye and walked back to the airplane they had left on the ramp near the hangar. "Come on, Dad. Let's go to your house. You can cook me dinner."

Wyatt Earp V would always remember the days he had spent with his father prior to taking his post as Village Public Safety Officer for Iliamna and surrounding area.

Chapter Four

By mid-November Wyatt Earp V was finished with his orientation classes and had been issued all the personal gear he was to use at his new post. He had been instructed to coordinate with the Wildlife Officer at Iliamna for use of the state Super Cub posted at the Iliamna Airport. His supervisor would be Captain Griffin in Fairbanks. His nearest backup officer would be from Soldotna, but most likely his help would come from the trooper in King Salmon and the local Wildlife Enforcement Officer. Wyatt flew on the local airline to King Salmon where he had left his Cessna parked while he was attending classes in Anchorage.

The elder Earp met his son at the terminal in King Salmon to help transfer his newly issued gear and equipment to the Cessna and take him to dinner that evening. The daylight hours are short this time of year necessitating the new VPSO to remain in King Salmon and stay with his father until the morning hours before flying the short distance to Iliamna in his Cessna. The two chatted the evening away like old friends. Both Earps, father and son, had become close in recent weeks.

The morning air was crisp requiring Wyatt to preheat the engine before attempting to start it. It was zero degrees, not extremely cold, but preheating it made the engine acquire better lubrication and suffer less metal shock when the engine fired on its own. An insulated cover was placed over the engine cowling and a small propane heater was used to circulate warm air around the engine cylinders and oil pan. Once the oil temperature gauge began to move upward he shut down the little Red Dragon heater and pulled off the engine cover, stowing both items in the rear of the Cessna. Climbing inside the cabin he started the 300 horsepower engine to let it idle and warm the oil before attempting to take off. He used the time to check the weather and advise flight service of his intended route to Iliamna. Minutes later the King Salmon tower gave him permission to take off. An hour later he walked into the hangar where Tom Dempsey greeted him.

"Hi, Tom, do you have room inside the hangar for the 206?" asked Wyatt.

"Sure do. Taxi on over here and I'll open the hangar door. I'll help you put her inside."

Wyatt stopped, returned to the airplane, started the engine and moved it to the front of the hangar where Tom was waiting to help push the Cessna inside. Once the plane was inside Tom closed the door to maintain the heat inside the hangar. Wyatt unloaded his equipment and gear to be taken to his little room and office in the front of the hangar, next to the office where Maggie was working.

"There are several messages waiting for you. You can get them from Maggie. I'll bet she has fresh coffee on, too." Tom helped carry the items to the front of the hangar where the office was located.

"Thanks, Tom. Was there any excitement while I was gone?"

"Not much. Lonnie Davis, the local Wildlife Trooper took a couple of calls about drunks raising cane at the hotel, but nothing major." Tom suddenly had a sad look, "You remember the Weaver boy we brought in from Pedro Bay?"

"Yes I do. How is he doing?"

"They couldn't save his leg. You remember how badly it was injured? The doctors tried to re-attach everything, but it didn't take. They said it took too long to get him to the hospital in Anchorage and the tissue was too damaged. Too bad, but his dad said he's going to have an artificial lower leg and foot. He's a commercial fisherman like his dad."

The two men entered the front office where Maggie was working.

"Hi, Wyatt, welcome home," said Maggie.

"Thanks Maggie. I hear you have been taking my calls while I was a way. I hope I'm not going to be a problem for you while I'm here."

"No problem at all, Wyatt. I'm not that busy as a rule and I've been doing this for years. I'm kinda used to it."

"I have a new cell phone now, one with the VPSO number. I should be taking all my own calls as long as I'm within cell range. My trooper captain, Griff, will be down here in a few days to make sure everything is going OK. If you need anything from us, let him know and he'll try to get it."

"Grab a cup of coffee and I'll get your messages and help you settle in. The little office over there is yours. Your living quarters are behind the office. I supplied fresh sheets and towels. There is a TV in the back with satellite reception. If you need anything just ask me or Tom and we'll get it for you if we can."

"You have done more than I ever expected, Maggie. Thank you, so much." Wyatt moved off with his arms loaded with gear and suitcases full of uniforms and clothing. The rooms behind his little office were larger and more comfortable than he had expected. It took more than an hour for him to stow and arrange his living space. It took a little longer for him to arrange all the office supplies he had brought with him. Once done he returned to the air taxi office for his cup of coffee with Maggie.

"I didn't expect to have this nice a place to live. I want you to figure out a rate for rent and I'll pay you every month. Add on a little for taking my calls while I'm out of range. This is wonderful, Maggie." Wyatt was beginning to relax now, feeling at home in his new surroundings. He was sitting in a chair next to Maggie's desk when his hand-held radio chirped. It was the voice of Wildlife Trooper, Lonnie Davis.

"VPSO Unit 16, go ahead."

"This is 41, I need backup in Nondalton. I have a local, drugged up or drunked up making threats and shooting off a gun. I've told the neighbors to leave the area, but I can't see the back of the house from my position. I have the Cub here with me. Do you have a way to get up here?"

Wyatt pressed the talk button. "I can get my Cessna out of the hangar, but Tom is gone so it will take me a few minutes to get there."

"OK, just ask one of the men at the airstrip where I am. They'll bring you up here. I'm not in danger at the moment, but I don't want this guy running out the back door."

"I'll be there as quickly as I can. I'll call you when I arrive."

"10-4," replied Lonnie.

Turning to Maggie Wyatt said, "Gotta go, Maggie, trouble in Nondalton. See you later." With that he stood, returning to his little office to get his duty belt with his tools of the trade. Only recently have VPSOs been allowed to carry weapons, one of the items on his duty belt.

Minutes later he had his Cessna 206 out of the hangar and running. He took off in the northerly direction toward Nondalton. It was a short flight and landed ten minutes later. One of the locals met him when he landed and offered to give him a ride to where Lonnie was waiting for him.

Lonnie was behind an old disabled pickup when Wyatt arrived. "Hey, Wyatt, sorry to disturb you on your first day, but you know how it is. I don't intend to go in after this guy. This is his home and he'll go to sleep sooner or later. My worry is that he may get more crazy and sneak out the back door and start shooting and injure one of the neighbors. I want you to go around there to the left, behind the other cabin and watch the back of the house in case he tries to come out that way. If he does come out, call me on the radio. I'll try to go through the front door to get behind him. Just keep him talking if you can."

Wyatt nodded his understanding and began to move cautiously around some outbuildings in an attempt to conceal his position. Lonnie continued to call to the man inside as a distraction, but it drew an occasional gunshot fired in his direction. It took only three or four minutes for Wyatt to get into position. The only window on the back of the house was the one in the rear door of the cabin. Wyatt was hidden behind the south wall of a woodshed where he could see the back of the cabin clearly. He waited.

Lonnie continued to call to the man inside the cabin. After about an hour there was no longer any reply from the man, no shots nor any shouting. He finally called Wyatt on the radio.

"Sit tight, I'm going to try the front door. I think he's asleep inside. If I draw fire when I move I'll wait a little longer. Moving now."

Wyatt continued to watch the back of the cabin. Nothing stirred.

Lonnie moved slowly to the front steps of the small cabin, keeping low and moving quickly. He stepped quietly to the front porch; putting his back to the front wall, he tried the door. He was amazed when the knob turned and the door swung open. There were no sounds from the inside. Lonnie quickly poked his head around the corner of the doorway for a look. He could see the resident on the couch in the front room; he appeared to be sleeping.

"I'm going inside," Lonnie said quietly into his radio. "Move up to the back door."

"Roger," Wyatt replied and began to move toward the cabin.

Lonnie stepped inside the open door, walking quietly toward the sleeping man. When he was close enough to reach the rifle on the man's chest he picked it up and stepped back. The movement awakened the older Native man.

"Hey, Lonnie," greeted the man, "whatcha doin' in my house?"

"I just came to visit, Rufus. It looks like you've been drinking quite a lot. Are you OK?" Lonnie was still holding the rifle he had taken from the man.

"Whatcha doin' with my gun? Ain't that my gun?" mumbled a still intoxicated Rufus.

"Your neighbors were complaining you were shooting out the front of your cabin. They were afraid you would hit someone. I'm going to have to keep your rifle awhile."

It was then Wyatt made his way into the front room from the small kitchen in the back.

"You OK, Lonnie?" he asked.

"Yeah, old Rufus here just drank too much." Lonnie turned to Rufus Donavan to introduce Wyatt. Rufus, this is the new VPSO in Iliamna. His name is Wyatt Earp the fifth. He's a good guy. You need to be nice to him."

Rufus sat up on the couch, put out his hand and said, "Pleased to meet you Mr. Earp. Come on in and have a drink with us."

Wyatt took the man's hand and shook it. "I think you probably drank enough for one day, Rufus, but thanks anyway."

"We're going to leave now, Rufus, but I'm going to have to keep your rifle for a few days. I'll bring it back the next time I come to Nondalton. You lay back down and get some sleep. Don't be waking up the neighbors again, OK?" Lonnie had seen this situation many times as he travelled the small Native communities. Rufus was one of the regulars, but usually only verbal, not shooting. This was a troubling escalation of his behavior.

"OK, Lonnie, I won't cause any trouble. Thanks for coming to see me. And it was a pleasure meeting you, Officer Earp." With those short comments the old Native man lay down and closed his eyes. The two lawmen exited through the front door and left him to sleep.

"Is this a usual case?" asked Wyatt as the two walked back toward the Nondalton Airport.

"I'd say about fifty percent of my calls are like this. Most of them end the same way. They get crazy when they drink and get friendly again as soon as they get a little sleep. I hate to say this, but that's the way it is in the bush. I want to caution you about getting too used to a friendly outcome. A drunk can kill you and never remember he did it. Don't take any of these calls for granted, especially if you know the guy. I had a friend out here a few years ago, a trooper from King Salmon. He came out on a call like the one we just had. He knew the guy inside and started talking with him through the front door. My trooper friend tried to reason with him, but the guy got more hostile, started cussing him and yelling. My friend tried to calm him down by talking him out, but the man kept getting even more angry as time went on. The trooper called him by name and asked him to come out of the house.

"The man inside said, 'OK, I'm coming out.' He opened the door and shot my friend in the gut with a 12 gauge shotgun. Blew him off the front porch." There was sadness in his voice, "He died in the front yard. When the drunk woke up he didn't remember shooting my friend. He said he was sorry, but my friend was still dead. Don't let this happen to you, Wyatt." They finished the walk in silence.

Chapter Five

When he returned to Iliamna, across the Newhalen River, he parked near the hangar and put the engine cover on the cowling of the Cessna before going to the office. It was his intention to return to the office and complete the reports for his first call. That all changed when he reached the air taxi office.

"You have three calls waiting for you, Wyatt," said Maggie as he entered. "Here are the messages." She handed him the three pink message slips.

"Are any of them emergencies?" asked Wyatt.

"No, two theft reports and one call about finding some drugs in town," Maggie said without looking up.

"Thanks, Maggie, I'll take care of them right away." He took the slips and walked to his little office space. He decided to document his call to Nondalton before returning the three new calls. It was nearly an hour before he got to them. Using his cell phone he dialed the first number.

"Hello," came the first answer; a friendly voice.

"Hello, this is VPSO Earp. Is this Mona Worthington?"

"Yes, it is. Thank you for calling back. I called to report someone has stolen our Honda four wheeler," she stated.

"Do you know when it was stolen?"

"Yes, sometime last night. It was parked in the front yard. We were having a party and had the music going. We didn't hear anyone start it and drive away. We didn't notice it was gone until this morning," stated Mona.

"Do you have any idea who may have taken it?"

"No, not really. It could have been anyone."

"OK, Mrs. Worthington, I'll come to your home in a little while to investigate. In the meantime, would you make a list of the guests at the party last night? I'll need to talk to them. I should be there in about an hour. Give me directions to your house."

He wrote down the directions and moved on to the next call.

"Yeah," was the short greeting to his next call.

"Hello, this is VPSO Earp calling in reference to your complaint. Is this Dick Stafford?"

"Yeah, thanks for calling back. Sometime last night someone came to my place and stole two five-gallon cans of gasoline. There were three in the shed, but they only took two."

"Tell me where you live and I'll come out and see if there is any evidence as to who took the cans. Give me directions to your place." Wyatt made notes, realizing this address was on the same road as the stolen Honda.

The third complaint was from Linda Mason. "Hello, this is Linda," said the pleasant voice.

"Hello, is this Ms. Mason? This is VPSO Earp."

"Oh, yes, I called earlier. I found something near my home I think you should come and look at. I think it's a package of drugs. I teach school here and I would hate for one of the students to find it."

Wyatt remembered meeting Ms. Mason on an earlier visit to Iliamna. "Do you have the package in your possession?"

"Yes, and I want to be rid of it as soon as possible."

"Please give me directions to your residence. I have two other calls, but I'll come to your place first. It should be only a few minutes, depending on where you are." Wyatt was prioritizing his list of calls and taking possession of possible drugs was the most important on his list of things to do.

After ending the phone call, he reached for his coat and walked through the outer office, speaking to Maggie as he went by, "I'm going on some calls. Call me if anything important comes in while I'm out."

On the street side of the hangar was an older GMC pickup once belonging to the Wildlife Trooper stationed in Iliamna. It was now the official vehicle for the Iliamna VPSO. Wyatt drove the truck to the road leading from the airport to the main town site about two miles east of the airport. He found the house as described by Linda Mason, parked at the end of the short driveway and walked to the house. He tapped on the door and heard footsteps coming from the inside. The door opened to reveal a very pretty Alaska Native lady probably in her early 40's.

"Hi, I'm Linda," she said as she opened the door.

"Hello, Linda, I'm Wyatt Earp, the VPSO. May I come inside?"

"Certainly. It's too chilly to be standing on the front porch." She stepped back to allow him inside. "You look familiar to me. Do I know you from somewhere?"

"We met once, at the restaurant in the hotel. I was with my father. He comes here quite often, but he lives in Naknek. His name is also Wyatt. Can we sit and talk a few minutes?"

"Yes, of course; let's go to the kitchen and I'll make coffee." He followed her to the kitchen area where she went about making fresh coffee. He took a seat at the table, placing his notebook on top in front of him.

When she finished and returned to the table he asked, "You said you had found what you thought was a package of drugs. May I see it?"

She reached into a drawer in a cabinet behind her and retrieved the package, wrapped in plastic and sealed with duct tape. It appeared to be about three by four inches and two inches thick and was in some sort of plastic bag, though not a freezer bag. The clear plastic revealed what appeared to be white or off-white powder. Wyatt examined the package.

"I doubt there are any fingerprints on the package after being handled like this, but I think you're right. It looks like drugs. It doesn't look like cocaine though. I think it may be heroin or some other opioid. I'm glad you found it instead of one of your students. I'll send it to Anchorage for testing. I can test it for general classification, but the lab can tell us exactly what's in the package. Do you have any idea where it came from?"

"No, I don't. I was walking to my car at the school and saw it lying in the bushes by the parking lot. I have been to a lot of classes where they show us how to identify drugs and such, but this is the first time I have ever found anything like this." Linda showed her concern with the problem of drugs in her community.

"The trooper office will probably send an investigator out here and he will want to talk with you. I'll try to find out when he's coming and let you know. In the meantime, if you hear any rumors about someone losing his drugs, get in touch with me right away. It could be dangerous for you if they think you still have the drugs. Don't hesitate to call me, day or night. Here's a card with my cell phone and office numbers. Please be careful who you mention this to for your own safety." Wyatt knew this was a large enough amount, if it was heroin, to be a major loss to someone—a loss large enough to get Linda Mason hurt. He would have to make it a point to keep an eye on her. It didn't seem like an unpleasant chore, after all.

"The coffee is done; can you stay a few minutes and have some with me?"

Wyatt checked his watch, "Only a few minutes, I have two other calls to make. Thank you, I've been on the run since early this morning and haven't had my coffee yet. It would really taste good."

Half an hour later Wyatt had finished his coffee and said good bye to Linda then drove off to the next call a half mile further down the same road. As he approached the location of the second house on his list, the home of the missing Honda four wheeled ATV, he again parked near the end of a short driveway and walked the short distance to the house. The owner of the home had seen him coming and came out to greet him.

"Hi there, I'm Dusty Alowon, Mona Worthington, my girlfriend, called you about the missing Honda," he said as he stepped off the porch

"Hello, Dusty, I'm Wyatt Earp, no jokes, please," said Wyatt as he approached the man.

Dusty grinned, "I'll bet you do get a lot of jokes."

"Where was the four-wheeler parked when it was taken?" asked Wyatt.

"I'll show you." Dusty was born in Naknek and raised in Iliamna. He was a commercial fisherman and trapper of Alaska Native descent. The two men walked to the shed near the house. "I always left the key in it. We've never had any problems like this before. I guess I'm going to have to be more careful from now on. What with all the new folks around here and them working on the new resort over there," Dusty pointed down the road toward the lakeshore.

"I suppose; I heard all the rentals were taken with workers hired to build the new lodge. Do you think one of those workers took your Honda?"

"I have no idea. Like I said before, we've never had this kind of trouble before."

The two men had walked to a small pole-barn style building, one end of which was piled high with commercial fishing nets. The other end was vacant.

"Right here is where it was parked. I tried to follow the tracks, but lost them just a few feet down the main road." There was frustration in Dusty Alowon's voice.

"Which way did they turn when they left your driveway, toward town or toward the lake?" asked Wyatt, making notes on his pad.

"Toward the lake," said the fisherman. "I drove down to the building site, but didn't see it anywhere. It's red, so it's easy to see."

"Do you know how much fuel was in the tank?" asked the VPSO.

"Not much. I had been hauling these nets up from the lake with it but didn't fill it up when I parked it in here."

"I have another report to check on where some gasoline was taken. The owner said the thief took only two of the three cans in the shed. I think it's possible they took the fuel to put into the Honda. If so, it must be someone who knew where to find the gas. I'm going there next and I'll see if I can follow any tire tracks from there. Can you give me the license number on the Honda?" requested Wyatt.

"It doesn't have a license on it, but I have the title with the serial numbers. It's new. I just bought it this spring. It cost me a lot of money. I would like to get it back all in one piece. Let's go up to the house and I'll get the numbers off the title."

Wyatt followed Dusty back to the house and waited on the porch while he went inside to get the title to the Honda. When Dusty returned Wyatt copied down the numbers on his note pad. "I'll let you know if I turn up anything."

It was only a half mile down the same road to the next complainant. Wyatt climbed the steps to the elevated porch and knocked on the door.

A very tall, red haired man about 30 years old answered the door. "Are you Dick Stafford?" asked Wyatt.

"That's me," said the young man. "I'm the one you talked to on the phone earlier. Follow me and I'll show you where the gas cans were. I can't figure out why they only took two of the cans. If they were out to steal gas I would have thought they would have taken it all."

"A Honda ATV was stolen last night and the owner said it was almost out of fuel. I suspect they only took enough to fill the tank. Did you hear anything like an ATV engine, during the night?"

"No, but I have the TV turned on most of the time and seldom hear anything outside, unless it's really loud."

The two men were now at a small shed at the side of the house. Wyatt looked for tracks in the dirt, but found none.

"Have you looked for your gas cans?" he asked.

"I walked up and down the road a couple of hundred yards in both directions, but didn't find anything."

"All right, then. I'm going to drive around and see if I can spot anything before I return to the office. I'll let you know if I find anything. Are the other two cans like the one in the shed?"

"Yup, just like it. I don't expect to get the gas back, but I don't like having anything stolen. I guess I'll have to start locking up my shed. Thanks for looking into it for me."

Wyatt returned to his pickup, jotted a couple more notes in his notepad, and backed out of the drive. He turned down the road toward the new lodge being constructed near the shore of Lake Iliamna. The log structure was huge. It was a beautiful log lodge with huge windows on the lake side. A veranda style deck was built on the front and two sides with several sets of wide steps allowing access from every side. The outside of the structure looked to be completed, but through the windows he could see scaffolding and materials piled around the ground floor. It was obvious construction was still in progress. When completed it would be an impressive lodge. Wyatt guessed the daily rate in the lodge would also be impressive. He was backing up to turn around to leave the grounds when a man in brown bib overalls came out of a door in the back of the lodge.

He walked directly to the pickup, held up a hand and called out, "Hold up a minute."

Wyatt stopped the truck and shut off the engine.

"Oh, I didn't know it was the police. Is there something I can help you with?" asked the carpenter.

"I have a report of a stolen Honda ATV and came down here to see if I could spot it anywhere. I just came to Iliamna this week and had never been down here to the lodge. By the look of things it will be world class."

"I'm Harry Porter, the foreman on the job. Pleased to meet you," he held a calloused hand up to the side window to shake the hand of the VPSO. "Mr. Douglas, the owner isn't here right now. I'm sure he'll be happy to give you a tour when he gets back from Anchorage."

Wyatt shook the offered hand. "I'm the new VPSO, Wyatt Earp the fifth. I have a temporary office in the Lake Air Taxi hangar." He gave the carpenter one of his cards. "If you need anything just call me at either of the numbers on the card. And when your boss returns, I would like to meet him. I'm headed back to the office now. Sorry I disturbed you. See you around."

When he returned to the office he found Tom sitting there, sipping a cup of coffee. Maggie was still busy behind the desk.

"Hi, Tom. Busy day, eh?" he inquired. Tom nodded, still sipping his coffee. "Were there any more calls, Maggie?"

"No, but Captain Griffin called and asked to have you call him when you returned"

"Thanks, Maggie. I'll call him right now."

Wyatt took off the heavy duty belt and hung it on the back of a chair, then took off his jacket and hung it on a hook near the door. He took out his notebook, placed it on his desk, and put the small plastic wrapped package he was carrying on the desk next to the notebook. He sat in his chair trying to organize his thoughts before calling Griff. Finally, he picked up the telephone receiver. "Captain Griffin, please. This is VPSO Earp in Iliamna."

"Please hold," said the lady on the other end.

A male voice came on the line, "Wyatt, I'm glad you called. I tried to reach you earlier, but the lady said you were out on a call. I'm glad you're finding things to do. How do you like it so far?"

"I like it here, Griff, uh sorry, Captain Griffin. I was about to call you anyway. One of the calls this morning was from the local school teacher. She was leaving the school grounds yesterday and found a small package in the brush by the parking lot. She turned it over to me and I agree with her identification, though I haven't tested the substance as yet. She thought it was heroin. I wore gloves while handling it, but she used bare hands. I don't know if there will be any prints on the outside of the package, but I have it here on my desk and will mark it for evidence. It looks to be about a quarter pound. It's a lot of stuff for this small community. How do you want me to handle the investigation?"

There was a short silence, then he replied, "I think I'll call the drug unit in Soldotna and have the sergeant come out to your office. You can work out a strategy with him. Just mark the package and lock it up for now. I'll call you back and let you know when he'll be there. This is pretty big stuff for your first day."

"And you thought VPSOs were just glorified crossing guards. I read a book once. I know what cops do." Both men laughed.

"I'll get back to you as soon as I talk to Sergeant Turner. I'll call you right back."

After the call, Wyatt placed the suspect package inside an evidence envelope and locked it in the small safe in his office, making appropriate notes in his book. He then went back to the air taxi office to speak with Tom.

Maggie poured him a cup of coffee as he approached her desk. "You have had a busy day, Wyatt," commented Maggie.

"It makes the day go fast when you're busy. Say, Tom, when you fly around the local area would you keep an eye out for a new, red, Honda, four wheeled ATV? One was stolen last night, down the main road toward the new lodge. I drove the road, but didn't see it from there. It's probably parked in the brush just off the road somewhere. I'll go out in my plane and scout around later, but I have to wait on a call from the Captain."

"If you're hungry there's some stew in the crock pot on the break room table. Help yourself, Wyatt." Wyatt took a large bowl of the moose meat stew and a slab of home-made bread back to his own little office area to await the call from Griff.

Chapter Six

Wyatt finished his lunch before beginning to work on the official reports he had to make in regard to the four calls he had made during the morning. The second report was finished when the phone jingled. "VPSO Earp," he answered.

"Please hold for Captain Griffin," said the pleasant female voice.

A moment later Griff came on the line. "Do you have anything on your schedule this afternoon, Wyatt?" he asked.

"Not much, I was just finishing the reports from this morning."

"Good, Sergeant Gene Turner is flying out to meet with you. He will fill you in on what he knows about drugs in your area. Try to be nice to him, Wyatt. He takes everything too seriously. He will be flying one of the state Super Cubs. He's supposed to leave the plane with you and come back on a charter, unless you want to fly him back to Soldotna."

"I already have one flight in the Cessna today. You buy the gas and I'll take him home. Do I need another check-ride before flying the Cub?" asked Wyatt.

"No. I'll have the check pilot sign you off. Leave a space on your log book and he can write it in when he gets out there. Is there anything else you need right now?" asked the Captain.

"I don't think so, Griff. I don't have any drug testing equipment here, but I'll try to get the sergeant to get me some." Wyatt thought a moment, before asking, "Ah, Griff—I know money matters are above my pay grade, but Tom and Maggie have me housed in a nice little area and furnished me a small, but adequate office space. They fed me lunch today. Is there any way we can pay them rent or lease money for being here? I don't even pay for my spot in the

Wyatt Earp V

hangar to park the Cessna. It cost them a lot for electricity and heating fuel. Since I can't get a place of my own until spring, I think it would be only right to pay them for those services."

"Let me talk with the Colonel and I'll see what I can do. Remember, use the local Wildlife trooper if you need back-up." Griffin was becoming concerned for the new VPSO. "Have Sergeant Turner call me when he returns to Soldotna."

"Thanks, Griff." Wyatt hung up the phone and returned to the reports he had been working on when the call came. Being a VPSO was like being a cop in Fairbanks; you spend more time on the paperwork than on police work. Wyatt was finished with the reports when he heard the engine of a Super Cub as it taxied to the front of the hangar. He placed his papers in a desk drawer, slipped on his jacket, and walked out through the big hangar to meet Sergeant Gene Turner. Turner was securing the engine cover when Wyatt walked through the man-door at the ramp end of the hangar.

"Sergeant Turner?" he called.

"Yes. You must be the VPSO," said Turner with an outstretched hand. The two men shook hands.

"Let's go inside where it's warm," said Wyatt.

In the front office Wyatt introduced Turner to Maggie. She offered him coffee which he accepted. He thanked her and carried the hot coffee down the short hall to a door where Wyatt's office was located. Inside Wyatt closed the door in order to talk with the drug cop privately then went to the safe to get the small packet of drugs he had placed inside. He handed the package, marked with red letters as "Evidence," to the sergeant.

"Captain Griffin said you thought the package contained heroin. I think you're correct in your identification. I have a test kit in my briefcase. Is it OK with you if we open the evidence bag and get enough material for a sample?"

"Sure, Sergeant, but let me get a legal pad and make note of the time and what we will be doing."

"Call me Gene," said Turner. "Have you been trained in drug testing?"

"Yes, I have. I was a street cop in Fairbanks for more than twenty years. I'm new to the VPSO position, but I've been a cop a long time," explained Wyatt.

"I'm surprised we haven't met before. I've worked in the Fairbanks area many times. I was a road trooper years ago and patrolled the pipeline road north of Fox. I never spent much time in Fairbanks though. I have been doing drug enforcement for the past seven years. They keep asking me to take a promotion and a post commander position, but I like my job and I always turn the offer down."

. . . 36 . . .

"I don't blame you. I'd go nuts sitting in an office all day." Both men chuckled. "I guess I'm ready now. You do the testing and I'll do the documentation. Is that OK with you?" Wyatt had moved a second chair to the desk.

Turner reached into his large brief case for the drug testing kit. He used a knife to cut a small slit in the plastic wrapping and used a sterile wood stick, like a Popsicle stick, to take a small amount of powder from the package and dropped it into a small bag, sealing the top with the plastic clip. The testing fluid is housed inside a small glass vial inside the heavy plastic bag used for testing. Turner broke the vial and instantly the powder changed color. Wyatt used cellophane tape to re-seal the small hole in the drug package before placing the package inside a fresh evidence bag.

"Wow!" exclaimed Turner. "This is some really pure stuff. It's heroin all right, nearly pure stuff from the looks of this test. I'll send it to the state crime lab in Anchorage for detailed testing. You say someone found it near a school?"

"Yes, the school teacher was leaving the school and saw it near her car in the parking area. I went over there and saw where she found it, but didn't see anything else. No footprints or tire tracks, nothing. Has your team heard any rumors about someone dealing heroin in this area?"

Sergeant Turner let out a huge sigh before continuing. "What I'm about to tell you is for your information only. We have no evidence to support this thinking, but we think John Douglas, the man building the lodge down the road, got rich dealing drugs all over the western states, including Alaska. He owns a fairly large trucking company and uses it to distribute his products in all the western states. The feds are following that lead, but I don't know what they have uncovered. I do know that Douglas never allows any amount of his product anywhere near his home, office, or properties. He owns and directs operations through intermediaries he hires. Nothing comes into direct contact with him. So far neither the feds nor we have been able to get anything on him. He's cagey and he's careful. He's also dangerous. The DEA has sent numerous reports of bodies of people associated with his business turning up dead all over the west. We think he's a major player in the drug trade down south and a dangerous one at that."

Wyatt thought a moment before speaking, "I don't understand, Gene. If he's so smart and elusive, why would he bring drugs to this little community where everyone knows everyone else's business?"

"Good question, Wyatt, but I doubt he brought it here. My guess is that someone working for him did. Why it was left in the parking lot of the school is beyond me, but I think if word about it gets back to Douglas he'll take quick action with whoever did bring it here. He won't tolerate anyone bringing the law to his doorstep. I think you will have a disappearance in this area as soon as Mr. Douglas learns about it."

"I haven't been at this post long enough to be familiar with the locals, but if you're right, the locals won't know anything about it either. It sounds like my quiet life in the bush is about to come to an abrupt end." The two men chatted for more than another hour before Gene Turner said he would have to go back to Soldotna. "Talk to Maggie at the front desk. If Tom has time I know he would be happy for the charter."

"Good, I'll ask. Is there anything else I can do for you while I'm here?"

"Probably, but I can't think of anything right now. Oh, yes, there is. Can you leave me a few drug testing packets? I don't have any here in the office," asked Wyatt

"Sure, I'll give you all I have in my briefcase. There's a couple of each of the ones I use on a regular basis. Are you certified in the testing procedures?"

"Yes, from my days with the Fairbanks Police Department. You can check with the Captain for copies of all my certifications."

"I am also going to give you my card with my personal phone numbers on it. If you have questions or need help, call me." Sergeant Turner was both friendly and helpful. Wyatt felt comfortable working with him.

"This was a good-sized package worth a lot of money to someone. I doubt this is a one-time deal. I'm still learning who's the good guy and who's the bad guy. This is a small community, but I haven't had time to get acquainted. I know a few folks here, but, of course, someone with this amount of heroin in his pocket hasn't taken the trouble to introduce himself to me. Give me a few days and I might come up with a suspect. I'll be in touch."

"You have only been on the job a couple of days and already you have uncovered a major drug deal, pretty impressive, Wyatt." Gene gathered his personal items, put his jacket back on and said, "Let's go see if I can get a ride back to Soldotna."

"If Tom is busy I'll take you back. I need a break from the paperwork anyway." Wyatt was about to speak again when his phone rang. "Go ahead and talk to Maggie. I'll be there in a minute after I answer this call." Gene walked away making his way to the front desk in the air taxi office while Wyatt answered the call.

"VPSO Earp," he answered.

It was Linda Mason, "Hello Mr. Earp. This is Linda. I was thinking about you being new here that you might be interested in coming to dinner tonight."

"That sounds great, but it will be a few minutes before I know if I'm free this evening. Can I call you back in a little while?"

"Certainly. I'll wait for your call. Do you have my number?"

"I wrote it down this afternoon. I'll call you back, I promise." Wyatt hung up the phone and joined Gene Turner at the front counter. Maggie was speaking to Tom on the company radio. Tom said he would be back in half an hour, but would need to fuel up before making the trip through Lake Clark Pass to Soldotna.

"Will you take a voucher for payment?" asked the sergeant.

"No problem," said Maggie, "Let me write you a trip ticket with the amount and you can make out the voucher to the company name, Lake Air Taxi. It's going to be dark, but the weather is good so I think Tom will be going over the top instead of through the Pass."

By the time Turner had finished writing the voucher slip they heard the airplane on the ramp in front of the hangar. "Wyatt, I'm going out to the plane and help Tom fuel up. Stay in touch and let me know if you learn anything new. I'll send you the reports when the lab is finished testing." He stuck out a big hand and shook the hand of VPSO Wyatt Earp V.

Wyatt returned to his office to call Linda Mason.

Chapter Seven

They arranged to have dinner at her house at 7:00 p.m. Wyatt told her he would have to put the airplanes inside the hangar before leaving for the day. By the time he finished his office duties, Gene Turner and Tom had taken off for Soldotna. Maggie was closing up her office and getting ready to go home for the night. Wyatt went into the hangar bay to open the big door. It took nearly a half hour to put the Cessna and the Super Cub in the corner of the hangar. It was a tight fit in order to leave room for the Lake Air Taxi company plane.

Once the hangar was closed Wyatt returned to his own little office and living quarters to wash up and comb his hair before leaving through the front door of the office. He was pleased Linda had asked him to dinner. He liked the lady. She was easy to look at, educated, and cared about her job and the children she taught. She was a nice person, in his opinion.

Minutes later he parked in her front yard, stepped up on the front porch, and knocked on the door. Her Native blood reflected in her physical features. When she answered the she looked nice.

"Come inside before you freeze," she beckoned.

Wyatt stepped into the living room and removed his heavy coat. "I would have stopped to get a bottle of wine, but I didn't know if you indulged."

"As a rule I don't, but once in a great while I'll have a glass of sweet white wine. Come into the kitchen. I have fresh coffee, and dinner is nearly ready. We're having moose pot roast, potatoes and gravy along with the veggies cooked with the roast. Does that sound good to you?"

"It sounds delicious. I have to admit I probably don't eat a healthy diet. I cook when I'm home in the evening, but it's mostly something quick and out of a package. Your dinner sounds and smells wonderful. He sat at the kitchen table while she dished up the food and set the platters on the table.

"Help yourself, Wyatt, and let me know if you need anything else." She handed him a bowl of steamed potatoes.

The two ate dinner without much conversation, but once they had finished they sat at the table sipping coffee. "Thank you for dinner, Linda, it was delicious. I could get used to meals like that."

Linda lowered her head a moment, planning her next words. "I'm glad you liked it, Wyatt, I don't often get a chance to cook for someone else. I don't mix with the locals very much, only the parents of my students. We have pot luck dinners at the school from time to time, but I don't socialize much. So many of the men my age are heavy drinkers and using drugs. I don't like that and do my best to avoid such things.

"My family lives in Pile Bay. That's where I was raised and went to school. When I started high school I was sent to Homer as a boarding student. I came home on holidays and in the summer, but went to school in Homer. After graduation, I went to college in Anchorage and became a teacher. I took this job in Iliamna and I like it here. I still go up the lake to home in the summer to fish with my dad." Linda lowered her head again. Wyatt remained silent. "I'm telling you this because I like you and I didn't want you to think I'm some floozy trying to get you into my house. I'm so embarrassed. I'm not very good at this."

Wyatt smiled a huge grin. "I've been a cop nearly all my life. I've spent my entire career chasing bad guys. I've never taken time to have a personal life. I took this VPSO job because I needed something to do. I'm too young to sit on the front porch in a rocking chair telling stories about my life. I have had a few lady friends in my life, but they always got tired of me working all the time and not spending enough time with them. You and I have only just met, but, already, I feel closer to you than I have to anyone. I like you very much, Linda. I don't know where this relationship will go, but in this short time you have become a dear friend. We have a lot in common, you and me."

"Oh, Wyatt, I am so relieved to hear you say that. I didn't want to scare you away." She was now grasping his hand in both of hers.

"After all I am a cop," he chuckled. "You realize we are both from Native American backgrounds, and we are both from commercial fishing families. We both went off to college to make a career of helping others. I think fate put us together and the gods are smiling at the result.

"It's getting late and I think I had better get out of here before I start telling you what a wonderful person I am." He stood, pulling her to her feet.

"Thank you for being so understanding. I'll get your coat." She followed him to the front door his coat in hand.

Wyatt took the coat and wrestled it on. He took the door knob in hand, paused and turned around to give her a small kiss on the cheek. "I'll call you tomorrow," he said, adding, "You're a great cook."

"Thank you, and I'll look forward to hearing from you."

The youngest of the Earp clan smiled as he drove back to the hangar and his small living quarters. Linda Mason could be a welcome addition to this life, he thought as he drove home.

Surprisingly there were no new calls while he was out. Back in the office he reviewed the reports he had prepared earlier in the day. They seemed to be in order, so he made copies and prepared them for mailing to Captain Griffin's office at State Trooper Headquarters in Fairbanks. It was late now and time to call it a day. He wondered if this new post would always be this busy. It was certainly more than he had expected, but he liked the pace.

The following morning Maggie came to his office with a plate of fresh baked cinnamon rolls. "I baked this morning," she explained. "I hope you like the buns. Oh, you already have coffee."

"They sure smell good, Maggie. Do you bring baked goods to the office every day?"

"Almost. Sometimes I sleep late, but the regular customers look forward to coming in and having coffee and some kind of rolls each morning. Tom will be here in a little while. He has a trip to Port Alsworth on Lake Clark and wanted me to see if you want to ride along this morning?"

"Do I have any calls pending this morning?" Wyatt asked.

"None I know about," she responded.

"Let me make a call to Soldotna and check in with Sergeant Turner first. If he doesn't have anything for me I'd love to make the trip." Wyatt picked a large roll from the plate and took a bite. "Oh, that's good," he said with his mouth still half full of the sweet goodie.

An hour later he was seated in the right seat of the company Cessna, wearing headphones and listening to Tom recite his checklist. They received clearance and took off toward Lake Clark. The day was clear and the air smooth as they flew low and enjoyed the scenery, the wandering caribou and moose, as well as several big brown bears foraging for last minute salmon along the small streams. Both men spoke into and listened through the intercom system of the aircraft.

"It sure has been a beautiful fall this year. The 'termination dust,' is creeping down the mountains, but the first snow is late." Termination dust is the snow line on the mountains foretelling the progress of 'old man winter.' Tom made his comments while sightseeing along the route.

"After spending all those years in Fairbanks, I'm looking forward to winter here," said Wyatt. "I remember, as a boy, how much I liked the winter time. We trapped and played on snowshoes. Now everyone uses snow machines. I guess it makes me a weirdo, but I still like the winter."

"Me, too," commented Tom as the plane passed over the Tanalian River, approaching the Port Alsworth Airport. "I'm going to park near Alsworth's hangar. I have some freight to load. I'm taking the load back to Iliamna for loading on the daily plane to Anchorage. There's a little shop a little way down the runway where they sell burgers. I think you should go up there and have a cup of coffee with Leon MacKammon. He's the owner and does the cooking. He's a nice guy and I think you might be interested in a story he has to tell; remember, I didn't tell you to go there."

The runway is gravel, but well maintained. The little settlement is named for one of the families who founded the business here, a homestead family wanting to live on the lake. The Alsworths still run the aircraft fuel pumps, terminal, maintenance hangar, freight business and have a great deal of land on the shore of Lake Clark. Tom stopped the Cessna in front of the Alsworth hangar and shut down the engine. His first act was to put an engine cover over the warm Continental engine.

Wyatt left Tom to his business and walked the two hundred yards to the little blue building with a sign depicting the menu nailed beside the only door. Inside was warm with two small tables and two stools at the counter. The cook was sitting at the counter smoking a cigarette and reading the newspaper. He turned to see who had entered.

"Want something to eat?" he asked, turning back to his newspaper.

"It's a little early for a burger, but I'll have some coffee. I'm the new VPSO in Iliamna and rode over from there with Tom. I just came in to introduce myself. I was told you know everything that goes on around here and I need to know someone like that. The name's Earp, Wyatt Earp the fifth."

The older man gave him a wary glance.

"No, I'm not joking. That's my name. We're related to the original. If you have lived here a long time you may know my dad. He, too, is named Wyatt."

"Oh, yeah, I know him, commercial fisherman, ain't he?" The old man put a cup of steaming coffee on the counter in front of Wyatt.

"Yes, that's him." The two men shook hands.

"Tom said you knew everyone around here. Since I'm new I'd like to get to know you…in case I need to find someone over on this side of the lake."

"Used to be a cop, you know," mentioned the old man. "Leon MacKammon's the name."

Wyatt reached into his shirt pocket to get a business card to hand to Leon. "You can call me Wyatt, Leon. My office and cell phone numbers are on the card. If you ever need to contact me just call one of those numbers. I'm sure you see some strange things from time to time."

"Quite often, as a matter of fact. Gotta pencil?" asked Leon, still looking at his newspaper.

Wyatt fished his pad and pen from his inside pocket.

"November 8816 Alpha, red and white Super Cub, flies all around these parts. Don't trap or guide, just flies around and stops at different strips on the lake. He does the same over on your lake, too. Has a cabin over on your lake, down by the mouth of the river. A de Havilland Beaver on floats stops at his place on a regular basis, but nobody knows why. Folks who know him say he's bootlegging liquor. I don't believe it; ain't enough money in it. I think you might want to find out what this guy is selling." Leon was still studying his newspaper.

Wyatt was writing the information in his notebook. "You wouldn't happen to know this fellow's name, would you?"

"Rick Buntz. Been in the area about two years. Don't like him at all," said Leon.

"Thanks Leon, I'll let you know what I find out." Wyatt reached for some money for the coffee.

"Coffee's on me this time," said Leon, not looking up.

Wyatt chuckled to himself as he walked back to where Tom was waiting near the airplane, his cargo loaded. Tom removed the engine cover when Wyatt came closer and climbed inside the warm plane. "That Leon is quite a guy," said Wyatt before Tom started the engine.

It was late morning as they flew back to Iliamna and, it seemed, the game they had seen had fled back into the brush. Back at the hangar Wyatt helped move the freight to a pallet inside the hangar door to await the Anchorage flight. Back inside the building he returned to his small office and called Sergeant Turner. "Hi there, Gene," he greeted in a cheerful voice.

"If it isn't the famous Wyatt Earp V. How are you this morning?"

"I've been to Port Alsworth and back this morning. It was a beautiful flight."

"I haven't heard from the lab on that package. Have you found anything new?" asked Turner.

"I don't know, Sarge, but, can you run an aircraft number for me?" asked Wyatt. "I don't want to do it through the local FAA office."

"Sure, I can do it from my desk while we talk. Hold on a second while I find the site." The line was silent for about two minutes before Turner returned with another question. "OK, what is the aircraft number?"

Wyatt read the number from his notebook. "I would also like to get a criminal history on a man by the name of Rick Buntz. He supposedly has an Iliamna address."

"Is this connected to the package?" asked the sergeant.

"I really don't know for sure. I just heard he was involved in some suspicious activity and wanted to check him out."

"I'll copy all this info and send it to your computer. You should have all the information in a few minutes. Anything else?" asked Turner.

"Nope, that's it for now. Have you got anything new for me?" asked Wyatt.

"No, not now. Thanks for the call." Both men hung up and waited.

Wyatt was waiting for the computer to bring him his information when his cell phone rang. "VPSO Earp," he answered.

"Hello, Wyatt, this is Linda, Linda Mason. Class has let out for lunch and I wanted to call and tell you I had a wonderful time last night. I hope we can do that again, soon."

"I'm glad you called, Linda. I had a very good time, too. You're good company." Wyatt felt a little awkward in this conversation. "I was thinking, if you have no plans for the weekend, perhaps you would let me fly you into King Salmon and have dinner in the restaurant? The weather is supposed to be good all week and it would be a fun trip. Sort of a three-hour vacation…are you interested?"

"I think it would be wonderful, Wyatt." The idea, in fact, excited her.

"Good, I'll get a weather check on Saturday and we can set a time." He stopped talking when the computer in front of him beeped. "I have to go now, but I'll get back with you. Thank you for calling. You can call me anytime."

"Goodbye, Wyatt, I'll be waiting to hear from you."

Chapter Eight

Wyatt gave the computer a few pokes and the messages from Sgt. Turner came on the screen. The first one was the air aircraft registration information on Piper Super Cub number N8816A. The aircraft was registered in a company name, Newhalen Resorts Inc. The corporate officer name on the title is Richard Buntz with an Iliamna, Alaska address. Wyatt pushed the print key to make a copy of the information.

The second message was a copy of a police record for Richard "Rick" Buntz. He was born in Wisconsin in 1989. Not yet 30 years old he had a lengthy police record. As a juvenile he had been arrested six times, but his juvenile record was sealed and not available. At the adult age of eighteen he was arrested in Wisconsin for burglary. He was not sent to prison for that crime when he promised to leave the state and never return. The judge was happy he would no longer be committing crimes in Wisconsin.

His next arrest was in Fairbanks, Alaska for burglary, robbery, eluding police, tampering with evidence, and assault on an officer. His public defender made a deal with the District Attorney in Fairbanks for dismissal of charges if he left Fairbanks. There were no further arrests, but a year after leaving Fairbanks he was identified as being at the scene of a shooting in Anchorage, Alaska. In this case he was listed as a witness. A few weeks later he was again listed as a witness to an assault near Merrill Field where he was taking flying lessons from a private instructor. In that case he listed his employer as Jimmy, 'The Con," Waterbury, a big time drug dealer in Anchorage. A few months later he was listed as a suspect in a drug related homicide, but no one was ever charged in that killing. It was shortly after this incident that he bought an airplane and moved to Iliamna. His aircraft had been seen in the area of several drug related cases, but he was never identified.

Wyatt read the reports several times, trying to imagine what kind of person Rick Buntz really was. Finally, he picked up the telephone to call Gene Turner.

"Sergeant Turner," he answered.

"Gene, it's Wyatt, in Iliamna. Do you have time to talk for a minute?"

"Sure, you must have read the rap sheet I sent to you. The one regarding a local resident; interesting read, isn't it?"

"I'm beginning to think not all the locals are nice, law-abiding citizens," commented Wyatt. "I have been sitting here thinking about it and I moved his name to the top of my list of folks who may have lost the package I sent home with you. This guy must be a smooth talker to have two arrests dismissed when he said he was leaving town. Do you know if he was ever a suspect for any crimes out here?"

"I haven't heard of any, but I'll ask around. King Salmon may have something, but I'm not aware of it."

"My first thought was to go down to the lake and have a talk with him, but I think I'll just wait a while. I can ask around about him, discreetly, of course. There are a few people I can ask without the word getting out. This is a very small and very close community. I don't want to tip him off as to my suspicions, especially since I don't have any proof he's involved in anything at all. I am surprised, though, no one has asked about the package we found. That's a lot of money to lose without someone asking around."

"I'm beginning to like the way you work, Wyatt. Just be careful; people disappear out there. You're probably dealing with a dangerous crowd. Don't hesitate to call me if you think there may be trouble. Don't take it on alone."

"I plan to do just that. Thanks for the help. I'll keep you posted."

"See ya," said Turner in a worried voice.

Wyatt was deep in thought when a rap on the office door startled him. "Come in," he said. It was Tom Dempsey poking his head around the door. Wyatt motioned for him to enter.

"Are you busy, Wyatt?" asked Tom.

"No, come on in and have a seat. I just got off the phone with Sergeant Turner and learned some interesting things. What have you been doing all day?"

"Moving some freight, driving folks around, you know, the usual."

"You get to have all the fun, Tom."

"And I like it." Both men laughed. "But I may have a bit of news for you. I was on my way to Newhalen and saw something in the brush over by the falls where the road parallels the river. I circled around and dropped down to see. I think it's your missing Honda. It's red and shiny, but it's in the bushes and I couldn't tell for sure."

"Thanks, Tom. I'll drive out there and take a look. In fact, I think I'll go get the owner to ride out there with me. It's probably out of gas, but, hopefully not wrecked. Show me on the map exactly where to look."

Tom pointed out the spot on the map which Wyatt recognized. "I'm headed out there now. I'll stop and see if Dusty Alowon will ride out there with me. I'll let you know if that's the one."

Wyatt slipped on his heavy coat and walked to his old pickup. He drove to the Alowon home and knocked on the door. Mona answered the door. "Hello, Ms. Worthington, is Dusty home? I'd like to speak with him if I could."

"Yes, he's in his office working on books. He never stops working. I'll get him for you." She stepped inside the house and moments later Dusty came to the door.

"Trooper Earp, good to see you. What can I do for you?"

"I have a report on something that might be your missing Honda. I wondered if you would mind riding out with me to take a look?"

Dusty smiled a big grin, "Let me get my coat. This is good news. I didn't think I would ever see it again. That machine cost me a lot of money. I'll be right out." Dusty went inside the house and Wyatt returned to his truck to wait. A couple of minutes later Dusty came out of the house and climbed into the passenger seat.

The road from the Iliamna Airport wandered westward, toward the Newhalen River then north along the high bank above the swift river flowing out of Lake Clark. There wasn't much conversation during the ride. Once the road turned to follow the river both men began to look into the brush for any sign of the Honda. A mile below the river falls Wyatt spotted tire tracks on the edge of the dirt road. He stopped the truck and stepped out and walked carefully to the edge of the roadway, looking for tire tracks or footprints and any other evidence the culprits may have left behind. After inspecting the area and finding tire tracks, the two men made their way down the steep bank and through the alders and willows to where the red, four-wheel, side-by-side seating vehicle was hidden in the brush.

After inspecting the site and taking some photos Wyatt asked Dusty to try to start the machine. His first thought after finding the key in the ignition switch was to check the fuel tank. The gauge read empty. He removed the gas cap to confirm it was, indeed, empty.

"I have a five gallon can of gas in the truck. I'll go get it," said Wyatt as he turned to climb back through the brush to the roadway. Ten minutes later he returned carrying the red plastic can.

Once the tank was filled Dusty was able to nurse the engine back to life. The dense brush made it a difficult chore to ride the Honda back to the open roadway. Once there the two men inspected the vehicle for damage. Other than some scratches in the shiny red paint, there didn't seem to be much damage.

"I'll ride the Honda back home. I'd appreciate it if you would follow me home in case something happens to the engine. I don't know if they did anything to the machine that I can't see."

"Happy to escort you home, Dusty. It's getting dark and it wouldn't do for you to break down out here without help close by."

"Thanks Wyatt, and thanks for finding my Honda. I owe you. See you at the house." He gave a short wave and sped off toward the village with the VPSO a short distance behind on the bumpy track.

After seeing Dusty safely home Wyatt returned to the office to write the report, but changed his plan when he reached the side road leading to the lower end of the Newhalen River where it emptied into Lake Iliamna. He drove down the side road a short distance before turning off his headlights. This was the first time he had driven along this route. He stopped when he saw lights in a cabin a short distance ahead. Wyatt stopped the pickup and shut down the engine. Stepping out of the vehicle he heard the flowing river. Lifting his binoculars to his eyes he could see the cabin and the airplane pulled out of the water onto the beach. Wyatt assumed Buntz was about to take the plane off floats and put it on skis for the winter. Having seen what he came to see, Wyatt backed his truck to a place wide enough to turn around. Driving carefully, with no headlights, he moved away from the area of the cabin until he could illuminate the road ahead without Buntz seeing the lights.

In the office he finished writing the follow-up report on the missing ATV and was about to go into his private quarters when he remembered he should call for an aviation weather forecast for this coming weekend. Learning that the forecast was for clear and cold, he dialed the number for Linda Mason.

She sounded sleepy when she answered. "Hello."

"Hi, Linda, sorry if I woke you. I just got back to the office."

"It's OK. I was sitting in my chair reading and fell asleep. I need to get ready for bed anyway. It sounds as if you've been busy."

"A little. Tom spotted the missing Honda in the trees over by Newhalen and I took the owner out there to retrieve it. Every time I do an hour's work I have to do two hours of paperwork. That doesn't seem right, but that's the way it is. The reason I called is I checked the weather and it's supposed to be clear, a nice evening for flying. Which night is best for you, Friday or Saturday? Keep in mind I never really have a day off. If there is an emergency I have to respond. That's the way this job is."

"I understand, Wyatt. I'll tell you what: let's try for tomorrow and if it doesn't work out we can go on Saturday. I'm excited about going."

"That sounds good to me. I'll plan on tomorrow evening, unless there is a call I can't ignore." They both laughed.

It had been a long, full day and Wyatt was tired. He went to sleep quickly. He was sleeping soundly when his telephone rang at 6:02 a.m. "VPSO Earp," he answered in a sleepy voice.

It was Harry Porter the foreman at the new lodge. "Good morning, Trooper. I'm afraid I have some bad news to report. One of my men was found dead in his cabin this morning. We need you to come to the lodge right away."

"How did he die?" asked Wyatt.

"He wasn't shot or stabbed as near as we can tell. But there are drugs on his table. We, one of the other hired guys and me, made sure he was dead and got out of there to call you."

"Keep everyone out of the cabin if you can. I'll be right there. How do I get to the cabin?"

Porter gave directions to the rented cabin. Wyatt was out the door in less than five minutes, buckling his duty belt as he walked. He felt a little guilty answering the call without a shave, shower or brushing his teeth. That's the way it is in the bush.

Chapter Nine

Wyatt had no trouble finding cabin. Porter and another man were smoking cigarettes in front of the company truck owned by the lodge. It was cold, but Wyatt took the time to check for fresh tracks near the front of the cabin. There were only those of the two men who had entered the cabin and called him. He told them to wait while he confirmed the man inside was deceased. They returned to their truck while Wyatt climbed the steps and opened the front door. The light was on in the living room/dining room area.

The body was cold, dead for more than eight hours. The dead man was wearing a tee shirt and jeans. His boots were near the door and he was wearing moccasins as slippers. He had been seated in a reclining chair with the back in a tilt position. A packet of powder, a spoon, a candle, cotton swabs, and needles were on the table beside him. The room was warm, heated by a thermostat-controlled, oil-fired heater. Wyatt took pictures of the scene and checked for any sign of violence but found none. Once the initial procedures were completed he called Sergeant Turner to report what he had found and what he had done to secure the scene.

"You say there are needles and signs of heroin use at the scene?" asked Turner.

"Yes, I have the pictures. The death looks like a drug overdose to me. He has a lot of needle tracks on both arms and on his ankles. He has no socks on his feet, only slippers." Wyatt was being as complete with his information as possible. "I think we need to send the rest of this powder to the Anchorage crime lab to see if it matches the big package we found the other day." Wyatt had seen many of these scenes in his career and none of them had a happy ending. "I guess my question is, how do you want me to handle this case?

I can do the investigation; I've done a lot of them in my career, but with the similarities between the drugs and the packet of drugs we found earlier I thought you might want to see the scene personally."

There was a short pause before Turner furnished an answer. "I think you're right, I want to see the scene myself. I'll come over in the Cessna 185. I should be there in about two or three hours. You had better put evidence tape on the entry door to keep out the onlookers."

"I did that while I was there. I'll be waiting for you." Wyatt was anxious to get to the lodge where the two witnesses were working. He needed more information about them and about the victim.

Two hours and ten minutes later Sergeant Turner tapped on Wyatt's office door. Poking his head inside he said, "May I come in, Wyatt?"

"Yes, come in. I'm just killing time waiting for you." He stood to shake hands with the sergeant.

Closing the office door behind him, Turner turned to Wyatt. "We need to have a talk before we go out to the scene. I want to share some information with you that I think will be useful. You already know some of it, but the rest is confidential data from the feds. It's about the owner of the lodge they're building down by the lake." Turner was now reading the papers he had in his hands. "The owner is a guy named John Douglas. He has no criminal record in Alaska, but he has a lot of money to spend and no known source. We have suspected for a long time he's been involved in the drug trade. We've never connected him with any drug deals in this state, but he travels a lot and owns several companies in the lower 48. His largest interests are in several trucking companies with huge terminal facilities. The feds can't prove he's transporting drugs in his trucks, but he hauls freight from Mexico every day. His trucks get searched regularly, but no drugs have ever been found."

"So, the federal investigators think he's a major supplier?" inquired Wyatt.

"Have you ever heard of a South American drug lord by the name of Pablo Escobar?" asked Gene Turner.

"Sure, he's in jail now, but was once the largest drug supplier in the Western Hemisphere. Super rich; had his own zoo."

"That's the one. Only he wasn't just super rich, he was like the sixth wealthiest man on earth. He controlled the government in several South American countries and influenced the Mexican government. Escobar is credited with killing or, having killed, hundreds of people. It's said he would go to a business man and want to rent his warehouse. If the man refused he said he would kill the man and all his family or even everyone in his town. I'm told he had warehouses full of cash, wrapped in plastic and stacked on pallets. It was brought to him in semi-truck loads."

Turner paused a moment before continuing. "He experimented with ways to disguise drugs for shipment. He had his own research and development department. At one time they found a way to dissolve heroin and cocaine, put it inside snow-globes, you know, the ones you shake and see the snow falling on a country scene. They shipped the globes by the thousands to the U.S. without detection. Once here they had a way to evaporate the fluid and recover the drugs. Pretty ingenious if you ask me."

"With that much money he could afford to experiment. Smart guy," said Wyatt.

"That was nothing. I've heard he built those high-speed ocean racing boats called 'cigarette boats' and found a way to infuse the drugs into the fiberglass of the hulls. The Coast Guard would board the boats and not find anything. When they got to where they were going they, somehow, melted down the hulls and extracted the drugs from the melted plastic. He built mini submarines the same way. He was responsible for long tunnels under the border fence, hiring pilots to fly drugs across the border, and who knows all the ways he smuggled his drugs into the United States."

"You have to admire the man's ingenuity," commented Wyatt.

"You've got that right," said Turner.

"What does all this have to do with our man John Douglas?"

Turner nodded at Wyatt's understanding. "John Douglas owned several fleets of trucks many of which travelled in and out of Mexico. Somehow, we think, he was hired by Escobar to transport drugs across the border and all over the United States. The feds think that's how he made his money. He's a rich man now. But, knowing and proving are two different things. He has never been arrested or convicted of any felony crime. I think a lot of that has to do with his association with Escobar and the protection he provided."

"Do you think he's still connected with the drug cartel?"

"He is still operating his trucking companies in the lower 48 and is still alive which leads me to believe he is still in the drug business. That's only speculation, of course, but I don't think this leopard has changed his spots."

"I've been told he doesn't allow any drugs on the job site. I'll bet if you check out his trucking companies you will find his drivers are all as clean as a whistle. That's why I don't understand his employee dying of a drug overdose a mile from the lodge." Now Wyatt was speculating. "I guess we had better get out to the cabin and have the body removed."

"I have a body bag in the airplane. We can bag it when we are finished documenting the scene and I'll take it to the crime lab in Anchorage."

"OK, then, let's get at it. We'll need to go to the lake and interview the foreman and his hired hand about finding the body."

Turner walked to his Cessna at the back of the hangar to get the body bag and returned to the office. The two men exited on the front side of the hangar where the old pickup was parked. Five minutes later the two lawmen were at the cabin. The evidence tape on the door was still intact.

Wyatt cut the tape from the door and stepped aside for Turner to take his own set of pictures and videos. They entered the cabin and closed the door for privacy and to preserve heat. It took nearly three hours to inventory and to document the contents of the cabin. The two men inspected the body of the dead man for any unusual injuries, but none were found. They finally loaded the deceased into the body bag and carried it to the truck parked in front of the cabin.

"I guess I'm done here for now," said Gene Turner. "You might as well take me back to the airplane and help me load the body bag. I'll fly it directly to the coroner at headquarters in Anchorage. The autopsy report should be interesting."

"How would you like to take a ride a couple of miles on a side trip to look at the cabin where Rick Buntz lives and keeps his airplane? I think he'll probably be taking it off floats within the next few days."

"Sure, I'd like to see it. I just don't want to linger too long. I should get through Lake Clark Pass before dark, if I can. Once through the Pass I can get to Anchorage and back to Soldotna without any trouble, but I just don't like flying through the Pass in the dark. I've done it, but didn't like it."

"I understand, Gene. I've done it too and feel the same way," Wyatt said in agreement with Turner.

Thirty minutes later the two men were loading the body bag into the Cessna 185. Gene pulled off the engine cover and shook the hand of the VPSO. "See you later, Wyatt. I'll be calling you."

Wyatt stood on the ramp and watched the airplane taxi to the end of the runway and take off, making a turn to the east and toward Lake Clark Pass. He returned to his little office and was greeted with a fresh cup of coffee as he passed Maggie's desk.

"No calls, Wyatt," she said as he walked toward his office door.

He waved a hand in acknowledgement and sipped the coffee as he walked. Inside the office he placed all his notes and camera on the desk before sitting in his office chair. Leaning back to relax, he continued sipping his coffee until it was gone, then turned to his office tasks. Once done with the reports he looked at his wristwatch. He still had enough time to return to the lodge site to interview the two men who had found the body this morning. He slipped into his coat and walked to the truck once again.

Harry Porter came out of the building as Wyatt drove to the front steps. He waved to the VPSO to come into the main building where the hired man was working.

"This won't take long," said Wyatt as he crossed the room. "Can we sit where I can take notes?" The three men went into the dining area where a large wooden table was arranged with eight chairs and a temporary overhead light. Wyatt sat, took his notebook from his pocket, and motioned for the other two men to be seated.

"Would you like something to drink?" asked Porter.

"No thanks, I just have a few questions and I'll be on my way. I have been at the scene all afternoon and I need to get back to my office. Trooper Sergeant Turner flew out to help me with the investigation. We sent the body with him to Anchorage for an autopsy. I'll try to let you know the details when I receive them."

"I appreciate that. I've been on the phone with John, the owner of the lodge, and he has asked to be kept advised of the details. How long do you think it will take to get the results?"

"If there are no complications I should have a report by the middle of next week. Do you have his employee file handy? I will need to get his information and next of kin for notification."

"Certainly, I'll get it for you." Porter left the room through the kitchen.

Wyatt turned his attention to the worker seated across the table from him. "Tell me your name again, will you?"

"Yeah, Don Zapo," answered the worker.

"Show me your driver's license or some form of ID, will you?"

"Sure, I got a Colorado license."

"Fine, I just need to get your information from the card. How long have you been in Alaska?"

"Couple o' years," said Zapo.

"You should get an Alaska driver's license if you're going to operate the company vehicles. I'm not citing you for it. But, the next time you go to town, stop by the DMV and get a new license." Wyatt finished writing the information in his notebook and gave the Colorado license back to Zapo.

"I'll get it done, sir," said the worker as his boss reentered the room.

"Here's the file you wanted. I can make a copy of it for you if you like."

"Thanks," said Wyatt, "I would appreciate it. I need the information for the report. Can you tell me what kind of worker he was?"

"He wasn't a ball of fire, but worked hard and did good carpentry work. Stayed to himself most of the time. He was a real craftsman when it came to fitting the logs together. He fit all the logs in these walls. You can see what a beautiful job he did. Not many men can do that kind of thing these days."

"Did he miss a lot of work?"

"No, almost never; he never went to town. He liked to work late here at the lodge. I honestly didn't know he was into drugs. I have orders to fire anyone caught using any kind of drugs at the site."

The interview lasted another few minutes when Wyatt asked Porter to make him a copy of the employee's file.

Back in his office, Wyatt took off his heavy coat and duty belt, pulled off his boots, and went to the kitchen area where he opened a can of chili to heat for dinner. He found some crackers and a glass of milk and was about to sit down to the not-so-wholesome dinner when the telephone rang. It was Linda Mason. The two talked for almost an hour and agreed both parties were looking forward to the trip to King Salmon tomorrow afternoon. When the conversation ended Wyatt found it necessary to re-heat the chili.

Chapter Ten

Friday began as a quiet day. The weather was cold and clear. The wind was not strong, only about 15 to 20 miles per hour, making it seem much colder than the 8 degrees Fahrenheit indicated on the thermometer outside the air taxi office window. No calls had been reported to him this morning giving him a little time to do some cleanup and rearranging in the small office. He was gathering the soiled laundry to be done when the phone rang.

"VPSO Earp," Wyatt answered.

"Good morning, Wyatt. Are you busy today?" It was Wildlife Trooper Lonnie Davis.

"Not at the moment. What's going on?"

"I just had a report of a big brown bear wandering around near Newhalen. I think I would like some backup with another shotgun if I have to shoot it. Several families live in the area and some of their kids are walking to school. The bear has been seen in the area for several days, but this morning he killed some dogs down there."

"Give me time to pull on my boots and I'll meet you at the schoolhouse. I'm not that familiar with that area, so you can lead the way and I'll follow."

"I'll be waiting at the school."

Wyatt pulled on his boots and tied the laces before putting on his heavy-duty belt. He found the shotgun and checked to make sure it was loaded and took an extra box of shells from a shelf. Wyatt stopped to tell Maggie where he was going as he walked to the truck. The engine block heater had been plugged in all night enabling it to start without any difficulty. He reached the school where Davis was parked and stopped with his driver side window next to Lonnie Davis.

"Have you heard anything more?" asked Wyatt.

"No, but the folks down by the lake are really spooked. They're used to seeing bears, so this one must be a nasty fella. I know the family who reported it and I'll stop to ask directions. The last report I had was that he was still near the dog yard where he killed some dogs. I don't know how many. In any case, the parents are afraid to let the kids go to school. Follow me down to Newhalen."

"I'll be right behind you."

Lonnie Davis rolled up his window and drove away in the direction of the big lake. When he came to a long driveway with a mailbox at the end, he signaled a turn and drove to a cabin at the other end of the drive. Wyatt waited in his truck while Lonnie went to the cabin and knocked. A Native man wearing a heavy coat and carrying a rifle answered the door. Lonnie conversed with the man a few minutes, convincing him to return to the home and wait. Once the man was back inside the cabin he came back to Wyatt's truck.

"He says the bear is still at the dog yard and makes threatening charges toward anyone getting near. It's the next drive toward the village. Follow me and see if we can get a shot at the brute before he runs into the bush. Stick close."

"I'm with you Lonnie. Let's go."

Lonnie returned to his truck, turning it around to drive back to the main road. A quarter mile down the road he turned right again and drove slowly up the drive until they could see a large house with several outbuildings. Lonnie stopped and quietly exited his truck. Wyatt followed suit, taking his shotgun in hand as he stepped out of his own truck.

"Stay behind me. I'll try to stay behind cover until we spot the bear. Usually they try to run for cover in the brush and trees, but this guy may try to defend his kill. I'll do the shooting, but if he doesn't go down right away step out and fire. Do you have slugs or buckshot in the chamber?"

"The first one is a sabot round the next two are 00 buck," said Wyatt.

Lonnie nodded and began to move toward the back of the big house. The men made their way slowly and cautiously to the back yard. A garage was on the right with a pole barn shed to the rear blocking the view of the dog yard behind the shed. As quietly as possible, the two men walked past the garage to the shed. Boats, nets and all manner of commercial fishing gear were stored inside the big shed. It was impossible to get to the back wall where they could see through the boards to view the dog yard behind. The Wildlife Trooper shrugged his shoulders and began making his way around the left end of the gear shed.

As they moved to the back of the building they could see the chain link fence surrounding the dog yard. Keeping their backs tight to the end wall they made their way to the back of the structure. Lonnie peeked carefully around the wall to view the enclosure. He saw seven dog houses in the pen. Five dead dogs lay in the yard, chained to the tether in front of each one's house. The bear had torn the metal fencing from the posts in order to enter the compound. He was in the yard, eating on one of the carcasses. The bear itself was thin, strange for this late in the salmon season. He should have weighed almost twice this much by now. Obviously, he was sick or injured and unable to feed normally.

"We need to try to get closer before we shoot. We'll have to move quickly across the open ground and shoot when he charges. Hopefully we can get him down inside the dog pen. Are you ready?" Lonnie waited for an answer from Wyatt.

Wyatt nodded as he pulled two more cartridges from his pocket and held them in his left hand for quick reloading. It was cold and three inches of snow covered the ground making the walk nearly silent. They were almost half way to the fence wire when the bear heard them. Instantly he sprang to life. When he heard the men he had been eating on one of the dogs. The bear jumped to his feet and spun around to face the threat. He stood on his hind legs and bellowed. Dropping to all fours he faced the intruders, bouncing on his front paws several times, clapping his jaws loudly.

The two officers continued toward the fence. When they were about 100 feet apart the bear charged, but was confused by the fence wire and had to change direction in order to get outside the fenced yard through the hole he had created to get inside. Lonnie stopped and held out a hand to stop Wyatt. It was amazing at the speed at which the bear made it through the fencing to charge the men. Lonnie pulled his Remington shotgun to his shoulder and fired a shot striking the bear in the chest. Immediately he jacked another round into the shotgun and fired again. The bear was hit once again in the chest, but did not slow. Lonnie inserted another shell in the chamber and fired the third time.

Wyatt now stepped to one side to fire his sabot round into the left shoulder of the huge bear. Each of the officers fired one more time at point blank range, Lonnie's round striking the bear in the face and Wyatt's round hitting the chest behind the shoulder. The bear staggered, but continued his charge. He struck Lonnie with a huge paw and five-inch claws just as he fired another shot into the face of the bear. Lonnie was thrown backward several feet. Wyatt was now beside the bear and fired three quick shots into the chest of the bleeding bear. With the last shot the bear collapsed and fell to the ground. Wyatt shot one more time placing the muzzle of his shotgun near the ear of the big grizzly, making sure it was dead.

Wyatt rushed to where Lonnie lay bleeding on the ground, unconscious. Luckily Lonnie had been wearing his heavy coat and ballistic vest, but the bear had done a great deal of damage in spite of it all. He pulled his cell phone from his pocket and called Maggie.

"Lake Air Taxi," she answered.

"Maggie, it's Wyatt, I need medical help right now. Lonnie was attacked by a big brown bear and is bleeding badly. I'll try to stop the bleeding, but I am going to need help right away. We're about a half mile from the dock at Newhalen, on the main road. When they see a mailbox with "Joki" painted on it, turn right at the next driveway. Lonnie is behind the main house. The bear is dead."

"Oh, Wyatt, that's awful. I'll get the medics on the way right now." The town had no doctor, but a Physician's Assistant and EMT personnel were available. She knew she would need to tell Tom to stand by for a medevac.

Wyatt searched his pockets for anything he could use to stop the bleeding on Lonnie's left shoulder and upper arm. The tear in the left shoulder was gushing like an arterial injury. In his jacket pocket he found a handkerchief and a pair of cotton gloves. There was no real way to tie a tourniquet on the shoulder to stop the bleeding so he opted for pressure. He folded the handkerchief to about a four-inch square and placed it on the wound. He then took one of the cotton gloves and placed it on the handkerchief. Using the heel of his left hand on the glove, the bleeding seemed to slow though it didn't stop completely.

With his right hand he covered the deep wound in the left arm with the remaining glove to hold tight until the medics arrived. It seemed like forever before they arrived. The PA drove his own SUV and the EMTs arrived right behind him in an old surplus ambulance. The PA dropped a canvas bag in the snow next to Lonnie's head.

"OK, keep pressure on the arm and let me look at the shoulder wound." The PA's name was Bill Stafford, but he and Wyatt had never met before. He carefully took the shoulder compress away to see the wound and immediately the gash began to spurt blood again. "Hold it tight again. I need to get some gauze pads from my bag.

Wyatt complied just as the two medics arrived on the scene. One of the medics opened his bag and moved Wyatt's hand from the arm wound. The three men worked feverishly for several minutes stopping the flow of blood as best they could. Finally, PA Stafford told one of the EMTs to get the ambulance. He said he would do his best to plug the bleeding wound, but the Wildlife Trooper was going to need surgery. Lonnie moaned a little, but was still unconscious.

Wyatt called Maggie. "Maggie, is Tom available to transport Lonnie to the hospital in Anchorage?"

"Yes, Wyatt, he's here waiting to see if you needed him."

"Tell him to warm up the plane. We'll be there in about 15 minutes. I'll call Sergeant Turner in Soldotna and he can make arrangements for an ambulance to meet him at the airport when they arrive. I'll let you know which airport and which hospital as soon as I know." Wyatt paused and said, "The PA just said he and one medic would go with him and tend to his medical needs on the trip."

"Tom just said he would take the twin. It's faster. I'll see you in a few minutes."

Tom and Maggie had stepped up when they were needed. Living in a small town has its benefits.

Wyatt followed the old ambulance back to the Iliamna Airport where they loaded Lonnie in the twin engine airplane. Tom had already started the engines. The stretcher was loaded in the rear of the cabin where two rows of seats had been removed.

"Do you want to ride along, Wyatt?" asked Tom before closing the rear door.

Wyatt just shook his head and motioned for him to go. He stood on the concrete apron and watched as the airplane rolled down the runway and lifted off. Returning to his office he called Gene Turner to tell him what had happened. Turner said he would have the colonel in Anchorage make the arrangements for Lonnie's arrival.

"I've got a dead bear in the complainant's back yard, Gene. What do you think I should do with it?"

"I'll call the State Fish and Game office in King Salmon and have them send someone out to skin it out and get rid of it. They should be there in a couple of hours."

Wyatt went to the front office to speak with Maggie. "Would you have a cup of coffee handy?" he asked.

"Sure do," she said as she reached for the pot. "You've had a busy morning."

"I was a cop for twenty years in Fairbanks and never had to shoot a grizzly. I'm still a little jumpy. I have to go back out to the scene and meet with the homeowner." He took a long sip of the coffee, "But I'm finishing this first." He held the coffee cup up high and returned to his office.

Chapter Eleven

In the office he set his coffee cup on the desk and took his cell phone from his pocket to dial Linda Mason. She was on her lunch hour when he called. "Well," said Wyatt, "Do you still want to go to dinner tonight?"

"Oh, yes, I have been looking forward to it all day. Should I meet you there at the office after work?"

"Yes, I'd like that. I have a lot of paperwork to get done this afternoon. And I have to go back out to Newhalen to talk with a homeowner about his complaint. Lonnie and I were there earlier and had to shoot a brown bear. The bear charged and slapped Lonnie with a huge paw. We medevacked him to Anchorage and he was still unconscious when we put him on the airplane."

"Is Lonnie going to be all right?" asked the school teacher.

"I think so, but he'll be off work for a while." Wyatt said goodbye and reached for his coat, now badly stained in blood, both from the bear and from Lonnie. He decided to wear it anyway and wash it when he returned to the office.

Back at the house where the bear was shot Wyatt tapped on the door. The owner had not stepped outside since he and Lonnie had arrived earlier. Wyatt had never met the man and thought it strange he never came out of the house during or after the shooting of the bear. The man didn't come out of the house after the bear was shot or while the medics were there. Wyatt thought he should ask about that behavior.

Wyatt rapped on the door for the third time before an elderly Native woman answered. "You the one who shot the bear what et our dogs?" she asked.

"Yes," said Wyatt. "I wonder if I could speak with you and your husband a few minutes, just to get information for my report."

"You take boots off and come inside. I call Art," she said stepping back inside to allow Wyatt through the doorway. She closed the door behind him and he kneeled down to untie his leather boots. He noted there was dried blood on them.

"My name is Nola; my husband is Art. He called the trooper." She turned to face a hallway and shouted, "Art, someone here to see you."

Art Swan was a short, muscular man appearing to be near 70 years old. He came from the direction of the hallway. "You the one with the trooper and shot the bear?" he asked.

"Yes, sir," remarked Wyatt. "I'm the VPSO and I need some information for my report. Do you have time to answer some questions for me?"

"Yes," was his short answer.

"Can we sit at the table?" asked Wyatt.

Swan turned to his wife, "Make some coffee," he said. "Follow me."

Wyatt followed the pair into the immaculate kitchen. The living room had been neat and very clean, but the kitchen was a showplace. There was not a crumb or drop of grease to be seen anywhere. "You have a beautiful place here, Mr. Swan."

"Nola likes to keep it neat."

Wyatt took a seat at the table and placed his notebook in front of him. "Have you been out to check on your dogs yet?"

"No, not yet. I looked out the back window and I see two dogs looking out of their houses. The rest must have been killed. That damn bear was a mean one."

"Fish and Game is coming to skin the bear and remove it from your property. They should be here in a couple of hours. I'll show them where the carcass is and help them get it out of here. I'm really sorry about your dogs, Mr. Swan."

"I'll go out and skin the bear for those biologists. They aren't very good at it. I am a guide for 50 years and I know how to do it. The meat ain't no good to eat, so unless they want it to study, I'll take it to the dump."

"Thank you, Art. That will be helpful." Wyatt didn't know what the Fish and Game officers wanted to do with the bear, but he thought having the bear skinned would save a lot of time. The skull and stomach will still be there if they want something to study. "Now, sir, may I see your driver's license to get some information for my report?"

"Nola, get my wallet," barked Art. She brought the wallet from the hallway area and placed it on the table where Art took out the license and handed it to the VPSO.

Wyatt made notes of numbers and dates before handing the license back to the fisherman. "Have you had trouble with bears in the past?"

"Sometimes, this time of year," said Art, while putting his wallet back in order. "They come by my place when they leave the river. Once in a while an older bear or a cub will come to the dog yard to get free food. This is the first time they broke into my dog yard. They usually just get in the shed for dog food."

Nola Swan set a cup of black coffee in front of Wyatt. "Drink it, it's good on a cold day," she said before returning to the pot for another cup for Art.

Wyatt sipped the strong coffee and visited with Art about his fishing season. When his coffee was finished he said, "Thank you, Mrs. Swan. The coffee was very good. I have to get back to the office now and wait for the biologists. I appreciate your offering to skin the bear, Art. It will save some time for them. I'll bring them to your place when they arrive and we will load the meat carcass and hide. I really don't know what they want to do with it." He returned to the tiled entry to retie his boots.

He had been in his office for an hour when the two biologists came in. Wyatt didn't wait for conversation but showed them to his truck to drive them to the Swan residence. On the drive they introduced themselves and asked about the incident. They admitted it was a pretty clear-cut case of a marauding bear taking advantage of free food in the dog yard.

When they arrived at the Swan home Wyatt turned his truck around and backed to the carcass. The hide had been removed and folded into a neat, but large bundle and bound with a rope. The biologists studied the bear for injuries, other than those caused by the many shotgun wounds, and checked his mouth to determine the age of the bear. He was old. They decided to take the skull and hide and dispose of the rest of the animal at the local land fill where other bears would likely scavenge the meat. Neither Art nor Nola came out of the house while the trio was there. Wyatt drove to the land fill to dump the bear carcass and on to the hangar where the biologists loaded the hide and skull into the Cessna 185 they had used. He returned his truck to the front of the hangar and plugged into the power to keep the engine oil warm, went inside to his office, saying hello to Maggie as he passed her desk.

By the time he finished the paperwork and called to check on the condition of Trooper Lonnie Davis, it was time to get ready for his date with Linda Mason. While on the phone with Turner he learned Lonnie had regained consciousness and had been taken to surgery to repair his wounds. A broken collar bone had punctured his artery causing the extensive bleeding from the shoulder. The gash in his shoulder had allowed the blood to exit the body. There was damage to the muscles and tendons in his shoulder as well. Lonnie would be off work for several months.

Wyatt finished his office chores and began to get ready for an evening off. He put his bloody coat in the washer along with his bloody shirt and jeans. He showered, shaved and put on clean jeans and a Pendleton shirt before going to the hangar to push the Cessna 206 outside and cover the engine. Linda arrived at the front of the air taxi office as he reentered the office. The temperature was dropping, but not severely. It was a clear and starry evening, a good night to fly.

Wyatt waited in the outer office, near Maggie's desk for Linda to enter. "Are you ready to go flying?" he asked as she entered.

"I'm ready." She and Maggie had been acquainted for a long time. "Hi, Maggie," she said over her shoulder as she walked by the desk.

Wyatt led her out through the hangar bay to a man-door leading to the flight ramp. He helped Linda get settled into the front passenger seat before going to the front of the plane to remove the engine cover which he stowed in the back seat of the Cessna before climbing into the pilot seat to start the engine. He let the engine idle a few minutes and used the time to fit a headset to his passenger. "Your mike is voice operated, so you don't have to push any buttons, just don't say anything while I'm on the com radio talking with someone. Are you set to go?"

"Yes, I am. This is so exciting." Linda had flown to King Salmon many times in the past, but this time was special. "Where are we going to eat?"

"Do you prefer the hotel or the big restaurant down the street?" he asked.

"I like the restaurant, but I'm hungry and the hotel dining room is more suitable for a first date, don't you think?"

"The hotel it is, then." They flew down the Kvichak River. It was dark, but with the snow on the ground and the half-moon shining, it was a scenic flight. Soon the lights of the King Salmon Airport came into view and Wyatt began his landing procedure.

In the transient parking area, Wyatt covered the engine and the two walked to the terminal where he called a taxi cab to take them to the hotel restaurant. Unlike the normal King Salmon winter evening there was little wind and the fifteen-degree temperature seemed balmy.

During dinner Linda told of her childhood and coming to teach school in Iliamna. Wyatt told of his days in Naknek and his college days as well as a short review of his 20-year career as a Fairbanks policeman. The prime rib dinner was excellent and the evening went quickly.

"I had thought about calling my dad to join us, but I wanted to spend our first date together, alone, getting to know each other. I'll have you meet Dad another time."

"Oh, Wyatt, this has been a perfect evening. It didn't seem fair, though."

"Why do you say that, Linda?"

"I was able to have a glass of wine with dinner, but you're flying and couldn't."

"Don't worry, I didn't miss it. Besides you're intoxicating enough. I've had a wonderful time. Is there anything you want to do while we're here in town?"

"No, I can't think of anything. I suppose we should be thinking of going back, but I hate for the evening to end. I really like you, Wyatt, and this has been a special evening for me. I don't date often. Thank you." Linda wiped her lips with her napkin, hoping she wasn't too forward.

"I've only known you a few days and I feel closer to you than to any woman since my mother. I have dated, but never found anyone I wanted to spend much time with, until now. We've only known each other a short time, but you're already special to me. I hope we can do this again—soon." Wyatt was unaccustomed to speaking like this to anyone, let alone a woman he had only known a few days. It just seemed right. He motioned for the waitress to come with the check, paid her, and asked her to call a cab to take them back to the airport.

The flight back to Iliamna was as enthralling as the trip over. The countryside was beautiful in the moonlight. The landing was smooth and he found Tom waiting at the hangar to help put the Cessna away for the night.

"You go ahead with Tom," said Linda. I'll find my own way home. Call me later." She waved to him as he tossed the engine cover over the warm engine and waited for the big hangar door to open.

"Maggie has some kind of message for you. I don't know what it is. She just asked me to tell you. How was your date?" Tom chatted as they moved the plane into its place in the hangar bay.

"It's been a long day," said Wyatt. "I hope I don't have to go out on a call tonight."

In the front office Maggie handed Wyatt a pink sticky note. "N8816A was here on skis this afternoon."
Wyatt read the note and turned to Maggie, "Is this all the message?"

"Yes, I think he just wants you to call him."

Wyatt looked at the time. "It's late to call tonight, but I'll do it first thing in the morning. Thanks for the help with the plane, Tom. See you folks tomorrow. I'm tired."

"Have you heard how Lonnie is doing?" Maggie called after him as he walked toward the door.

Wyatt stopped and turned. "Yes. He has a broken collar bone and torn muscles and tendons in his left shoulder. He had surgery and is doing well, but will be off work for a while."

"I saw the way he was bleeding, Wyatt. He was lucky you were there, first, to shoot the bear, and second to slow the blood loss. If you hadn't acted quickly he wouldn't have made it. Lonnie owes you his life.

Good job, Wyatt." Tom was being honest in his assessment and admired the way Wyatt had taken control of the situation which saved the life of Trooper Davis.

"Thanks again, Tom. I'm tired and I'm going to bed. See you tomorrow. I'll take care of that call in the morning. Good night."

Chapter Twelve

Wyatt didn't realize it had snowed during the night until he stepped out into the outer office. Through the front window he saw six inches of new snow on his truck. The sun was shining making the world a white, clean, pleasant place. A thermometer outside the window read 25 degrees making it a good day to be out of doors.

He turned to Maggie saying, "How about some of your coffee? I was going to fly up to Lake Clark this morning, but without skis on the Cub I don't think I'll try it."

Maggie handed him a steaming cup of fresh brewed coffee, "Here you go, Wyatt." He took the cup.

"Tom will be flying up to Port Alsworth sometime around noon if you want to ride along," said Maggie. "I know he would like your company on the trip."

"I have some phone calls to make this morning, but I may just take you up on the offer. I'll let you know in a short while."

There was an Anchorage newspaper on the counter and Wyatt read the front page while sipping his coffee. When he had finished his coffee, he set the cup on the end of the counter. "I guess I had better start earning my paycheck," he said, turning toward his own office.

"I'll let you know as soon as Tom gives me a time on his Port Alsworth flight," Maggie announced as he walked away.

Back in the little office he realized he had not taken his heavy coat out of the clothes dryer. He walked into the small living area behind the office and pulled the heavy coat from the machine. Seeing how wrinkled it was he stuffed it back in the dryer and turned it on for a ten-minute fluff, taking out the wrinkles.

Hanging the coat on a sturdy hangar, he went to his desk and began to make his morning telephone calls. His first call was to Captain Griffin.

"Good morning, Captain," Wyatt said in a cheerful voice.

"Hey, Wyatt, good to hear from you. Turner called to tell me about your bear encounter. Everyone I've talked with about the incident says you saved Lonnie's life. I'll see there is a citation letter in your file. I checked with the hospital this morning and they told me he's out of the woods now, thanks to you, and will be going home in a couple of days."

"I'm glad to hear that, Griff. Lonnie put two shots in the bear's face and one in the chest while he charged. He's a cool guy. I enjoy working with him."

"I don't know how soon he'll be able to come back to work. What else is on your mind this morning?"

"There is six inches of new snow on the ground this morning and I realized I don't have skis for the Cub. Do you think you could find a pair somewhere and send them out here? I may have to go somewhere that isn't plowed."

"I'll check with the Anchorage hangar and let you know if there is a set available. If there is, I'll send them to you on the first flight headed your way. Have a local mechanic install them and pay them with a voucher. Anything else?"

"Not right now, Cap." Wyatt hung up the phone and leaned back in his desk chair thinking about calling Leon MacKammon but decided to ride with Tom when he flew to Port Alsworth. He was about to call Gene Turner when Maggie tapped on his door.

"Tom will be making two stops on Lake Clark if you want to ride along. He'll be leaving in fifteen minutes."

"I'll be ready," replied Wyatt. He looked at the clock. Linda was at home today and should be near the phone.

She answered on the first ring. "Hello," said her cheerful voice.

"Hi, are you missing me yet?" Wyatt asked jokingly.

"Of course, after all it's been nearly twelve hours since I've seen you."

"I've been doing trooper stuff all morning. I'm going up to Port Alsworth with Tom in a few minutes. I won't be there long, though."

"Good, I was thinking about dinner tonight. Would you let me cook some moose steaks and have biscuits and moose meat gravy? I baked a cake this morning."

"If I keep seeing you I'll have to go on a diet." They both laughed. "I'll be there. What time should I show up?"

"Oh, around six I think. We could watch a movie after dinner, just to spend a little quiet time, together," she said pensively.

"That sounds wonderful. I'll see you around six. I have to go out to meet Tom right now. Bye."

Wyatt heard the 206 taxi up to the hangar door. He pulled his coat on as he walked. Tom had left the engine idling as he climbed out of the cockpit to get the mail sacks he was taking to his two stops on Lake Clark. Clouds were gathering again, moving up the valley toward Lake Clark.

"We had better get moving before the weather closes in. Climb in and buckle up." Tom spoke as he walked to the airplane with a mail pouch in each hand.

It was snowing lightly when they landed at Port Alsworth. Wyatt said he was going to the little burger shop to talk with Leon. Tom had his own business to mind.

Wyatt brushed the light dusting of snow from his shoulders as he opened the door, stamping the snow from his boots before entering. "Hello, Mr. MacKammon," he said as he entered to see one other customer in the dining area.

"Howdy, Trooper. Coffee?" asked the cook.

"Yes, please. I just stopped to say hello. I'm riding with Tom again today."

The customer apparently didn't want to stay while the VPSO was there and made his exit, leaving half a cup of hot coffee on the table.

Wyatt watched him leave before saying anything to Leon. "Maggie gave me a note she said was a message from you. You said that Super Cub had been here again?"

"Yeah, he met two guys from the lodge up by the Tanalian River. They only talked about a minute and the pilot handed something to one of the men. The other man gave the pilot something, I assume it was cash, and they climbed into their truck and drove off. The pilot climbed into his plane and took off. Looked like a drug deal to me." Leon seemed more friendly today, looking Wyatt in the eyes when he talked.

"Same pilot as before?"

"Yup, and same customers," stated Leon.

"Anything else?" asked Wyatt.

"Nope."

"Thanks, Leon, I'll see what I can find out and do about all this. How much for the coffee?"

"On the house," Leon said as he turned his attention back to the open newspaper on the counter.

"Thank, Leon, I'll be in touch. Gotta go. Tom is bucking weather this trip." Wyatt spoke as he reached the door and stepped out into the increasing snow to walk back to the airplane where Tom was waiting.

"Climb in; I need to make a stop at Hornberger's Lodge across the lake if I can see to land. This snow is beginning to affect visibility across the lake." He pulled the engine cover off and shoved it into the back seat before climbing into the left front seat.

Visibility was better than expected as they crossed the shoreline on the west side of the lake. Mrs. Hornberger was waiting on a four-wheel ATV. Tom carried the mail pouch to the ATV and spoke a few words to the lady. He climbed back into the seat and buckled up. The runway is dirt and runs uphill. Tom taxied to the top of the hill, revved the engine and released the brakes. The wheels left the ground near where the lady was sitting at the side on her ATV.

"Let's go home, Wyatt. This looks like it's going to get worse and I want to spend the night at home, not out here in a cabin on the beach."

Back at the hangar Wyatt helped Tom push the airplane inside before returning to his office to call Gene Turner. Sergeant Turner answered his phone, even though it was Saturday.

"Don't you ever take a day off?" asked Wyatt.

"Christmas Day. What can I do for you today?"

"I was just up at Lake Clark to take a report from an informant. He says he saw that Super Cub I checked on last week and it looked like a drug deal going down. The owner lives here in Iliamna, actually down by Newhalen, and he is my number one choice for ownership of the packet of heroin I turned over to you. I'm not exactly sure how to go about investigating this report. This area is pretty small and I'm pretty visible. I can't do anything covertly here. I'm going to need some help on this one."

"Hmmm, let me talk to my Captain and I'll see what I can come up with. It may take me a couple of days, but I'll figure out something." Turner had a couple of ideas, but didn't want to commit to anything before checking with the commander. "By the way, I talked to Lonnie this morning. He says he's doing pretty well, considering, and will be released next week. He is going to need some healing time and a lot of physical therapy. He told me he was going to call you in a few days, but wanted me to thank you for what you did for him. He said his last thought, before the bear slapped him, was that he was going to die. He said he remembers you shooting, but that was all. You should get a medal for that one, Wyatt."

"Just put ten bucks on my next paycheck and we'll call it square." Wyatt didn't consider himself a hero, just doing his job. "I think I'm going to take the rest of the day off, if the citizens will let me."

"You deserve it, Wyatt. I'll get back to you on this other matter."
Wyatt felt hungry and went into the small kitchen area to get a bowl of cold cereal and milk. He was sitting at his desk munching his Cheerios when the phone rang. It was Harry Porter calling from the new lodge.

"I just had a call from my boss. He said he'll be back in town on Monday afternoon. He wants to meet with you. Will you be available on Monday?"

"I should be. It depends on how many calls I get. If this snow continues at this rate I should have plenty of time."

"I'll try to set a time for his meeting. It depends on what time he can get a flight from Anchorage. I'll be talking with him when he gets a flight schedule. He wants to thank you for taking care of our hired man the other day. He won't stand for any drug use by the crew. He doesn't want the lodge to have that kind of reputation," Harry explained before ending the call.

Wyatt finished his reports and washed his cereal bowl. It was time for him to shower and change clothes before going to dinner at Linda Mason's house.

Chapter Thirteen

Monday morning Wyatt was up and dressed early. Maggie was not in her office yet. Looking outside there was more than a foot of snow that had fallen during the weekend, making the walk to the office of Lake Air Taxi difficult. Inside an office closet he found a shovel and began to scoop a trail from the parking area in front of the office to the steps. After shoveling a path to his truck and sweeping off the snow, he started the engine to warm the truck and defrost the windows. Back inside he found what was needed to brew the morning coffee. It had just finished brewing when Maggie and Tom came into the office.

"Thanks for shoveling the parking lot and walk, Wyatt. I thought I was in for a lot of work this morning."

"And even better, you made coffee," said Maggie. "I guess I won't have to raise your rent after all," she giggled.

"I see the state boys are out plowing the runway. It looks like you will have to work today after all, Tom." Wyatt made his comments while pouring coffee for the two new arrivals.

"I hire a fellow to plow the parking lot and clean out in front of the hangar doors. He should be coming by here soon. He does a nice job and saves me a lot of shoveling. I'll have you move your pick-up when he gets here. How was your weekend?" asked Tom.

"Quiet. I guess the snow had a lot to do with that. Linda fed me dinner Saturday night and I slept like a log when I got back here. Yesterday I finished some reports and did my domestic chores. It felt good to take a day off. As soon as the office in Soldotna opens I'll have to get busy, though." It had snowed most of the day on Sunday giving Wyatt a reason to stay inside to read and relax.

"Tom," Maggie addresses her husband, "Go out to the car and get the tray of cinnamon rolls on the front seat. They're still warm and I'll bet Wyatt hasn't had breakfast yet."

Tom returned to the office with a large plastic tray piled high with huge, aromatic rolls. He placed the tray on the tall counter. "Help yourself, Wyatt. You earned a treat this morning."

"They sure smell good," he replied. I'll take one back to my office with me. Thanks." The lawman relaxed while he finished his coffee and ate the tasty treat. When done, he went to the sink in his living area to wash the stickiness off his fingers before beginning his day. His first task was to call Gene Turner. He was about to make the call when the phone on his desk rang loudly.

"VPSO Earp," he answered.

"Wyatt, its Gene Turner. I think I may have a way to help your investigation into the drug trafficking."

"Good, what's your plan?"

"I have an undercover officer in Fairbanks who builds log cabins when he's off duty. I talked to him and he said he's willing to help."

"What did you have in mind, Gene?" asked Wyatt.

"That body I helped you process, you remember, he was a log home builder. The lodge owner will need someone to replace him on the work crew. If we can get him hired on to replace the dead worker it would give us an inside ear to what is happening down there at the lodge. And if nothing is going on there he can fit in the community and see if he can learn anything about the outside drug connection. What do you think?" asked Turner, "Will it work?"

"It should, at least we'll have someone working in town not known to the locals. I'm not sure how we can get him hired, though."

"If we send him out there, do you think you can get him introduced to the foreman at the job site?"

"I think so," said Wyatt. "John Douglas, the lodge owner will be back in Iliamna today. He's supposed to come to my office for a meeting. If Porter, the foreman, comes with him I'll try to plant a seed with him."

"Just be careful how you go about it. This Douglas guy is cagey, according to the federal narcs."

"Speaking of cagey, have you been able to learn any more about this Rick Buntz guy?" Wyatt inquired.

"No, but if we can get our man hired he can nose around and possibly make a buy from this Buntz character."

"Tom Dempsey, who owns Lake Air Taxi, knows the foreman at the lodge. I might be able to get him to approach Harry Porter about your man. I'll ask him if he is willing to do this for us.

"According to the federal agents, this John Douglas fella, is very particular about having any drugs around him. All that tells me is that this Buntz doesn't work for Douglas. We can try to find out who his suppliers are and bust him by doing a buy from him. It's worth a try." Gene Turner knew making long range plans on an arrest seldom worked. It was going to be up to the officers on the scene to judge when the time was right.

"I'll call you after I meet with Douglas."

"Do that, Wyatt. This is dangerous business. Try to keep from getting killed. I hate it when that happens."

"Me, too, Gene, me too."

After his phone call Wyatt walked from his office to the desk where Maggie was seated, putting the finishing touches on a billing for one of the clients. "Are there any of those cinnamon rolls left?" he asked.

"Just one...on the table over there. Someone had better eat it before it gets stale."

Wyatt found the roll and took a huge bite, then had to chew a while before continuing with his conversation. "When Tom comes back into the office, ask him to come see me," as he walked back to his office, carrying what was left of the sweet roll. An hour later Tom knocked on the door.

"Come on in, Tom. I have a matter I want to discuss with you."

Tom closed the door behind him. "What can I do for you, Wyatt?"

"You know about that packet of heroin found near the school. I have an idea I want to try, but I need a little help from you. This is strictly off the record. You can't tell anyone about what I'm planning. Can you keep a secret?"

"You know I can, Wyatt. I've worked with the troopers in the past. I know how it goes."

"I just wanted to be sure, Tom. I want to set up a sting of sorts. I need to get someone into the community without arousing suspicion. I'm going to meet with John Douglas and Harry Porter this afternoon and try to get Porter to say something about replacing the log builder who OD'd the other day. I'd like for you to comment that you know someone with log building experience who may be available to replace him. His name is Carl Lewis from Fairbanks. You don't have to add any more unless Porter asks a specific question. Do you think you can do that for me?"

"I can if that's all there is to it, Wyatt. I just want you to remember I have to live in this community and operate a business here. I don't want to jeopardize all that."

"I understand, Tom, and I agree there is a degree of risk, but I'll do my best to shield you from any blame. It's important, Tom."

"OK, I'll do it, but remember what I said. I have a wife, a home, and a business to look out for."

"If this works we'll take a major drug dealer out of the town. I think it's worth the risk." Wyatt hoped he wasn't making a mistake by pressuring his new friend.

"If it doesn't work I won't let Maggie bake any more cinnamon rolls for you." Tom had given his reluctant consent.

At that moment there was activity in the outer office. It was Harry Porter and John Douglas entering the front door. Maggie directed the two men toward Wyatt's office. Wyatt had opened the door to see who had come into the outer office and met the two newcomers as they approached.

"Hello, Harry," the VPSO greeted them. "This must be your boss."

"Yes," said Porter, "this is John Douglas. Mr. Douglas owns the lodge we're building."

"How do you do, Mr. Douglas, I'm the VPSO in Iliamna now. That new lodge of yours is going to be a real asset to the community. Pleased to meet you, sir." Wyatt shook the hand of the lodge owner. "This is Tom Dempsey. He owns Lake Air Taxi. You met his wife, Maggie, when you came into the outer office."

"Nice to meet you, Officer Earp. I've heard a great deal about you. I want to thank you for taking care of everything when my logsmith died. It was tragic. As you may have heard I don't tolerate any type of drugs on the premises. Had I known he was using drugs I would have fired him immediately. I run a clean operation and want to keep it that way. Harry tells me you did an excellent job of taking care of the details when he died." Douglas was a friendly man with a pleasant manner.

"Yes, he did, sir, which reminds me, I'm going to have to find another log builder to finish the construction job."

"Did you say you were looking for someone to finish the log construction at the lodge?" asked Tom.

"Yes, the man we had died recently," answered Porter.

"I might be able to help you out with that," replied Tom. "I know a fellow in Fairbanks who has been building log structures in Alaska all his life. He does really nice work. If you're interested I'll give you his phone number. He is always looking for a big job and that lodge is about as big as they come."

"That would be great; get me the number and I'll call him. What's his name?" asked Harry.

"Carl Lewis. He's well known in the Fairbanks area. I'll have Maggie give you his number when you leave."

"Thanks…you may have helped me solve a big problem."

Douglas was nodding his head in agreement with the conversation. "I just flew in from Houston and you have a lot more snow here than we had in Texas. I have other businesses down there, but my first love is right here in Alaska. I'm anxious to get the lodge open. We hope to furnish a true Alaska experience for our guests. It should provide employment for many of the local people and give local businesses an opportunity to make some extra income from our clients. I want the entire community of Iliamna to benefit from this venture. I plan to participate in local projects and help out wherever I can."

"This is a very small town and we welcome any helping hand we can get. I think you will find this a very nice and friendly place to live. Welcome to our town," said Tom.

"I'll be by to see you from time to time. If you have any problems out your way, just call me." Wyatt opened the door for the little party to leave the office.

When the three men had exited Wyatt quickly dialed Maggie on the in-house phone to give her the telephone number of Carl Lewis which Tom was about to ask her to give to Harry Porter. Just minutes later Tom returned to the office.

"Well? Did I do it right?" he asked.

"You sure did, Tom. It worked out perfectly. It's up to the other team now. I'm going to call Gene Turner and warn him of the call Lewis is about to get."

The rest of the day was routine: writing reports, shoveling snow, and waiting for calls of someone in distress. He had called Turner and warned him of a call Carl Lewis was about to get in regard to finishing the log work on the new lodge. Wyatt wondered if John Douglas was always as pleasant as he seemed today. He also wondered what business interests he had in Houston, Texas.

It was just noontime when his cell phone signaled an incoming call. It was Linda Mason.

"I have a big pot of soup on the stove. Can you come over for lunch?" she asked.

"I'm going to have to go on a diet if I keep hanging around with you." Wyatt liked Linda very much and felt good when he was with her. "What time is lunch?"

"Whenever you get here," she answered. "The fresh rolls will be out of the oven in ten minutes."

"I'll be there to help you take the pan out of the oven."

Wyatt had swept the snow off his truck earlier and it had now quit snowing, at least for a while. He drove directly to Linda's little house, stepped onto the porch, and stomped the snow off his boots. She greeted him with a smile and a kiss on the cheek. Inside he sat on the chair next to the door to remove his shoes, customary in Alaska, particularly in the winter.

"Come into the kitchen, Wyatt. I'll serve the soup. You can pour the coffee." This domestic invitation pleased the lawman very much.

The two didn't have much conversation while eating the moose meat soup and fresh baked dinner rolls soaked in butter and with a little honey on the side.

"You know, I'm beginning to like this homestyle living," said Wyatt as he leaned back in his chair and sipped the cup of coffee he was holding.

"I like having you here, too. I don't get a chance to cook for anyone but myself and it's nice to have someone who appreciates my cooking."

Wyatt smiled, "I've lived a solitary lifestyle my entire life. I never needed anyone but myself. I'm sorry to say I didn't even visit with my mother much when she was alive. I should visit my father more, but I've always liked being alone. I'm beginning to see what a mistake that really was. Just having this close companionship of another person at the dinner table is wonderful. I've always been self-reliant, but I can see now how much nicer life can be when you have someone to share it with."

"Thank you, Wyatt, but I really haven't done anything but cook a couple of meals for you. I want you to know my life's road hasn't always been smooth. There have been a lot of bumps along the way. I've sort of isolated myself since I took this teaching job, but since meeting you I just feel more relaxed in my life. I think it's only because you are around and I can count on you to protect me. I haven't said anything before because our relationship is new and untested. I didn't want to scare you off. The truth is I like you very much, Wyatt. I hope we will always be close."

"I guess I feel the same way, Linda," said Wyatt, reaching across the table to hold her hand.

Chapter Fourteen

During the week that followed, Wyatt Earp, VPSO, had few calls. His jurisdiction was quiet. There were reports of two dogs fighting, one domestic violence report which turned out to be a wife beating her husband (the man decided to take an airplane to Anchorage until she sobered up), and a wounded moose which Wyatt had to dispatch with his shotgun. The meat of the moose was claimed by one of the local citizens who butchered the moose and gave the meat to needy families in the area. Other than these calls his week was uneventful. It was mid-week of the second week when he had a call from Gene Turner.

"How's it going, Wyatt?" Gene asked.

"It's been quiet," was his reply.

"I have some news for you. Can you talk a couple of minutes?" asked the sergeant.

"Yes, I'm in the office."

"Good. I just had a call from Carl Lewis. He's been hired by Harry Porter to finish the log structure at the lodge building. Carl called me to tell me about the interview and said he was warned specifically about bringing any type of drugs onto the premises. He was told such action would result in immediate dismissal. He also said he met John Douglas while at the meeting and he issued the same warning. Carl said they were nearly paranoid about it. He agreed with the condition and was hired. He will start on Monday. He said he would come in to meet you when he had an opportunity."

"That's good news, Gene. At least he will be in Iliamna and get acquainted with the locals. He should be able to find out if there is a drug operation happening in town."

"I've checked on that suspect of yours, Rick Buntz. He's been off the radar for a while now. Has your informant given you any more tips?" asked Turner.

"No, none. Since the big snow things have been really quiet. Barking dogs and wife beaters is about it. I plan to go to Nondalton this afternoon to visit with an old friend and make an appearance in town. If there is enough daylight I might fly up to Port Alsworth and have a burger with my friend there. There's another big storm moving this way, so this may be my last day to fly for several days."

"Just be careful out there, Wyatt. You already know how hazardous winter flying can be," Turner cautioned the VPSO.

"One other item, Gene. Have you heard how Lonnie Davis is getting along?"

"He had another surgery this week. The doctors say this is the last one. Once he begins to heal they will let him out of the hospital, but he will still have several months of physical therapy ahead of him. He told me to tell you he intends to come back to Iliamna and King Salmon when he returns to duty. He told me the first thing he wanted to do was to thank you for shooting that bear."

Wyatt laughed, "Tell him I didn't do it for him, I thought he was going to eat me too."

Now Gene laughed. "I'll tell him when I talk with him again. Take care, Wyatt, and expect a visit from Carl, soon."

When he finished with his call he went into the hangar to pre-flight the state Super Cub before taking it out of the hangar. Outside he started the engine and let it idle a few minutes. The hydraulic wheel skis were in the up position for him to maneuver on the plowed surface of the Iliamna airport. When he landed at Nondalton he pumped the handle to lower the skis to allow the weight of the aircraft to land on the large flat skis. After shutting down the engine he placed the insulated engine cover over the cowling to keep the engine warm. Once done he hiked up the roadway to the cabin of Rufus Donavan. Rufus was surprised to see the VPSO and invited him inside for coffee and a short visit.

Rufus had nothing unusual to report to Wyatt, but said a Super Cub from Iliamna had made several trips to Nondalton in the past couple of weeks. Each time he had been met by someone on a snowmobile, but the pilot never left the airport. The number on the Cub was N8816A. There was nothing unusual about his actions but it seemed strange he never went to the home of one of the locals or unloaded any freight. All this was conjecture on the part of Rufus Donavan.

Wyatt chatted with Rufus and finished his coffee before walking back to his airplane to leave town. Upon takeoff he pointed the nose up the lake toward Port

Alsworth. He flew up the west shore of the lake past Keyes Point to Chulitna Bay before crossing the lake to the Alsworth airstrip. The runway had been neatly plowed and he was able to land with the wheels down. He taxied to the front of the little hamburger shop and stopped, once again putting the engine cover on the front of the little plane.

"Howdy," said Leon as Wyatt entered. "Want coffee?"

"No thanks, just water, but I'm hungry. How about one of your famous cheeseburgers and fries? Can't stay too long. I want to get back to the office before dark."

"Comin' right up," said Leon as he turned to the grill to cook the burger. "How ya been?" he asked.

"I've been great. The last couple of weeks have been mostly quiet. I thought it was time for me to come up and see what you were up to these days." Wyatt was making conversation, tempting Leon to volunteer what he knew.

"Since the big snow there ain't been much goin' on 'round here. Saw that Super Cub a couple of times, though. Don't know what he was doing, just talking with some guy from the camp across the bay. Didn't stay long, didn't even cover his engine, just talked a minute and took off."

"I had another report like that about the same plane. I'm looking into it."

The thick burger and hot French fries were placed in front of the customer with the badge on his coat. "Want ketchup with your fries?" asked Leon.

"Sure, why not. Nobody's looking."

"Heard you had an encounter with a bear some time back," inquired Leon, leaning on the counter.

"Yes, we did. Lonnie and I found the bear in a dog yard eating one of the dead dogs. The bear charged and Lonnie shot him several times, but the bear got to him and clawed a big chunk out of his shoulder. He's still in the hospital in Anchorage."

"Heard you shot the bear," stated Leon.

"Yup, I shot him four times before he went down, but that was after Lonnie had hit him at least four times. He was a tough old boar." Wyatt gave the information between bites. He finished his burger and wiped his mouth with the napkin.

"Want anything else?" asked Leon.

"Nope, it was good, Leon. Thanks, but I have to get back to the office. What do I owe you?"

"The usual," said Leon.

Wyatt tossed a twenty on the counter. "See you next trip," he said as he slipped off the stool to leave.

Wyatt flew down the Alsworth side of the lake in a straight line to the Iliamna Airport. Clouds were gathering over the west end of the big lake when he landed and taxied to the hangar. Tom opened the hangar door and helped Wyatt push the Super Cub into its place inside the big hangar.

"Another storm is on its way in," stated Tom as he turned off the hangar bay lights and the two men walked to the office.

"Hello, Maggie, any calls for me?" Wyatt asked as they entered the air taxi company office.

"Only one, a Captain Griffin called and asked to have you call him back when you came in."

"I'll take care of it, Maggie," answered Wyatt.

Tom was looking at the scheduling book, "I see we have some freight to go to New Stuyahok, but that storm is already there. It will have to wait until the snow stops. I'm going to the house for a while, Maggie. I'll come back later and let you take some time off." He called down the hall toward Wyatt's office, "See you later, Wyatt."

"OK," came a distant reply.

In his little office the VPSO dialed his captain in Fairbanks. "Captain Griffin, please,"

The call was forwarded to Griffin. "How are you doing out there, Wyatt?"

"Just fine, Cap. I got word that Carl Lewis was hired at the new lodge. I hope he can pick up some information on who is distributing the heroin locally."

"So do I. I instructed him to contact you when the time was right. We don't want him to blow his cover, though. Carl is a good man. You will enjoy working with him. Have you learned any more about the guy, I think his name was Buntz, and what he was doing in the villages with his Super Cub?"

"No, but I just came back from a couple of those villages and both places told me he had been there within the past few days. He didn't stay but a few minutes in each place, talking to one of the locals at each stop. Perhaps he was taking orders for another shipment or maybe he was explaining why he lost one of his shipments."

"Give Carl a little time to get acquainted and he may turn up some answers for you," commented Captain Griffin. "In the meantime try to keep the peace out there. Stay in touch."

Wyatt was sitting at his desk when his in-house line rang. It was Maggie. "You have some visitors out here," she notified him. He walked to the front office to see who they were and was surprised to see Linda Mason and a small group of school children waiting there.

"Hello kids, what can I do for you today?" he asked. A very small girl about twelve years old held up her hand. "Yes, what's your name?" asked the VPSO.

"My name is Deena Petrovich. Miss Mason said if we came down here you would show us your office and tell us what you do."

"Miss Mason is correct. I'll be happy to show you my police station. Let's all stay in a group and walk down the hallway to my office. Mrs. Dempsey has work to do so we will get out of her office. Thank her for helping you, please."

"Thank you, Mrs. Dempsey," was the unified response.

"OK, children, follow Trooper Earp to his office." Everyone lined up behind the officer to walk toward his little office down the hall. In the office the children formed a semicircle around his desk. Wyatt was patient and showed the kids his police radio and other communication equipment as well as his filing system and pointed out his police vehicle parked outside the other office. He answered all the questions the children posed with lengthy, official sounding, explanations. After several minutes Miss Mason interrupted.

"All right children. Officer Earp is a busy man and there is a storm approaching. We had better get back to the school in time for the bell to ring that lets us go home. Say thank you to the officer," she instructed the class and winked at Wyatt.

"Thank you, Officer Earp," another reply in unison. As they filed out of the room one of the boys turned to speak to Wyatt.

"I like your big gun safe. It's really neat. Bye," he said as he went out the door.

Wyatt chuckled to himself at the wonder in the minds of the children and the skill with which their teacher was able to get them to follow her lead. She was, indeed a school teacher right from the heart. He would call her later and possibly drive to her home if the storm wasn't too terrible.

An hour later the storm struck with all its fury. Heavy snow fell horizontally driven by a fifty mile per hour wind. Lake Iliamna was living up to its name, "mother of the wind." As the storm seemed to intensify he decided a trip to her house was out of the question. He waited another hour before calling her home number.

"That was a nice surprise, Miss Mason." They both laughed about the visit. "I had planned to drive out to your place this evening, but the storm is getting worse and I might get snowed in at your place. We can't have that; the neighbors would talk." Again, the couple laughed.

"You truly impressed the children. They had never been to a police officer's office before. It was my goal to relieve any fear they may have had about the presence of a policeman. You did an excellent job of gaining their confidence and introducing them to what a VPSO does here in the village. I was impressed with your presentation, especially since you had no advance notification of our visit. Thank you for being patient and taking the time to explain things to the children."

"I was happy to do it, ma'am," teased Wyatt. "If you like I'll make a trip to the school and give a short dissertation on my family history. You know, tell how Wyatt Earp the first came to Alaska during the gold rush and how I, Wyatt Earp the fifth, came to be a VPSO in Iliamna, Alaska."

"Oh, that would be wonderful, Wyatt. I would like to hear that story myself." Linda hated to end the call, but she had to get ready for the storm: Fill the lanterns and fill containers with water in case the power went out. There was plenty of firewood near the big stove in the living room. She would heat the house with the oil stove as long as the power was on and the fan would circulate the heat. "I have some things to take care of, but I'll call you later if the phones are still working."

"I'll come out and check on you in the morning when the road gets plowed. Good night." He wasn't worried about Linda. She could handle life in the bush and she was prepared for a long, windy, snowy, cold, night.

Chapter Fifteen

The storm raged on for two days and two nights. The third day the snowfall slowed enough to allow the local snowplowing trucks to go to work. Wyatt was out early to shovel the snow from in front of the office where his truck was parked and to clear the front walk and parking area for Maggie. Tom had hired a local man to plow the parking lot on an as needed schedule. He was definitely needed today. The wind had done a good job of moving the snow to the edges of the parking area, but the edges and area near the hangar were covered with snow drifts reaching five feet deep in some places. Wyatt didn't attempt to remove those drifts with his snow shovel. He had finished removing the snow from the entry and walk when Maggie pulled into her parking spot. Wyatt stood the shovel against the porch railing and stepped over to open the office door for her.

"Good morning, Wyatt," she greeted. "Thank you for shoveling. I thought I would have to do that before I could open the office. Just for that I'll make the coffee."

"I talked with flight service this morning and they say to expect a lot of freight traffic today since no one has been able to fly for two days."

"That's what happens when we get a big storm like this one. Tom sleeps most of the time and when the weather clears he doesn't get any sleep at all. I feel sorry for him."

"I plan to spend the day in the village checking on any locals who may be stranded or snowed in and can't get out. Sort of a public safety day, you might call it. I'll be in the area and I can help Tom load freight or whatever he needs." Wyatt felt it was only right to help Tom and pay for the kindness he and his wife had extended to him. "Have you heard if the school will be open today?" Wyatt asked Maggie.

"I haven't heard, but I'll give them a call and let you know. The coffee's done. Come and get a cup."

Wyatt took a cup of the fresh, hot coffee to his office. There had been no calls for two days, but daily reports must be filed. When he finished with his daily ritual he reached for his heavy coat and bundled up to go out into the snowy countryside. He cruised most of the local roads checking for stranded citizens or anyone who might be in distress from the storm. It was nearly noon when he made his way to Linda Mason's house. The driveway had been plowed and the front walk and steps cleared of snow. He stepped up onto the porch and knocked on the door. He heard footsteps inside. Linda opened the door wearing snow pants but no coat.

"Oh, Wyatt, I'm so glad to see you. Come inside and take off your coat. I tried to call you, but the land line is still out from the storm."

He stepped inside and Linda closed the door behind him then wrapped her arms around the big lawman. "I missed seeing you, too, Linda," said Wyatt. "I can't stay long. I have to check on the rest of the people living out this way. I haven't heard from the lodge down the road, but if the land line is still out they couldn't contact me either. Are you OK?"

"Yes, I'm fine. We get this kind of weather a lot and I'm prepared for it. Have you heard if this storm is done or just a lull?" she asked.

"Aviation weather says it isn't over, but it won't be as bad and the wind will diminish to about fifteen miles per hour. The FAA is expecting several planes to land this morning and Tom is anticipating a busy day."

"The school will be closed today but open tomorrow. I'll be home all day. How about I fix you dinner tonight?"

"I like that idea, Linda. I'll go anywhere for food…you know that."

"The phones should be working in a little while. I'll plan dinner for six. If that's a problem, just give me a call." Linda was excited to have the VPSO for company once again.

"Six it is then. I have to go now. There is a lot of the village I haven't patrolled since the storm. I had better get busy." He zipped up his coat, preparing to go back into the weather outside the warm cabin.

He continued along the same road, checking on those cabins with no visible foot traffic to or from the homes. It was just a welfare check on those folks who may be sick or injured and unable to get out of the cabin. He found no one in distress anywhere on the trip.

At the end of the road was the gate and private drive of the new lodge building. He entered the property and found the drive partially plowed. The walks had been shoveled, but the hired hand was still in the process of getting the road cleared. Wyatt stopped in front of the main lodge building, climbed the steps, and knocked on the door. It was opened by a man he had never met on the previous visit. The man was six feet tall, unkempt with blond hair and a week's growth of beard. His clothing was clean, as was he, but he gave a rumpled appearance.

"Hello there. You must be the VPSO I've been told about. I'm Carl Lewis. I was just hired to finish the log work on the lodge." The new man seemed friendly and articulate.

"Yes, I'm Wyatt Earp V. I'm new in the area myself. I just came by to see if everything was in order after the storm."

"Well come on in. Mr. Douglas and Mr. Porter are in the kitchen. The other guy is out plowing snow. We have some coffee on the stove. Do you want some?"

"No thanks, but I would like to speak with your bosses, if they aren't too busy."

"Sure, follow me." Carl led the way to the huge kitchen area where two men were seated at the kitchen counter, drinking coffee. They both looked up as the men entered.

"Ah, Officer Earp," greeted the owner.

"The road to town must be cleared if you made it all the way out here," said Porter.

"Yes, they're still working on it, but it's passable. The phones are out yet and I thought I should come out and check on the local citizens to be sure they're safe. How are you doing out at the end of the road?" asked Wyatt.

"We're just fine. We have been discussing the completion of the lodge. Mr. Lewis has pointed out some changes we should make to the structure to accommodate the hired help when we get up and operating." John Douglas was definitely in charge of the operation. "By the way, have you heard if there will be any flights out soon? I need to get back to Houston for a few days."

"There is going to be some freight delivered today, but passenger service won't resume until tomorrow morning. Visibility is iffy and some snow is still drifting on the runway in Iliamna."

"Thank you, Officer Earp. I'll come to town later and make arrangements for travel. Thank you for the information. I have been considering purchase of my own jet airplane for my commute between Alaska and my holdings in Texas and the southwest. This storm has made me wonder if it's worth the investment. Even my own jet couldn't influence the effects of this storm. If I don't see you before I leave, I will return in about three weeks. If you have any questions or requests please feel free to contact Mr. Porter." Douglas was speaking as if he was more than rich, but super rich.

"I'll do that, Mr. Douglas. Have a nice trip." Wyatt stood to leave, but was interrupted by Carl Lewis.

"Trooper Earp, would it be all right if I stopped by your office to say hello from time to time? I may have questions about places to go hunting and fishing in the local area," explained the logsmith.

"I don't know how much help I can be, but you can stop any time. I have to get back to the village now. I have a six o'clock appointment."

"Come back any time, Earp," invited Harry Porter.

Wyatt wondered what was so urgent that John Douglas, who had just returned from Texas, must schedule an immediate flight. He drove directly to his office to call Gene Turner in Soldotna. He gave Gene a report of his conversation with Douglas and asked if this would be useful to the federal officers who seemed to be watching the suspected drug lord.

"I think they will be extremely interested. Any time they can get ahead of him enhances the chance of catching him with his hand in the cookie jar. Did you know that Douglas was an acquaintance of Pablo Escobar and ran his distribution system in the U.S.? After Escobar was arrested the business of importing drugs from South America is still strong. Escobar hired scientists and engineers to devise ways to ship drugs. He had buildings filled with cash and paid them well. They built tunnels, submarines, speed boats and all manner of ways to get the drugs into the United States. Escobar experimented with ways to disguise the drugs by infusing them in fluids, plastics, fabrics and other powders like flour and corn meal. The man was relentless in his search for diversity.

"The system still exists, but without the leader they once had. We believe he still controls the business from prison, but without the imagination he supplied. One thing that has not diminished is the ruthlessness of the organization behind it all. John Douglas has aspirations to become the Pablo Escobar on this side of the border. I'll call and talk with a friend of mine involved in this case and let him know what you told me. After you find out when Douglas is leaving town, call me. Thanks for the heads up, Wyatt."

"Sure thing, Gene. Also, I met Carl Lewis today. He said he was coming to the office to talk about hunting and fishing. I've only just met him, but I liked him a lot. Tell Lonnie Davis I said hello." With that Wyatt hung up the telephone and checked the time. He had time to clean up and shower before going to dinner at Linda's.

He had just begun his drive to the school teacher's home, driving slowly, when an ATV sped from a driveway on the right, towing two young boys on a small dog sled. The ATV was traveling at a high rate of speed and the sled at the end of the long rope skidded around the turn to the main road, sliding across the road and nearly turning over when it hit the snow berm on the other side. Wyatt thought the sled would overturn and injure the boys, but it stayed upright. He turned on his red overhead lights to follow the boys, but they didn't stop. He chirped the siren several times, but the driver only went faster. Fearing for the safety of the boys on the sled he slowed his pursuit and turned off the red flashing lights. The boys sped away and disappeared around the next turn in the road. Wyatt gave up the chase, driving directly to Linda Mason's house.

During dinner Wyatt told Linda of the encounter with the ATV and the sled.

Linda chuckled quietly, "Where did you run into the boys?" she asked.

Wyatt described the driveway and the milepost reading and gave a rather sketchy description of the ATV and the three young boys.

"That sounds like the Akio boys. Timmy, the oldest was probably driving the ATV. He was one of the students I brought to your office this week. Of course, there is no way I can be positive about the identification, but they live in that area and match the description you gave. They're good kids, but you're right, it wasn't safe."

"I should find them and beat them with my night stick; they scared me to death."

"Oh, Wyatt, you are so funny. I'll tell you what. I'll have a little safety class at school tomorrow. Would you like to come to the school after lunch and help me with the class?" she asked, giving him a fake look of sadness.

Now it was Wyatt who was chuckling, "Yes, I'll come to the school. Can I bring my night stick in case I get a chance to beat one of the kids?"

"You may not, Wyatt Earp. Just come and be your own sweet self. The boys will get the hint they have been caught and take the lesson to heart."

The two went into the living room with their coffee. Linda put a movie in the player and the two sat close together while it played.

Chapter Sixteen

Wyatt had driven back to the office around nine last evening. There was a light snow falling, but the wind had subsided. He arose early this morning knowing there would be some shoveling to do in front of the office. It took nearly two hours to rid the parking area of snow and push it far enough away from the office that the plow truck would have no trouble removing it. Even now there was a light snowfall. Maggie pulled into her parking spot a little after eight o'clock. She had the coffee brewed by the time he finished his chore. Handing him a cup of hot coffee when he came inside, she said, "Thanks for doing my morning winter job."

"I have an emergency response vehicle. I am on duty at all times. I must be ready at all times." Both Maggie and Wyatt laughed at his humorous remark.

"Do you expect much in the way of calls today?" asked Maggie.

"No, just the usual, I have to go to the school to give a safety speech after lunch. I think the owner of the lodge is leaving today and he may stop by the office while he's waiting for his airplane. The snow has nearly stopped and the plow has almost finished clearing the runway. I have an idea Tom will be busy today." Wyatt refilled his coffee cup and turned to go to his office.

He sat at his desk attempting to organize his day when Maggie called to say John Douglas was in the outer office. Wyatt walked to the front desk to greet him. Maggie handed the new man a cup of coffee to take to Wyatt's office. Wyatt closed the door behind them and asked an off-hand question, "What kind of business interests do you have in Texas?"

"I have several," said Douglas. "I own a string of travel agencies across the state of Texas. I own several day spas and nine filling stations. My largest companies are four trucking companies. One of the trucking companies deals exclusively with moving household goods. That company is nationwide. Two are oil field service companies working both in the oil fields and tankers hauling petroleum products in the southwest. My offices are in Houston where I own a small mall building with storefronts on the first floor and offices on the second. My home is not far from the office."

"You are a busy man, Mr. Douglas. Whatever possessed you to build this world class resort out here on Lake Iliamna?"

"I came here on a fishing trip and fell in love with the place. The contrast in the daily pace is why I decided to build a lodge where executives could come to get away from the stress of their business routine. It's a gamble, but I think it will pay off. I've applied for a liquor license for on premises only. I don't intend to sell liquor to locals unless they come to the restaurant to have dinner. My prices are going to be very high along with the food quality which leads me to believe not many locals will be patronizing my lodge."

"It's a big dream, for sure, but it sounds like you've thought it out very well. I wish you all the luck in the world." Wyatt was, indeed impressed with the business plan described by John Douglas. "What time is your flight, sir?" he asked the visitor.

Douglas looked at his wristwatch. "In about an hour. Harry is due back here in a few minutes to take me and my luggage to the terminal. I just wanted to come by and tell you that if there is anything you need just ask. You've done a marvelous job of keeping the reason for my employee's death as quiet as possible. I thank you for that. I must go now. Harry will be arriving. I'll see you in about three weeks." Douglas handed Wyatt a business card. "Feel free to call me at any of these numbers if you want anything."

"I appreciate the offer, Mr. Douglas. Have a good trip."

Wyatt opened the door for the man to leave. Douglas shook hands with the VPSO as he walked out the door. Wyatt followed the visitor as far as Maggie's desk where he stopped to watch Douglas climb into the company truck with Harry Porter and drive toward the airport terminal building.

"I'm glad I'm not as busy as Mr. Douglas," commented Wyatt as he walked back to his little office.

Inside, he closed the door once again and sat at his desk. His next task was to call Gene Turner to let him know Douglas was on his way to Houston.

Turner explained, "Douglas has never broken the law in Alaska, as far as we know. That makes this a federal case all the way. They've been stymied at every turn so far. The information you've given me will enable them to get ahead of him, theoretically. You did a great job with this case, Wyatt. You know, the department doesn't expect the VPSO program to contribute much toward statewide investigations, but you, only being there a short time, have pushed your post to the forefront of state investigations." Turner laughed, "We expected you to quiet the drunks, stop domestic disputes and solve local problems. I guess we were all wrong about the scope of your talents."

"I'm just trying to keep the peace in the village," said Wyatt. "In fact, I'm scheduled to give a safety talk at the school this afternoon. By the way, since I'm doing such a bang-up job, can I get a raise in pay?"

Turner roared with laughter. "No, but I'll nominate you for sainthood."

"Let me know how it works out in Texas," said Wyatt as he signed off and hung up the phone.

Sergeant Turner, meanwhile, dialed Captain Griffin in Fairbanks to pass on the information given him by VPSO Earp. "Do you want to call the team in Texas or do you want me to do it?"

"You go ahead and call them. I'm trying to make arrangements to fly to Iliamna to inspect the post. They've had a huge storm over there, but it seems to be moving out. I think I can get there tomorrow. Let me know what the feds say to you about the information."

"Will do, Cap," said Turner.

In a small obscure office in a suburb of Houston, Texas a team of federal officers were meeting to discuss progress in a gigantic drug import case. The FBI (Federal Bureau of Investigation), DEA (Drug Enforcement Administration), and ICE (Immigration and Customs Enforcement) agencies were working together to stop the largest drug ring known to them. The FBI agent in charge of the task force, Darren Hatfield, had taken the call from Turner and called the meeting to formulate a plan of action.

Meanwhile Wyatt was gathering visual aids for his afternoon presentation to the school children. He found a box of plastic zipper pulls in a locker. These were reflective plastic bears wearing the symbolic trooper campaign hat. When attached to a child's coat zipper it would shine when struck by headlights, making the presence of the child known to any driver. They look like a cartoon character which makes them popular with school children. It was now past noon and time for him to drive to the school to meet with Linda.

Once in front of the class he was introduced by Miss Mason as Village Public Safety Officer, Wyatt Earp. "Yes, he is related to the famous lawman of the Old West." This fact got the attention of the class immediately.

"I will be happy to come back some other time and tell you about my family history, but today we are going to be talking about safety. Living in a bush community, we sometimes ignore the usual traffic safety rules that must be obeyed in cities and towns all over the country. I enforce the traffic laws less strictly here, but I must care for you and the other members of the village when it comes to safety." These pupils were twelve and thirteen years old and Wyatt tried to keep his speech on their level. "An accident in the village will leave you just as injured or dead as if you were in Anchorage or Fairbanks. Remember, a broken arm or leg or back may leave you crippled and unable to trap or fish for the rest of your life. So, let's talk about safety."

The class went on for almost an hour including the question and answer session at the end. When he finished, Miss Mason asked the class to write a one-page paper about what they had learned today. She walked Wyatt to the door where she thanked him for coming. "I'll call you later," she whispered.

He winked at her and walked from the school. He was driving back to the office when his cell phone rang, it was Captain Griffin.

"Hello, Wyatt, I hear you're making quite an impression on the locals in Iliamna."

"Just keeping the peace, Cap," said the VPSO.

"I just called to tell you I'm coming out to inspect the post. If the weather cooperates I plan to be there tomorrow afternoon. I'll spend the night if I can get a room. Can you arrange that for me?"

"It shouldn't be a problem, Captain. No one is very busy this time of year. I would let you stay with me, but I have nowhere for you to sleep." Wyatt apologized for his lack of accommodations. "How long do you intend to stay?"

"Just overnight; the days are too short this time of year to make a round trip in the daylight. It will give us a chance to talk. By the way, I have a gift for you from Lonnie Davis. I'll bring it with me when I come. I'll see you tomorrow. Let me know if there is a problem with getting a room for the night."

Later, after making reservations at the hotel, he called Linda. "I'm bringing makings for dinner. Can I use your stove?" he asked.

"Of course. What are you cooking?"

"I found a recipe for some Cajun shrimp and honey fried king salmon. I have all the ingredients. Do you have a frying pan I can use?"

"Oh, it sounds delicious. I have all the utensils you will need. I just got home, but you can come over any time at all."

"I'll be there soon." Wyatt found himself enjoying the time he was spending with the pretty school teacher. He thought it was time to take her to Naknek to meet his father.

An hour later he carried a large bag of fish, shrimp, cayenne pepper, garlic and other dry ingredients into the house where the kitchen had been readied for him to begin cooking. The recipe had many combined flavors and seasonings, but the secret was frying the fish in honey and butter, adding the other spices and more butter to the fry pan to cook the shrimp. The dinner was an instant hit.

"We must do this again, soon, Mr. Earp," said his admirer as he was leaving for the evening.

It was almost noon when the State-owned twin engine Navajo landed and taxied to the back of the Lake Air Taxi hangar. Captain Griffin climbed out and covered the engines with insulated covers and asked if he could plug the engine heaters into the hangar power. Once done, the two men walked into the hangar and on to the office occupied by the VPSO, Wyatt Earp. The initial meeting took less than an hour when Trooper Captain Griffin suggested they go to the hotel in order for him to check in and the two men have lunch.

Back in the office the mood was more relaxed now. "I'm extremely pleased with the job you're doing out here, Wyatt." The Captain was leaning back in an office chair drinking a Coca Cola. "Sergeant Turner gives me updates on happenings out here. You've turned out to be the perfect officer for Iliamna. Which reminds me, I have something for you." He reached into a briefcase for a small gift-wrapped box. "Lonnie sent this to you with his thanks." He handed the box to Wyatt.

"What is it, Cap?" he asked.

"You will have to open it to find out," the Captain teased.

Wyatt tore the wrapping paper from the box and lifted the lid. Inside was a leather necklace strung with ivory beads and bear claws…grizzly bear claws. "Holy smokes, Cap, look at this."

"Yes, I saw it when he had it made. The claws are from the bear you killed. Alaska Fish and Game let him have the claws, saying they could have wooden ones made for the mounted hide. Lonnie said he wanted to do something special for you, since you saved his life."

Wyatt held the necklace up to his throat and walked over to a mirror to view the new possession. "I don't know what to say…this is fantastic. Is it OK for me to accept this gift?"

"In this case, yes. Approval came from the Governor. I have a letter with me," said Griffin. "Now, let's talk about the overdose death and that suspicious pilot you have been watching."

The discussions went on all afternoon and ended when Captain Griffin invited Wyatt to have dinner at the hotel with him. He explained he would be leaving in the morning, but would continue to give him any assistance he needed in his remote post in the bush. Finally, he addressed the presence of Carl Lewis. Carl had notified the captain he was attempting to make acquaintance with your friend, Rick Buntz. Carl said he met the man in a local bar, but had not yet had an opportunity to approach him about drugs.

"We've had good men in this post in the past, but you seem to have a way of sniffing out possible crimes that we didn't know existed. I credit your past police experience with making that possible. You're doing a great job, Wyatt. Try not to get shot in the process." He laughed and said, "I'll see you in the morning before I go back to Fairbanks."

"OK, Cap, and give my thanks to Lonnie for the gift. See you in the morning."

The following morning Captain Griffin came to the office to meet with Wyatt. "Is there anything I can send you or do for you, Wyatt?"

"No, I think Sergeant Turner is taking care of all my needs and wants. Have a good flight back."

The two men pulled the covers from the engines and stowed them in the back of the airplane. Captain Griffin started the engines while Wyatt watched him call the flight service station to file a flight plan. It was time for him to get to back work.

Chapter Seventeen

Darren Hatfield, of the FBI, headed the task force formed to investigate the activities once belonging to Pablo Escobar. With Escobar in prison his empire should have faded away, but this particular empire was too lucrative and too powerful for that to happen. Escobar was still the head of the cartel, but his designated CEO or Operations Chief was a Columbian by the name of Carlos Mendoza. Mendoza had worked as Pablo's right hand man for many years. He was a vicious man, ruling his throne with a steel hand. He had ordered hundreds of murders in his career and had ordered many poor cocaine farmers and their families killed when they refused to do his bidding. He ran a private prostitution ring employing hundreds of kidnapped young girls which he sold or traded through the cartel.

It was Carlos Mendoza who had devised the cash storage methods used by Escobar and the drug cartel. Mendoza built warehouses on small farms where cocaine was harvested and processed. The cartel had so much cash on hand, semi-truck loads, that it was impossible to store it all in one place. No one ever knew exactly how much cash was stored in the countryside. Any time there was a hint that a farmer had entered the storage building or refused to have one built on his property, he was killed along with all his family—women, children, aunts, uncles, the entire family. This was all done in front of the farmer before he too, was killed in a slow and painful way.

Carlos was the man responsible for seeking out John Douglas, a small-time business man with a trucking company moving products out of Mexico into the United States. His trucking company used second hand, old, trucks. Once the deal was made with Mendoza, Douglas began to upgrade his fleet of trucks to new, powerful Freightliner units. He also acquired a trucking company licensed to move household goods throughout the entire United States. As time went on Douglas became the main link between Mendoza and the distribution network in America. Douglas also hauled many truckloads of cash into Mexico for the cartel.

Early on Douglas hauled snow globes from a manufacturing plant in Mexico through the border, where they were inspected by customs officers, to a network of distributors in the Southwest. Cocaine and heroin were dissolved in fluids inside the snow globes and was undetectable. Once on the north side of the border the globes were taken apart and the drugs recovered through an evaporation process. This same system was used to infuse narcotics in fabrics used in tee shirts and other products. Such ingenuity was the secret to the success of Pablo Escobar and his cartel. Douglas became the primary transportation facility for the cartel. He also became a very wealthy man.

The beauty of this operation was that it had never been detected. It had been suspected of transporting drugs, but the method was never disclosed. Douglas and his trucks had moved billions with a 'b,' of dollars, in drugs and cash across the border in both directions without discovery. Douglas was the lifeline for the cartel. He never allowed use of, dealt in, or sold drugs. His company policies were to never have any type of drugs on his premises or in his vehicles. Never had one of his drivers been stopped at the border or at a weigh station because of an officer or a dog sniffing out drugs in the cab or on the trucks. All his companies operated under these policies. Any driver or employee violating the policy was terminated at once.

In return for this trouble-free service, Mendoza paid very high transportation costs. Douglas's company trucks delivered shipments to warehouses owned and operated by the cartel, and in return protected the delivery sites and his trucks during their journey to the delivery point. The protection had paid huge benefits and not once during his years of doing business with the cartel had a truck been stolen or hijacked. This is remarkable since the hijacking rate, especially on the Mexican side of the border, is extremely high. The cartel had obviously put out the word to leave these trucks alone.

Douglas operated the trucking companies without competition. His companies had a reputation for obeying traffic laws and load limits. The drivers never ran a set of scales and always had complete paperwork for both the trucks and their loads. He had, long ago, eliminated troublesome drivers. Today most of his drivers were older family men who enjoyed the good pay, safe trucks, and great hours.

John Douglas sat in his modern office with his trucking company managers having one of the monthly meetings in which any problems that might arise were discussed. The meetings usually lasted about two hours after which Douglas treated them all to a prime rib dinner at a local restaurant. If there were any individual problems to be undertaken they would be discussed in a private meeting the next day. There were four of these managers, all experienced trucking company executives. His companies were running smoothly.

As was his practice, Douglas kept an open phone line exclusively for Carlos Mendoza. Carlos called on a regular basis to discuss products to be shipped and new warehouses to be serviced. Mendoza had been instrumental in the cartel disguising the products they shipped, and, like Pablo, kept a research and development lab and facility operating. When a new item was developed Carlos called John Douglas to discuss shipping details.

"Douglas Enterprises," he answered the private line.

"Ah, Mr. Douglas, you have made it back to Texas. I hope you had a pleasant trip to Alaska."

"Yes, I did, Carlos. The business was unpleasant, though. One of my employees died and I had to deal with the local policeman. He's new up there, but did an excellent job of taking care of business and keeping the lodge free of any scandal. The lodge is coming along and should be finished in another year. I hope you will make a plan to visit when it's complete."

"I would like that very much. What happened to your employee? Was it an accident?"

"Unfortunately, it was a heroin overdose. My manager didn't know he was a user. The employee was a logsmith. He built log structures. He was responsible for fitting all the logs in my lodge and outbuildings. We hired a new man while I was there. Construction should proceed without delay. If I can find the person who brought the drugs to the job site I'll eliminate him."

"I am calling to inform you that we have a new product to export. We have a new line of small cactus plants to sell in California. The plants are very beautiful and come in a colorful decorative adobe pot. The new warehouse is in southern Nevada. This is the address for the delivery." Carlos quoted the address and GPS coordinates. "We think there will be a problem with the adobe pots and plan to send extras. There will also be small plastic pots in the shipment in which to transplant the cactus plants, if we are unable to correct the problem with the bright color pots."

"How soon will the shipment be ready, Carlos?" asked Douglas.

"In about two weeks. We are working on the adobe pots and the potters are a little behind. The ingredients are being shipped from Colombia and should be at the greenhouse by the end of the week. I assume the usual fees will apply?"

"We will be using the same routes, though the new warehouse will have a slightly different mileage, but we can assume the same freight rate will apply."

"Good," said Carlos. "There will be a return shipment from this warehouse from time to time. I will try to let you know when that will occur."

"Thank you for the business, Carlos."

"I think it must be different weather in Houston from that at your lodge in Alaska," Carlos laughed.

"Yes, indeed," said Douglas. "There was a big blizzard while I was there; even the airplanes couldn't fly. The snow came down and the wind blew until the roads were impassable making it impossible to leave the lodge for a couple of days. Winter days in Houston are much more comfortable."

"The winter time here in Columbia, even more so. Stay well, my friend."

John Douglas was fully aware that his trucking company was the link between the modern-day world and the backcountry, donkey cart world of the farmers who grew and harvested cocaine. The same primitive methods were being used in the fields where the Mexican brown heroin was produced. All this product was gathered at central points in South America and moved by oxcart, backpack, boat, and sometimes aircraft to manufacturing points in southern Mexico. Douglas didn't know where the plants were located that turned the harvested products into products for shipment to the United States, but he was given the names of warehouses in Mexico where the items were loaded on large semitrailers licensed to the trucking company owned by Douglas. When each load was ready he was notified and it was up to him to schedule the needed trucks and replacement trailers to make the pick-up.

The manager of his trucking company operating in Mexico was a tall, thin, red haired man by the name of Dillon Dixon. His office was in the same group of offices as the one occupied by John Douglas. Douglas summoned his manager. "Hello, DD, John. Bring the dispatch book and come to my office, will you?"

"Sure, boss," was the reply. Five minutes later Dixon entered the office carrying a large ledger under his left arm. "Good to see you back in town, Boss," said the trucking company manager.

"Thanks. It's good to be back where the weather is warm. How is everything going? Any problems I should know about?" asked Douglas.

"No, nothing important except that plant south of Mexico City, where we pick up the tee shirt loads for Nevada. It's closing down. We got notification yesterday."

"Yes, I know, but there will be a new outlet opening soon. That's what I called to ask you about. We will be picking up our loads at a new location in that area. The new warehouse is only twelve miles from the old one, but the move will require the first driver to drop a trailer at the new location and move all the other trailers from the old location to the new one. The move will take an entire day for one truck and driver. Once he has all the trailers moved he can use his best judgement on whether to stay overnight or hook up and stop somewhere on the road. Do you have a good driver for this one?"

Sitting on the other side of the desk, Dixon opened the ledger now lying on the desk. "Yes, one of the regular Mexico route drivers, Ray Thiel. He's been running that route for a very long time and knows the countryside. He's a good man, married to a Mexican lady from that area."

Douglas slid a piece of paper with directions to the Mexican location as well as the new delivery address in Nevada. "Here are the directions to both the new locations. Pay him extra for the hosteling trailers at both sites. Tell him to stay in touch with the office. I don't know how secure these routes will be. So, until we test them, we need to be vigilant. Carlos usually takes care of that angle, but I want to know for sure how safe it is."

"How soon do you want this to be done?" asked Dillon Dixon.

"It's a two-day drive to the new terminal; start him early tomorrow morning. Get him a new Mexican cell phone in addition to the company cell phone he has, just in case." Douglas always worried when one of the locations was moved.

"I have some good news for you, Boss. The trucks and trailers all have our new logo painted on them. They look great. We had all the trailers acid washed and they're shiny as new. The new Amerimex name is on everything, including shirts and jackets for the drivers."

"Good. It should make it easier for Carlos to keep an eye on the trucks. Double check the licenses, registrations, and permits for every truck we send down there. We don't need any kind of screw up at the border or with the local police along the way." Such details were what made John Douglas successful.

"That oil field service company, you know the one in Wyoming with only four trucks, is about to lose its contract. The local pipeline company is shutting down. I'm bidding on another job in the area, but I have no idea if we will get the job. If we don't get the contract, what do you want me to do with the trucks? Bring them home? Sell them? What?"

"What are the chances we will win the new contract?" asked Douglas.

"Pretty good, I think. We have a good reputation up there and we spent a lot of money keeping gas field bosses happy."

"Let's wait until the contract is let to make that decision."

"OK, but the four drivers are going to be uneasy about their jobs." Dixon, too, was a detail man.

"If we don't get the contract I'll bid on another one up in North Dakota, but it would mean the drivers would have to move out of Wyoming."

"At least they would be working," said Dixon.

"OK, DD. Do you have any other questions for me?" asked Douglas.

Dixon closed the big ledger and stood, "No, I think we covered most everything. I'll get the ball moving on this stuff. I'll get Ray briefed on his trip for tomorrow morning."

Later that afternoon Darren Hatfield was sitting in his office, frustrated at the progress being made by the task force, when the phone on his desk tinkled a musical note. "Hatfield," he answered.

"I've been dispatched to a change of location in southern Mexico. I'm leaving in the morning, early."

"Where?" asked the FBI agent.

"I copied all the directions and put them in the mail a few minutes ago. I'm headed home now. The rest is up to you," said Thiel as he hung up the phone.

In the process of investigating all the companies regularly crossing the border Hatfield had met Ray Thiel who agreed to help the federal officer in his investigation, but warned the FBI agent he was not aware of any wrongdoing by his firm. Hatfield had asked to be notified of any changes in his schedule or types of loads. This was the first time Thiel had called with any information.

Hatfield received the letter the following morning. Inside were the instructions to find the new terminal in Mexico and for moving the trailers. It also included directions to the new warehouse he was to deliver the load to in Nevada. He passed the information on to the head investigator, Greg Hansen for DEA, working on the task force. Hansen, in turn, passed the information on to his team with instructions to check out the new terminal.

Two DEA officers found the warehouse in a secluded area away from town and on a dusty back road. This seemed unusual as a delivery destination for large tractor-trailer rigs coming from Mexico. The two men watched the large building from a distance for two days without learning anything except that there was a great deal of activity at the warehouse. After discussing a way to get into the operation the younger of the men, Stan Andrews, thought he could go there and apply for a job as laborer.

The following morning Andrews drove to the warehouse in an old 1978 Ford pickup. The engine used a lot of oil and blue smoke poured from the tailpipe. The driver, Andrews, stopped near the loading dock and asked one of the men working there where he could find the boss. The worker pointed to a man on the other end of the platform. Andrews was wearing tattered jeans and an old tee shirt with old boots on his feet. He looked as if he hadn't worked in a long time.

Chapter Eighteen

The man he had been directed to see was almost six feet tall, wearing a hard hat and carrying a very large beer belly. "Waddya want," asked the man as he approached.

"The name's Stan. I'm looking for work and I heard you were opening a new shop and thought I might could get on here. A laborer, like, you know?"

"We're still installing our equipment and we ain't hiring yet, maybe in two weeks. You belong to the union?"

"Not any more, used to, though," replied Stan.

"Gimme your name and number and I'll call you when we get open."

"What kinda stuff you handle here?" asked Andrews. "I don't wanna do hazmat stuff."

"Nah, we're just repackaging desert plants and stuff. Regulations say we have to inspect and repack the plants before we can ship them to stores. We got Mexicans to do that work. We might want extra help on the docks, though. I'll let you know."

"Good enough," said Stan as he wrote a phone number on a piece of note pad. "Gimme a call." He walked back to the other end of the loading dock to where his old Ford was parked and climbed in.

The warehouse was located near Nevada State Highway 165 just outside the small town of Nelson, a short distance south of Boulder City. Andrews drove into town and stopped in front of the local tavern, Buddy's Place, and went inside. He quickly evaluated the dive before walking to the bar to order a beer. It was early and he was the only customer.

"Is this where the big guy from the new truck terminal comes to drink beer?" he asked the bartender.

"Tony Bucco, yeah, but he won't be in until later this afternoon. Are you friends with Tony?"

"Not really, I just went out to see him about a job."

"I don't know what they do out there. His company just bought the old warehouse." The bartender was a friendly sort, "You a truck driver?"

"No, warehouseman and hostler; got hurt on the job over in California. Union won't let me go back to work over there no more," explained Stan Andrews.

"The first beer is on me. Come back later and Tony will be here."

"Thanks, appreciate it," said Stan as he tossed back the last of his draught beer. "See you later."

Stan backed out of his parking space and turned right on 165 and on toward Boulder City. Once away from the roadside tavern he used speed dial to contact his office.

"Greg, Stan. I made contact at the warehouse, but didn't get inside. I met the foreman and asked for a job. He said they were repackaging desert plants for delivery to retail outlets. I didn't see any sign of drugs, but, like I said, I didn't get inside the warehouse. The foreman's name is Tony Bucco. Run him through the checks and see if he has a rap sheet. I think I'll hang around here a couple of days and see if I can turn up anything. Bucco told me they weren't up and running yet, but shipments were coming in soon."

"You be careful out there, Stan. You don't have backup." It was Greg Hanson's way to express concern for his officer's safety.

"I'll be careful, and I'll call you tomorrow."

The road south through Mexico is difficult and in some places, treacherous. The Amerimex logo on the truck and trailer was a warning to local bandits to leave these trucks alone. Mexico does not enforce the same hourly restrictions as the U.S. Department of Transportation. This allowed Ray Thiel to travel more hours of the day governed only by how much sleep he needed to keep going. The trip is long, almost two thousand miles to a small town named Puebla. The truck terminal and warehouse are located on the outskirts of the sleepy town. The plant where the pots, mixed with cocaine or heroin, were manufactured was twenty miles away at a large vegetable farm and trucked to the Puebla location. The crew at the warehouse was busy completing the load of plants, but it would take another day to fill the van. Thiel would need the extra day to move all the other trailers to the new warehouse. It was hot and he was tired from the long trip, but the pay was good.

It had taken three days to make the journey, but the new company trucks were air conditioned and the seats comfortable. The sleeper compartment was spacious and air conditioned. The cost of operation for these trips was very high which made Ray wonder how any money could be made by shipping these goods such a long distance since the individual sale price of the products was so small. He had no other reason to suspect anything unlawful was taking place at his company, but it bothered him enough that when he was asked by a federal enforcement officer if he suspected anything, he had to admit he wasn't sure and volunteered to inform him when he was to pick up a load in Mexico. Now, here he was and still had no idea if he was doing anything illegal in either country.

His first full day in Puebla was spent moving trailers and resting. The second morning he backed under a loaded trailer and collected the weigh bills and shipping manifest from the dock foreman. It was still cool in the morning hours when he drove out of the yard and pointed the load north toward the U.S. border. The return trip was much slower going than the trip south due to the fragile nature of the cargo. The trailer was air conditioned and the plants needed no additional water during the transport, but the rough and narrow, snaking roads required more care during the drive. He checked the time of day on the clock in the dashboard of the new truck. When he was sure Dixon was in the office he reported in.

"I moved all the trailers to the new location. They have a big crew working inside the warehouse. It's all desert around there. Hotter than heck; it's a nice loading dock, though. The foreman down there doesn't look much like a warehouseman, but he knew his job and got me out of there on time. I'm on my way north now. I hope to be through Mexico City by evening. I'll pull off and stop for the night in one of the small towns along the way. The refrigeration doesn't work as hard at night, but it needs the airflow of the moving truck in the heat of the day. Once I pass Mexico City the traffic shouldn't be bad and I think I'll make good time. The packaging for the cargo isn't very good and I can't make very good time on the rough and crooked roads without damaging the plants." Thiel gave his report to the boss as he drove.

"Good job, Ray. That's why I picked you for this move. Just keep moving and let me know exactly how much time to allow for each leg of the trip for the other drivers. Let me know when you deliver in Nevada."

Dixon was pleased with the smoothness of the changeover to the new warehouse in Mexico and with the efficiency of Ray Thiel. He made a note to give Ray a bonus for his efforts. Money worked better than a letter in his personnel file as incentive to any employee.

Thiel kept notes and documented fuel stops, rest stops, services and danger spots along the trip. The next driver would not know what to expect in case he had an emergency, and these notes would aid him in seeking help if he needed it. It was mid-afternoon on day eight when Ray backed his trailer up to the loading dock and handed the paperwork to the dock foreman. Bucco read the documents and checked the customs seal on the door of the trailer. Everything was in order. He pointed to another Amerimex trailer parked near the perimeter fence.

"I'll have one of the dock boys help you hook up to that one. Mr. Dixon said you could go home for a couple of days and he would schedule you out after he talked to you." Bucco looked more like a union exec than a dock foreman, but knew his business and directed the process with efficiency. He ordered the yard man to assist Ray with hooking up and inspecting the trailer.

The yard man pulled the handle to disconnect the trailer and hoses before walking to the trailer Ray was to back under. With only one truck in the yard it was not a complicated process.

Ray pulled out of the yard and pointed his Freightliner East toward Houston. At the first Flying J truck stop he stopped to eat and to call Stan Andrews from his personal cell phone. He gave the DEA Agent a report of the trip he had just completed and again told him there was nothing suspicious to report. Once he had eaten a good meal and filled his truck with fuel he crawled into the sleeper for a much-needed rest before driving home to Houston. Thiel was a single man, never married, but enjoyed his time at home just the same.

Rodeo was his hobby and though he no longer competed he liked watching the bull riders on television.

Stan Andrews had been waiting for Ray's call. Once he talked with the truck driver and learned a load had been delivered to the Nevada location near Nelson, he put on his tee shirt, jeans and boots before driving the old Ford to the warehouse to see Bucco and inquire about work. He saw Tony Bucco standing on the dock behind a large cargo trailer painted with an Amerimex logo. He stepped up on the dock to speak with the foreman.

"Hello, Mr. Bucco, Remember me?" asked Stan.

"Yeah, I do. We just got our first truck in today and should start to get busy soon. Have you ever run a dock like this one?"

"Sure, over in California. But that one was union and I'm guessing this one isn't. The union won't let me work on their docks no more, 'cause I got hurt and sued 'em. I lost the lawsuit and my job in the process. How many trucks will you be turning around?" Stan really didn't know what to ask, but it seemed like a relevant request.

"Hard to tell at this point, but we expect about one incoming load each day, like this one," he said pointing at the large refrigerated van, "and, once the inspections are started, we will be shipping at least six delivery vans each day. Five-day week, payday on Friday, miss a day and you're fired. Your schedule will depend on the time of day the trucks arrive from Mexico. Your job is to load and unload trucks. You don't do the work. You just keep the flunkies working. You keep your mouth shut and the dock boys working. I run the plant, inside and outside. You work for me. You tell no one what we do here and report any nosey visitors to me. You still want the job?" asked Bucco.

"What's it pay?" asked Stan.

"I'll pay you $1,500 a week, but you work when the trucks are here, whatever time of day that is. Seven days a week, but you're off when there ain't no trucks. OK?"

"Yeah, I like it. When do I start?"

"Right now. Go into the office and tell the girl what size uniform you wear. You can't run our docks looking like that. I have the crews processing the plants from Mexico and we should start loading delivery vans day after tomorrow. Where ya livin'?"

"Gotta room over at Boulder City," replied Stan Andrews.

"The company has a motor home you can use. Park it out back and hook up to the power, water and sewer. We won't charge you for it, but you have to keep it clean. That way you will always be here when a truck comes."

Stan was amused that Bucco never smiled when he talked. "I'll go get my stuff out of the room. Want a beer at the tavern in town later?"

"I always stop there around 5:30. See ya there. Don't forget to see the girl about a uniform."

Stan climbed into his old Ford and drove off toward Boulder City. Once away from the warehouse he poked the speed dial to call Greg Hanson. "I got the job. They gave me an old motorhome to live in behind the warehouse. I don't know how often I'll be able to call you, but I'll do the best I can."

"Have you seen inside the warehouse yet?" asked Hanson.

"No, but the back doors were open on the unloaded trailer. It was full of paper boxes that looked like cases of smaller boxes. Bucco said they were repackaging desert plants from Mexico, so I assume that's what's in the paper boxes. The trailer was completely full all the way to the rear doors."

"I'm going to send someone out to back you up. I don't like you being there alone."

"I'll be OK, Greg. Give me a chance to learn what they do inside the warehouse before you have anyone start nosing around. This Tony Bucco seems like a tough bird. I don't want him to become suspicious."

"OK, Stan, if that's the way you want it, but I don't like it. If there is even a hint of danger I want you to get out of there, understood?"

"I hear you, 'Daddy,'" said Stan.

Chapter Nineteen

In Boulder City, Stan packed all his regular wardrobe and equipment in his duty sedan and moved it into an enclosed parking garage at one of the large hotels. He hitched a ride back to Nelson where his smoky old Ford was parked. The girl in the office had told him to come back by five in the afternoon to pick up his new set of working clothes. He drove back to the terminal yard and located the motorhome.

The girl in the office handed him a box with two sets of uniforms inside and asked him to sign for the motorhome keys. Within minutes Stan was at home in his new quarters. It would be handy for watching the activities around the yard and the warehouse. Once finished with the move it was time to drive into town for a beer with Tony Bucco.

Bucco was sitting on the end stool at the bar when Stan arrived. When he saw Stan enter he waved a large arm for him to take the next stool. "Come on, Stan, have a beer. We never talk shop here, so we can both relax. I'm buying this round. What kind of beer do you like?"

"I want to thank you for taking a chance on me, Mr. Bucco. I only got enough cash to buy you one round in return and I needed the job."

"No shop talk, Stan. You can buy next week after payday," said Tony. "Are you an Arizona Cardinals fan?"

"Will I get fired if I tell you I'm a Seahawks fan?"

"No, but if we have this discussion when I'm drunk you could get hurt." Both men laughed and shook hands. It was the first time Stan had seen Tony Bucco smile.

"Do you live close by, Tony?" asked Stan.

"Yeah, in the motel across the street, the company moves me around a lot, so I just rent a motel room and charge it to the company. Did you get moved into the RV?"

"Yup, all moved in. Nice place. Handy, too. I can see the trucks coming and going. It'll work out good for me."

"Have another beer, man, but don't get arrested on the drive back to the terminal."

Stan would have never guessed his boss would be this friendly away from the loading dock. This relationship should make it a little easier for him to snoop around inside the warehouse.

The home place for Ray Thiel was a twenty-five acre parcel where he had originally intended to raise bucking bulls for the rodeo. His dream collapsed when he learned it would require far more than twenty-five acres and far more than his total savings account to finance such a project. He had nearly used up his savings when he gave up and took a job driving truck once again. He had no wife, no kids and a bad leg he acquired from injuries while bull riding in his rodeo days. His second love was driving truck and he liked the man, John Douglas, he worked for and who paid him very well for doing his job. This long trip to Mexico had made him feel guilty about forsaking his company loyalty to help that DEA agent, Stan Andrews.

Ray parked his truck and opened the house before going back to the yard to get what he needed to wash his truck. Like the old-time cowboy taking care of his horse, Ray never put his truck to bed without cleaning it, inside and out. Two hours later he entered the house to take a shower and relax. He fell asleep in his recliner.

It was exactly nine a.m. the following morning when his phone rang, interrupting his breakfast. It was his boss, John Douglas. "Hello, Ray, sorry to bother you, but I would like you to come into the office and meet with me. I need a first-hand report on the operation in Puebla. Can you come in this morning?"

"Sure, what time?" asked Thiel.

"The earlier the better for me," said Douglas.

"I can be there in an hour. Is that good for you?"

"Yes, and I'll have DD here for the meeting, also."

An hour later, Ray climbed the stairs to the second-floor offices of John Douglas Enterprises where he was met by the shapely office manager, Shirley. "Mr. Douglas is waiting for you, Mr. Thiel." Shirley ushered Ray into the boss' office, closing the door as she left the room.

"Good morning, Ray. Sorry to bother you on your first day home, but I need to hear your opinion of the terminal operation in Puebla." Douglas pointed to Dillon Dixon. "I think you know DD."

"Yes, I do. Good to see you again, Mr. Dixon," said the truck driver.

"The reason we picked you for this initial trip to Puebla was that you have a reputation for being thorough and trustworthy. I want an honest opinion of the terminal operation in Mexico. Is it a safe operation?"

"It seems to be, Mr. Douglas. The dock boss there gave me the help I needed to get the trailers moved to the new location and helped me get hooked up to the new load. I didn't see the inside of the warehouse, but there were a lot of people working there. The only thing I saw out of the ordinary was the two guards with AR-15s at the gate. They didn't hassle me or anything, but I wondered about armed guards at a trucking terminal."

"That bothered me, too, when I was told about it. I'm told there is a great deal of bandit activity in the area and the armed men are to protect the property and crew from them."

"Was there anything else there that made you suspicious?" asked Dillon Dixon.

"No, sir, I was told at the outset that the Amerimex logo on the trailers and trucks would keep the bandits away and it seemed to do just that. I never had any trouble anywhere, fuel stops, rest stops, or restaurants.

"Customs looked at the manifests and opened the trailer to look inside, but closed it up and waved me on. It was a pretty trouble-free trip. The packaging for the cargo is pretty fragile for the rough roads, making it difficult to make good road time on the return trip. I took it easy to protect the shipment, but I don't know how much damage might have been done."

"My initial report is that the cargo arrived in good shape, thanks to you. I'll see to it you are compensated for your care. Mr. Dixon and I were worried because of the long distance to the new terminal. Thank you for being so cautious, Ray." Douglas had been making notes of the conversation while Dixon listened intently and nodded from time to time.

"We realize this is a long trip, Ray, and want you to take some extra time off between trips. I think a week between trips is fair, considering the long hours you spent on the road," Dixon offered.

"Thanks a lot," said Ray as he stood to leave the meeting. He was reaching for the door handle when he turned to say something, "Ah, Mr. Douglas, I have a confession to make."

"Oh, and what is that?" asked Douglas.

"A while back I was approached by a DEA agent to report if I suspected any drugs being transported in our trucks. I told him there wouldn't be any in our trucks. He wanted the delivery schedule for this load and I gave it to him. At the time I didn't think it made any difference, but I feel guilty about it. I'm sorry Mr. Douglas. I know there isn't any chance of our trucks transporting drugs. I know your policies on that. I hope I didn't do anything wrong."

"Do you know this agent's name?" asked Dixon.

"Stan something, he showed me his credentials when he talked to me, otherwise I wouldn't have agreed."

"Can you tell me what he looks like?" inquired DD, while taking notes. Ray described the agent for Dixon.

"It's all right, Ray. As long as you're sure he was a DEA agent. We'll check into it. I appreciate your telling us about it. Now, take a few days off. I hear the national finals for bull riding are in progress in Las Vegas. You should go and see the show. We'll be in touch with your next dispatch."

Once at home, Ray checked on the computer to see if he could get box seats for the bull riding competition. He paid for a box seat and made plans to drive his SUV to Las Vegas.

Dillon Dixon had long been the fix it man for John Douglas. This was definitely a problem needing fixing. DD's first call was to Tony Bucco in Nevada where he learned of a new hire at the Nevada terminal using the name Stan. The problem had now become serious and must be dealt with as quickly as possible.

"The immediate problem is the DEA agent," remarked Douglas. "I think you had better deal with this one personally. We can't take any chances with this. Rent a car and drive up to the new terminal in Nevada. Try to make it look like an accident. In any case get it done quickly."

"What about Ray?" asked DD.

"He can wait for now. The DEA agent is the priority."

"I'll take care of it." Without further conversation Dixon left the office to call the rental company to order a pickup. He called a cab to take him to the car rental office.

It was going to be a long drive to Nevada using Highway 10 the entire way. It was all open country and freeway speeds, but a long distance, nonetheless. It was very early morning hours when he arrived in the small town of Nelson. At a rest stop outside of town he stopped to relieve himself and get a couple hours of sleep before contacting Tony Bucco. The sun was warm and the sky clear when he awoke to begin a search for somewhere to eat breakfast. The local truck stop was convenient and the food was good. After breakfast he refueled his rental truck and contacted Tony.

"I need to see you, Tony. We've got a problem. I'm here to correct it. Meet me at the Flying J. I'm driving a green Chevy pickup and parked in the truck lot."

"I'll be there in twenty minutes," said Tony.

Bucco found Dixon's truck and pulled alongside, their driver side windows facing each other. "Does this have to do with the phone call yesterday?"

"Yes, it does. One of our drivers—you met him a couple of days ago—passed information to a DEA agent by the name of Stan. I'll take care of him later, but for now I need to see that your new man has some kind of accident. Have you got any ideas?"

"Hmm," wondered Bucco, "maybe; he moved into the RV behind the warehouse. I think it could develop a propane leak."

"Sounds like it could happen that way. Is he there now?" asked Dixon.

"Yeah, he doesn't have to be on the dock until ten or eleven to meet the next truck."

"OK, you go back to work and try to keep my visit private, if you know what I mean." Dixon was good at his job and had done this kind of thing in the past.

Chapter Twenty

Dixon parked outside the fenced area and walked to the office entry. Tony was on the loading dock speaking with one of the employees. Once close to the huge warehouse building Dixon made a quick turn and stepped around the corner of the warehouse, out of sight of the guards at the gate. He walked directly to the motorhome behind the big building and tapped on the door. Stan Andrews, half asleep, opened it from the inside.

"Oh, hello, I thought it was someone else. What do you want?" he asked.

"I need to speak with you a minute. Can I come inside?" asked DD with a pleasant smile.

"Sure, come on in. Want some coffee?"

"That would be nice," said DD.

When Andrews turned toward the cupboard where the coffee pot sat, Dixon pulled a short piece of pipe from under his shirt and struck Stan on the back of the head knocking him unconscious. He then reached behind the propane cook stove and disconnected the pipe allowing the propane gas to flow into the interior of the RV. He had rigged a barbecue igniter with duct tape and attached the switch to the back of Stan's shirt, thinking that when he came back to awareness he would roll over on his back and reach for the lump on his head. His body weight on the igniter would trigger enough spark to ignite the gas trapped inside the motorhome causing a deadly explosion. An accident....

After carefully taping the trigger to the back of Stan's uniform shirt, Dixon quickly exited the motorhome, closing the door carefully behind him. He walked to the corner of the warehouse building near the office door, then directly to the gate and his rented truck. He was nearly a mile from the gate when he heard the sound of an explosion and saw a plume of smoke and dust rising behind the warehouse. He drove directly to the intersection with U.S. Highway 10 and turned left, driving east toward Houston. Once on the freeway he called John Douglas with news there had been a terrible accident at the warehouse in Nevada.

It was the next morning when Greg Hansen saw the report of the explosion at a warehouse in southern Nevada. An unidentified man had been killed in the explosion.

Shocked and upset he called Darren Hatfield. "I told him, Darren, I told him. He just wanted to snoop around a couple of days before he would let me send him a backup. I knew better, but I let him have his way. Can you put a team together to investigate the explosion?" asked Hansen.

"Yes, Greg, I'll send a team over there right away. I'm really sorry about Stan. He was a good man and I liked him a lot. If you have time I'll come by your office and take a look at any reports Stan had made. I think we can take a walk through the warehouse and see if there is anything suspicious. There has to be something going on there for them to want Stan dead. I'll get a warrant and we can take a legal look."

The warrant process would take too long and any evidence that might have been there would be long gone by the time it arrived.

In the meantime, Tony Bucco stayed with the Nevada State Police while they investigated the explosion and death of their employee. They gathered evidence all afternoon, questioning many of the employees at the warehouse and in the office. The troopers were gathering to leave when he was notified the FBI was sending a team of investigators to the scene. Bucco called John Douglas immediately.

"I don't know why the feds are coming in, Mr. Douglas. The Nevada State Police are leaving and taking lots of evidence with them. The body was taken by the police and they have sealed the scene with evidence tape. I heard this Stan guy I hired was a DEA agent. That's the only reason I can see for an investigation by the feds."

"I have talked with our associate, Mr. Dixon, and he assures me there is nothing for them to find. Just answer all the questions they ask and keep them out of the warehouse. I don't want them to see the inside and start asking questions. Let me know if there's a problem." Not waiting for an answer or another question, Douglas hung up the phone.

Two days later, the FBI investigators had finished their evidence gathering. There had been little to find as the Nevada State Police had done a very thorough job in their initial search. Bucco had insisted the investigators stay out of the warehouse area and only enter the office portion of the building. He told the investigators there were perishable plants in the warehouse and the temperature changes, caused by traffic in and out of the entry doors, were enough to cause damage to the plants inside. He gave the lead investigator a quick tour of the work area inside the big warehouse, allowing him to see the work being done, and offered to answer any questions he may have about the work being done there. The investigator seemed to be satisfied with the information and told Bucco he and his team would be as careful as possible if it became necessary for them to enter the warehouse.

Greg Hansen, DEA investigator, had contacted the Nevada State Police to have them coordinate their investigation with his team now on the scene. He also volunteered to have the FBI lab take care of all the analysis to be done on the evidence taken from the scene. Since this would relieve the State Police of the cost involved they were more than willing to turn over the evidence to the FBI team. The head investigator for the Nevada State Police informed Hansen the local investigators concluded this was an accident and nothing more. Hansen thanked him for his efforts and added that he would forward a report of the analysis to him and his department.

Dillon Dixon was now in Houston, rested and ready to report to his boss. He met Douglas in his office to report what he had done and assured him there was nothing for the investigators to find that would make them suspect anything but a tragic accident. Douglas was pleased with the result.

"What about Ray Thiel?" asked Dixon.

"He is definitely another problem. I'm torn between having you arrange a trucking accident for him or to call Carlos and have him provide it for us. I don't like depending on others to do this kind of detail work. It leaves too many open possibilities. I know Mendoza has competent people, but I still don't like it." John Douglas was thoughtful in his comments. "What do you think, DD?"

"How soon do you plan to send Ray back for another load?" asked Dixon.

"I'm working on the schedule now, but I think the end of next week will be as soon as he needs to go out again. Why?"

"I have an idea about doing this remotely. I can plant the items we need on his truck while he's gone to Vegas. If you can get him to call in on his second night on the road, when he's about to call it a day and crawl into his sleeper, I can trigger a remote agent while he sleeps. I can set it off with only a cell phone and he'll never wake up. The gas will dissipate in a few hours and not be detected. The Mexican police will find him dead in his truck of natural causes." Dixon smiled, "New technology is great, and simple. We can send someone down to recover the truck and eliminate any chance of finding the cause of his passing."

"His truck will be parked at his home until he returns from Las Vegas. Take care of the details and I'll make arrangements for him to make another trip." Douglas was making notes on a pad on the left side of his desk. "I'll make a note to have him call in when he stops for the second night."

"I'll get on it right away, Mr. Douglas. Just let me know when to make the call." Dixon gathered the items he needed and made his way to the little farm owned by Ray Thiel. He planted the items under the bunk in the truck's sleeper and connected the power source to the wiring of the Freightliner. There was nothing to find inside the compartment except the end of a piece of plastic tubing protruding through the floor under the bunk. The tank of gas and the electronic trigger were hidden under the floor in a compartment containing Ray's tool box.

Dixon closed up the truck cab and the tool compartment, wiping any fingerprints away with a shop towel he had found in the compartment. Where the truck was parked had been paved and clean which meant he didn't have any worry about footprints. He inspected the area carefully before getting back into his own truck and driving away. All he now had to do was to wait for Ray to call.

Nine days later the call came. Douglas notified DD who made the electronic call to the device beneath the sleeper compartment of the truck parked alongside the highway in southern Mexico.

John Douglas received a call from the police south of Mexico City two days later to report the death of one of his drivers. Captain Ramirez reported the driver had apparently died of a heart attack while sleeping in the truck. Ramirez asked about disposition of the body and the truck.

Douglas breathed a huge sigh of relief and said he would send someone down to claim the truck and asked Ramirez to ship the body to his office in Houston. Amerimex Trucking would pay for the shipping.

"Ray was a good man. One of my most trusted drivers. I'll send a driver to get the truck. I thank you for taking care of this matter for me. Please let me know if there is ever anything I can do for you, Captain."

Douglas then called DD. He said: "I just had a call from a police captain in Mexico. He said Ray Thiel had died of heart problems. I'm sending a driver to complete the run the truck was making since the police said the truck was in good condition. I'm having Ray's body sent back here. I think he has some relatives, and I'll see they're notified."

"Are we back on schedule now?" asked Dixon.

"It appears so, yes. I will have to call our friend in the south to let him know what has happened." Douglas didn't like the notoriety being generated by his company in recent days. "Once things are back to normal I'm going back to Alaska for some rest. You know how to contact me."

"How soon are you leaving, Boss?"

"The end of next week, if everything is going well," said Douglas. "I've moved those other four trucks to North Dakota and given the drivers a small pay raise, making them happy. I'll leave this for you to manage if there are no further problems by next week."

Weather had kept most residents off the roads and nearly all travelers out of the air during the past two weeks. Wyatt was very bored with the lack of activity and spent most of his time organizing his filing system and cleaning his office and living quarters. There had been a lot of snow to shovel in front of the air charter office, but almost no official business for him to tend. Tom Dempsey's flying schedule had been sporadic to say the least.

The only official call for Wyatt during this period had been a bar fight at the local hotel. Two nights a week he drove to Linda Mason's home for dinner. Had it not caused the local tongues to wag he would have liked to spend every evening with the school teacher. He had begun to gain a little weight from the regular home cooked meals he consumed while visiting her.

Late the second week, Wyatt was sitting at his desk early in the day when his cell phone rang. It was Leon MacKammon. "Hello there, Leon, what's up?" he asked.

"Flying weather in the Pass ain't too good, but your favorite Super Cub just took off headed for Lake Clark Pass. Said he was goin' to Anchorage on business. Might want to check him out when he comes back from his business trip."

"Thanks, Leon, I'll look into it." The VPSO thought about it a few moments and dialed Gene Turner.

"How's the weather, Wyatt?" asked Sergeant Turner.

"Not great, but flyable. It looks like we may have a little break for a few days. We could sure use it."

"Just hunker down and wait it out. It will get busy soon enough. What's on your mind this morning, Wyatt?" he asked.

"Do you remember that suspicious Super Cub we talked about?"

"Sure, don't tell me he's been up to his old shenanigans in this weather."

"No, but I just had a report he is headed toward Anchorage on a 'business trip.' I was wondering if you could have someone in Anchorage learn where he went while he was there. It might be interesting to know."

"Sure thing, Wyatt. I'll call one of my associates up there and have them keep an eye out for the plane and watch to see where he goes. He might just hook up with one of our old friends in town." Gene chuckled, "I don't understand how you can be that far off the beaten path and still learn this much about what goes on in the big city. You're amazing,"

"This is a very small community and I'm such a nice guy everyone wants to be my friend. You should try to be nice, Gene. It might improve your image." Now both men laughed.

Chapter Twenty-One

Captain Wilson, head of the narcotics investigation team, had called Sergeant Bill Cook to ask him to check out the Merrill Field area for a red and white Super Cub with a certain tail number and report back. Cook had the numbers and was near the airfield when the call came in. Bill Cook was a pilot himself and had many friends with the FAA on Merrill Field. He drove directly to the flight service office to speak with an old friend there, Tommy Goodson. Goodson agreed to call Cook if this particular Piper reported in to land at this airstrip. Two hours later Cook got the call.

Sergeant Cook, driving an unmarked pickup truck, found the plane parked in the transient parking area near the tower. An old Chevy Camaro was parked in front of the little Piper and two men stood near the front of the yellow car. Cook parked nearby in front of an aviation electronics dealer's shop to watch the pair. One of the men wore street clothes while the other wore a heavy parka and insulated boots. The investigator took pictures of the men and the airplane as well as the old yellow sports car. He was not able to hear what the men were saying, but the man in the parka handed the other man a large cloth shopping bag. The other man put it in the front seat of his car and came back carrying a medium size priority mail box to give to the man in the parka. Cook was able to video the entire transaction until the men parted ways. The man in the Chevy drove away to leave the airfield while the man in the parka climbed into his Super Cub and started the engine.

This information was relayed to his boss and eventually to Gene Turner and on to Wyatt in Iliamna.

"It looks like our dealer just bought another shipment to bring out here," said Wyatt.

"It sure looks that way. Bill Cook said he didn't recognize the man in the Chevy, but he must be a regular dealer to have a meeting at the airport. Our team is keeping an eye on the dealer to see what he's doing. How do you intend to deal with this on your end?" asked Turner.

"I'm not sure, Gene, I don't have a warrant to seize his shipment, but that would be nice. If I could say for sure there were drugs in the box there would be no problem, but since we don't know for sure I can't do that. I really don't want to tip our hand and let him know we're watching him." There was frustration in his tone.

"How about this, Wyatt?" asked Gene Turner. "Why not contact Carl Lewis and let him work on this Buntz guy?"

"That's probably the thing to do, since I stick out like a sore thumb around here. He can do it without tipping our hand. At least we might find out for sure if he really is a drug dealer or if he's bootlegging alcohol or something else." Wyatt thought a few seconds, "I'll try to contact Carl and let him know what we want. I'll let you know how it works out."

Lewis had made a habit of coming to town to check his mail each morning. This gave Wyatt a way to stop him on the road from the lodge if there was a reason to talk. The following morning Wyatt drove out the main road past the school and stopped his truck. He stepped out of the pickup and opened the hood. He sat in the driver's seat until he saw the SUV owned by the lodge coming from the opposite direction and stepped out to lean on the fender, looking under the hood. Carl stopped his vehicle and stepped out to speak with the VPSO.

"Howdy, Officer. Need help?" asked Carl as he stepped out of his car.

"No, I just heard a funny noise from the engine and stopped to check it out. Good to see you again," Wyatt answered as Carl walked closer to the pickup.

When the men were side by side Carl asked, "What's up, Wyatt?"

Wyatt gave the undercover officer a short rendition of the situation with Rick Buntz. "Gene and I thought you may be able to learn what he bought in Anchorage, without tipping your hand, since you already know the man."

"I'll see what I can do."

"How are things going out at the lodge?" asked Wyatt.

"I've been busy with the logs. The last guy did a really good job of fitting the logs together and it takes a while to match his handy work. It's a great place to work, though. They leave me alone and let me do my work. The helper is kind of a half-wit, but he works hard. Mr. Douglas called yesterday to tell Harry he will be coming back the end of next week and will be here for two or three weeks." Carl had been speaking quietly.

Wyatt reached up to close the hood of his truck, "Thanks for stopping to help, Carl. Good to see you again."

Lewis turned to walk back to his SUV, calling back over his shoulder, "See ya 'round."

Wyatt drove to the end of the road and stopped in front of the lodge. He climbed the steps to the porch and knocked on the big solid wood door. Harry Porter answered the knock.

"Officer Earp, good to see you. Come on in and have a cup of coffee."

"Thanks, Harry, I can use one today. How have you been?"

"Things are good. We seem to be getting things done around here in spite of the weather. We're getting a lot of finish and trim work done inside the lodge. I want to thank you and Tom Dempsey for helping us find a replacement for the worker who died. The new man may be even better with the logs than the other one. He's a real craftsman and easy to get along with."

"I didn't know your new man until he came here. All that was Tom's doing. I'm glad you like him and he's working out OK. I was stopped on the side of the road a while ago and he stopped to see if I needed help. He seems like a nice guy. By the way, where is the other helper today?" asked Wyatt.

"Oh, he's around. I have him splitting firewood right now. He, too, is a good worker, but lacks motivation." Harry set two cups of hot coffee on the table. "How are things in the village?" he asked.

"It's been pretty quiet since the storm moved in. It was good for me. I was able to get my office organized and usable." Wyatt sipped his coffee, giving a satisfied sigh.

"I've heard you're seeing the school teacher. Is that true?"

"News does get around out here on the tundra. Yes, but I haven't seen her much since the storm. I plan to stop over there this evening if she is free. She's a nice lady...a local girl, you know." Wyatt didn't want to get into details.

"I envy you. There aren't many single, attractive, young ladies around here."

"That's life in the bush, Harry," commented Wyatt, taking another taste of the hot coffee. "I have to be getting back to town now. I just wanted to come out and check on you folks at the lodge, to be sure you're doing all right."

"Yes, we're doing fine. Thanks for checking. The boss called and said he planned to come back up here by the end of next week."

"Does he give you a lot of orders while he's here?" asked Wyatt.

"You know, he doesn't. He is probably the easiest employer I've ever had. He wants production, but never grumbles if he sees we've been working at something. I don't know if he will want me to stay on after the construction is completed, but I would really like to stay and run the lodge. I sure don't miss the bustle of the city life," Harry gave a short chuckle, "except for the ladies, of course."

Wyatt finished his coffee and put the cup in the sink before leaving. "Call me if you need anything, Harry." He waved and walked out to his pickup. Spotting the other hired hand in front of, what looked like, a woodshed, he waved as he drove out the gate.

On his way back to town he checked the time and realized Linda should be getting home about now. He stopped at her cabin and tapped on the door. There was no answer. He was climbing into his truck when she pulled into the yard. She greeted him with a huge smile.

"Do you have time to come inside for a while?" she asked.

"Sorry, girl, I'm still on duty. I just came by to say hello."

"I'll cook dinner tonight if you can come back and eat."

"I would like that, but I can't get here before six. Is that too late?"

"Six will be just fine. I'll heat up some of that stew and make some fresh dinner rolls. Sound good?" she asked.

"It sounds wonderful. I'll be here." He put his hand on hers and held it for a moment while looking at his own feet.

Linda covered his hand with her other hand and squeezed it gently. "I like you, Officer Earp."

"I like you, too, Linda." He was becoming uncomfortable. "I'll see you around six."

"Don't forget," she said, stepping back to allow his door to open.

Maggie Dempsey stopped him as he walked through the office. "A man came into the office and left a note for you. Said his name was Carl." She handed the note to him over the top of the tall counter.

"Thanks, Maggie," said Wyatt, taking the envelope to read in the privacy of his own office.

The note said Carl had contacted Buntz and the two were to have some drinks this evening at the hotel bar. Carl said he would contact the VPSO if he learned anything worth reporting. Wyatt thought about it for a few minutes before lighting up his computer screen to finish his daily report and add notes to his list of information he kept there. It was nearly six p.m. when he finished his paperwork.

He showered and changed into different clothing for his dinner date with Linda Mason. Suddenly, he realized how much he was looking forward to spending an evening with the school teacher. He went to his upright freezer to take out a half gallon container of triple chocolate ice cream. There was nowhere to get flowers tonight but he thought ice cream would have the same effect. Maggie was still seated at her desk when he walked out to his truck.

Chapter Twenty-Two

The next several days were quiet in the village. There had been a report of a moose poached near the swamp north of the village. Since Lonnie Davis was still off work with his injuries it was Wyatt's task to investigate the case.

An old Alaska Fish and Wildlife Trooper named Dan France had once told Wyatt; "Look at everything; they always leave something behind. Poachers are always in a hurry and careless. You will find something, a knife with initials carved on the handle, or a gasoline credit card receipt with the poacher's name on it, or an imprint of a license plate in a snow bank. They always leave something."

Wyatt found the carcass near the small swamp. Everything was frozen and snow covered. The blood in the snow looked like a neon sign. He began to take pictures of the area, the boot prints, and tire tracks. The tracks indicated the vehicle was another four-wheel ATV. He found where the ATV had been parked and the meat loaded. On the snow behind where the vehicle had parked was a small fanny pack with butcher tools inside. A liquid ink pen had been used to write the name of the owner on the canvas pack, Rufus Donavan. Wyatt grinned and picked up the pack. He followed the tracks of the ATV toward the lake where it crossed on the ice. The VPSO drove his truck across the frozen lake and on toward Nondalton where Rufus Donavan lived. He hated having to write his old friend a ticket for poaching, but it was his job.

Wyatt stopped his truck in front of Donavan's cabin. He could see an ATV parked near the back corner of the house. There was blood in the snow near the small vehicle. Wyatt knew this man and knew he was not ordinarily a violent person so he stepped up onto the front porch and knocked on the door. Rufus answered, wiping blood from his hands on a towel he carried.

"Whatcha doin' here, Wyatt?" asked the Native man.

"I had a report of a moose poaching over on the other side of the lake. I found the site and followed the tracks here to Nondalton. Would you know anything about the case?"

Rufus gave the officer a huge grin, "I guess you caught me, Wyatt. The neighbor lady is old and was out of meat, so I went over there to get some meat for her. Come on in. Want some coffee?"

"Sure, I'll take a cup. You say you got the meat for the neighbor lady. Who would that be, Rufus?"

"Mrs. Ootok. She lives in the house just down the hill. She's old and her husband passed away, so I get her meat when she needs it."

"I saw the kill site and I could tell you didn't waste any of the meat."

"No, I don't waste it. She will use it all this winter. I'm cutting it up for her now." They were now in the kitchen where the meat was piled on the cupboard. "Come on and sit down and drink your coffee. I need the rest anyway. I lost my best knives somewhere and the ones I'm using aren't very good."

"Were they in a green fanny pack with your name on it?" asked Wyatt.

"Yeah, they were. Did you find them?"

"You left it lying on the snow behind the ATV when you loaded the meat. I am going to have to walk over to the Ootok house and talk with her. If what you say is true and she backs your story I'll give you the pack. Rufus, you know there are rules about this and you can get meat for her, but you have to follow the rules."

"I know, but it takes too long to get permission and she was gettin' hungry." Rufus stared at the floor, "I know you have to write me a ticket. I got it coming, but don't take the meat, please. She needs it bad."

"I'll walk over there and talk with her. I'll make that decision afterwards. Thanks for the coffee, Rufus."

It was all Wyatt could do to control a good laugh about the case before he made it out the door. He walked the hundred yards to the neighboring home and tapped on the door. An elderly lady answered.

"Are you Mrs. Ootok?" asked Wyatt.

"Yes, what is this about?"

"I've heard you were running short of meat for the winter. Is that true?"

"Yes, but how did you find out about that?" she asked in a quiet voice. "My husband died this spring and I can't hunt any more. Sometimes one of the neighbors will get a moose for me. The law says they can do that for me."

"Yes, it does and that's why I'm asking you about it. I am just checking to be sure you can have it. I'm going back up to Rufus' house and help him finish cutting up the meat. We'll bring it down to you when we finish."

"That Rufus is such a nice man," she commented.

"Yes, he is. We have been friends for quite a while. It's a good thing for him to look out for his neighbors. You go back inside and we'll be back soon." Wyatt stepped off the porch and walked back up the hill to the Donavan house.

The two men spent another hour cutting and packaging the meat. It was much easier after Rufus had his good knives back in his possession. When the two men finished the meat cutting project they loaded it into the back of the VPSO pickup and delivered it to the neighbor lady. They were instructed to place the packages in her chest type freezer located on the back porch.

Wyatt took Rufus back to his cabin, but remained in his truck where they talked a few moments.

"Well, are you writing me a ticket?" asked the older man.

"I guess not this time, Rufus. I'll make out the proper forms for this charity moose, but, please, if you are going to help a neighbor, call me and let me know. It'll save us both a lot of trouble. I have to get back to my office and take care of all the paperwork you caused me." Wyatt knew how it worked in the bush. People looked out for the elderly or disabled. It was a good system, but was hard to justify in the modern world.

Rufus climbed out of the truck and Wyatt made his way back across the frozen lake to return to his little office. He called Captain Griffin in Fairbanks to report the subsistence moose kill and to ask how Lonnie Davis was progressing.

"Good to hear from you, Wyatt. How is everything going for you?" asked the Captain.

"Things seem to be moving along smoothly, Captain. Carl Lewis is lending a hand in an attempt to learn what that Buntz guy is up to. All indications say he's dealing drugs, but I still have no evidence. I faxed you the report on the moose kill I investigated and just called to be sure I did the right thing in letting the poacher off with a warning. He was helping an elderly neighbor get some moose meat for her freezer."

"Yes, I read the report. It seemed like the thing to do. I'll be glad when Lonnie is back on duty and you won't have to deal with these cases."

"Do you have any idea when Lonnie will be back?" asked Wyatt.

"In about two weeks, according to my last talk with him. He seems to be healing up well, but says he won't be 100 percent when he goes back on duty. That means you will be helping him for a while." Griff knew Wyatt would be helping the Wildlife Trooper as much as he could without instruction from the boss. "I hear you're seeing the local school marm. I'm glad; Iliamna can be a very lonely place."

"Yes, we have dinner together a couple of times a week. She's a very nice lady. She was raised on the lake near Pedro Bay. It's nothing serious yet, but it may be one day."

"How is your dad, Wyatt?"

"He's doing really well. He's leaving for Seattle next week to take care of the fish business he has down there. He asked me to go with him, but I can't get away right now. My mean ole boss wouldn't like it."

"Yeah, I know him and he's a hard man." Both Wyatt and Captain Griffin laughed.

After the call Wyatt was making entries in his daily report when the in-house phone rang. It was Maggie telling him there was a message for him at the front desk and it needed his immediate attention. The VPSO went out to the front desk to retrieve the note.

"You were on the phone when it came in. Someone found a local man dead in his cabin a mile past the school. The mailbox says 'Shaffer' and his friend is there waiting for you to come to the home." Maggie quoted the information in order to speed the response.

Wyatt walked quickly to his truck and started the engine. He drove quickly the two miles to the cabin where Dick Stafford was waiting at the end of the drive. Wyatt turned into the driveway and stopped in front of the small cabin.

"Hello, Mr. Stafford. Are you the one who called this in?"

"Yes, Bob and I do some trapping together and I came over to get ready for a trip we were planning. I knocked on the door, but he didn't answer. His truck is in the driveway, so I tried the door and it opened. Bob is inside on the couch, stiff as a board. Once I saw he was dead I called you and came back outside to wait. There are needles and stuff on the table next to him. I didn't know he was into drugs. We both like to drink a little, but I didn't know he used any drugs."

"OK, Mr. Stafford, I am going inside to check on him. I'll need some information from you, so please wait here until I get finished and come back." Wyatt stepped up on the front porch and tried the door. It opened and he entered the cabin. He could see the occupant sprawled on the couch with the left sleeve of his shirt rolled to above his elbow. Wyatt checked for a pulse, but it wasn't necessary, the man had obviously been dead for several hours. He returned to his truck to get his crime scene pack and begin documenting the site. While in the truck he used his cell phone to call Gene Turner and report the death.

Back in the cabin the VPSO began to photograph the scene and gather evidence. There was evidence of recent drug use, probably heroin, on the table next to the body. A small packet of brown powder lay open on the table. The contents looked remarkably like the powder found at the last, similar death scene. It took several minutes to log his evidence and photos before exiting the cabin to seal the doorway with evidence tape. Dick Stafford was waiting near his vehicle when Wyatt had finished closing the cabin.

"Come sit in my truck, will you Dick?" asked Wyatt. "I will have to see your ID and get some information from you."

Stafford agreed and took a seat inside Wyatt's pickup. The information gathering interview took nearly an hour when Wyatt asked, "Do you have any idea where your friend Bob got his drugs?"

"Nope, I didn't even know he used drugs. I can make a guess, though. He recently took up acquaintance with a guy by the name of Rick Buntz. I didn't like the guy, but Bob had started meeting him at the bar quite often. I never asked him what they talked about; it was none of my business. Did you ever know Bob Dilly?"

"I never met him, but I've heard his name a few times. He never came up on my radar as a drug user, though."

"He was a good guy. He liked a beer or a whisky sometimes, but I never suspected he used heavy drugs. We ran a trap line together for many years. We were just about to start trapping this season and that's why I came to see him. He was a good trapper and a smart guy about the wilderness." Stafford obviously liked Bob Dilly and respected his knowledge.

"Do you think Bob bought his drugs from Buntz?" asked Wyatt.

"I don't know. I never saw him buy any, but I knew most of Bob's regular friends and this Buntz guy is a new one. Maybe he just started using. I don't know."

"I'm going to have to call the sergeant in Soldotna to come help me remove the body. I would appreciate it if you not tell anyone about his death until I can get the body removed."

"Sure thing, Officer Earp. Thanks for taking care of this. Let me know if there is anything I can do to help." Dick Stafford opened the door and stepped out.

Once he was alone, Wyatt used his cell phone to call Gene Turner. "Hello, Gene," he said, "We have another death here in the village and it looks like the same cause. I'm going to need your help again. How soon can you get here?"

"Two hours," said Turner.

Wyatt stayed in front of the cabin for over an hour before returning to his office to wait for the State Cessna to arrive. Not knowing how long the sergeant would be in Iliamna, the two men covered the warm engine and plugged the engine heater into the outlet outside the hangar. Wyatt had moved his pickup to the ramp side of the hangar and they now loaded Turner's equipment and the body bag into the truck.

"So this looks like another heroin overdose?" Turner asked as he climbed into the pickup.

"The paraphernalia on the table is identical to that we found at the other death a few weeks ago. Two deaths from heroin in that period of time in a village of 120 residents could be considered an epidemic. Everything we know right now points to Rick Buntz, but we don't have one shred of evidence. I would like to talk with Carl Lewis, but I didn't want to blow his cover. He sent me a note to the affect that Buntz had hinted to him he had drugs for sale, but I haven't talked directly to Carl." Wyatt was referring to the note Lewis had left for him at the office earlier in the day.

The two men parked the truck in front of the cabin and began the work of documenting everything at the site. After photographing the exterior of the cabin Turner removed the evidence tape from the doorway and stepped inside while Wyatt brought all the equipment to the front porch. It took Turner nearly two hours to document and catalog all the items to be used as evidence. Once done Wyatt helped the sergeant load the body into the plastic body bag and zip it closed. Using a folding stretcher the men carried the body to the truck, placing it in the back, and loaded the evidence containers and other equipment into the cab of the pickup.

Wyatt drove directly to where the Cessna 185 was parked and the two men loaded everything, including the body bag, into the airplane.

"I'll take the body directly to Anchorage for the crime lab and the coroner to take care of," said Turner. "I'll also give Captain Griffin a call and have him contact Carl Lewis to arrange a meeting with you. You have done a great job out here, Wyatt. I'm glad we have a man with your experience here in the village. Usually I have to come out from Soldotna and do the investigations myself. We lose a lot of evidence in the process. You have made my job much easier and I thank you for that."

"That's why I'm here, Sarge," said Wyatt as he pulled the engine cover from the cowling.

Turner waved as he closed the door of the airplane and started the engine. Wyatt watched him taxi to the runway and take off toward the east and Lake Clark Pass. Once the aircraft was out of sight he drove his truck back around the hangar and parked in his spot in the front of the large steel building. Maggie handed him a cup of coffee as he entered.

"Busy day, eh, Wyatt?" she commented as he took the cup from her hand.

"Any calls while I was out?"

"Nope, none," she said as she continued her accounting tasks and Wyatt went to his office to catch up on his reports.

Chapter Twenty-Three

It was after five and Wyatt was still at his desk when the telephone rang. "VPSO Earp, how can I help you?"

"You can come to my house and kiss me," said the sweet voice on the other end.

"Oh, hello, Linda. I've been busy and lost track of the time. How was your day?"

"Cold. The heat went off in the school for a while today. I was ready to send the children home when Mr. Cooper got it going again. Are you coming over tonight?"

"Sorry, but I've had a busy day and I still have a couple of hours to finish paperwork. Can I get a rain check?" asked Wyatt in an apologetic tone.

"Well, of course. Was it something important?" she asked.

"Yes, unfortunately, there's been another heroin death in the village. I have got to find out where these drugs are coming from. I don't want anyone else to die."

"Oh, Wyatt, I'm sorry, I didn't know. You finish up your duties and call me when you get done."

"Thanks, Linda. I'll call you before you go to bed," said Wyatt. "By the way, I had a note from Dad and he's going to come out to Iliamna for a visit the end of next week. I'll try to think of something to cook for him while he's here."

"We'll talk about it later. Get to work. Bye," Linda giggled as she hung up the telephone.

It was late and Maggie was leaving the office when Carl Lewis came in to visit with Wyatt. She let him into the office and locked the door behind her. Carl made his way back to the VPSO office and tapped on the door. Wyatt was still working at his desk, but stood up and opened the door, thinking it was Maggie. He was surprised to see Carl.

"I had a message from Griff to stop and see you. He said you had another OD in the village."

"Come on in to the office, Carl. Want some coffee or a soda?"

"No thanks, I'm just on my way to the café for dinner."

"Like Captain Griffin said, we had another overdose death. The substance appears to be the same as the heroin used in the first one. Gene is having it tested to be sure. I was wondering if you had made any inroads with Rick Buntz?" asked Wyatt.

"I'm working on it, but he's a tough nut to crack. He never volunteers anything. I hinted a couple of times that I wanted to buy some stuff, but he hasn't said he could fix me up. I've seen him have private conversations with some of the locals at the bar, but he won't allow me to hear what he's saying."

"I suppose the Captain told you he was in Anchorage a few days ago and we think he made a buy there. It all took place at the Merrill Field Airport, in the transient parking area near the old tower. If he did make a buy he has product on hand right now. It looks like the stuff we found is Mexican brown and potent. Probably never been cut and that's why the two ODs. This stuff is dangerous. I just wanted to have a talk with you to see if you had learned anything from Buntz, but I didn't want to contact you in public." Wyatt was frustrated with the lack of new information.

"I'll try to press him a little harder," said Lewis. "I need to be careful, you understand, since he isn't the one I'm here to investigate. I'm here to learn what John Douglas is up to. The DEA is financing this operation, so I have to keep my head down. I hope you understand."

"I do understand, Carl. I was just checking on what you had learned. I don't want to get in the way of your main investigation. I had word that Douglas was returning to Iliamna the end of next week."

"That's the word I got, too. I came into town to have a beer with Buntz and to socialize a little. Douglas is paranoid about any connection with his lodge or his employees being associated with drugs and I can't jeopardize that investigation, but I'll see what I can come up with. I don't mean to be hard-nosed about it, but I'm in a tricky position. I hope you understand." Carl was apologetic and sincere with Wyatt.

"I do understand, Carl. Just let me know if you come across any information on my cases. Thanks for taking the chance and coming here tonight. Let me know if you need anything." Wyatt reached out to shake the hand of the undercover officer.

Once Carl Lewis had gone Wyatt finished his reports and turned off the light on his desk before stepping into his small kitchen to heat a can of soup for dinner.

The following ten days were mostly uneventful for the VPSO. There had been nothing from Gene Turner in regard to the death of Bob Dilly. The weather had been cold and windy giving most local residents cause to stay indoors. There had been a lull in the air charter business for Maggie and Tom as well. Most of the down time had been caused by the bad flying weather. Rufus Donavan had driven across the frozen lake and stopped at the office to visit with Wyatt on Wednesday. There was nothing for him to report from Nondalton either.

Wyatt had been to Linda's for dinner twice this week. They were very pleasant visits, indeed. His father had planned to visit by this weekend, but wind and snow had interrupted his plans. He had called to say he would be out to see him on the first good day which was predicted to occur on Saturday. Wyatt was looking forward to the visit.

Carl Lewis had not reported back to him since the evening he had stopped at the office. Wyatt was becoming bored with just sitting in his little office waiting for the telephone to ring. He was sitting at his computer playing solitaire when his phone jingled. It was Harry Porter.

"Hello, Officer Earp. I need to know if there will be flying weather on Saturday. Mr. Douglas plans to be in Anchorage on Saturday and is checking to see if he can get to Iliamna during the day."

"I talked with Tom Dempsey earlier and he said there will be a break on Saturday, actually late Friday night. He should be able to get a charter on Saturday."

"Good. Mr. Douglas doesn't like to sit around and wait. He has no patience," Harry laughed.

"How are things at the lodge?" asked Wyatt.

"They're coming along. We have nearly finished hanging all the trim and doors inside the lodge building. That Carl Lewis is a whiz. He surely knows about woodworking. I'm glad we got him. The main lodge is shaping up really well now and we have Carl to thank for that. He's a hard worker."

"I'm glad he's working out for you. I've talked with him a couple of times and he is certainly a pleasant fellow. I liked him, too." Wyatt was bored enough to chit chat with Harry.

"Well, thanks for the information. I'll pass it along to the boss. Stop by when you get out this way and have coffee."

"I'll do that, Harry. Be seeing you."

With that Wyatt went back to his card game. He soon tired of it and wished Linda could get home from her teaching job. He suddenly remembered two very nice steaks he had in his freezer and thought it would be a good night to take them to Linda's kitchen and cook them. In the freezer he also found a bag of frozen cauliflower and some grated cheese for topping. He also looked through his small library of movies and found "Taken" with Liam Neeson, the trilogy. He put all the items in a grocery bag to take out to Linda's when she arrived at home. He was beginning to think this relationship was pretty nice and wondered if she had considered making it permanent. Tonight, would be a good time to discuss it, he thought. She called him at 4:30 to let him know she was home.

"I have dinner planned if I can use your kitchen, and I have something I want to discuss with you and tonight would be a good time. It has to do with our relationship. Do you still want me to come see you?"

"Of course, silly, I was going to ask you what you wanted for dinner anyway."

"I'll see you in an hour. You remember, Dad is supposed to visit this weekend?"

"Yes, I remember. I'll see you in an hour." Linda had an inkling as to what Wyatt wanted to discuss and was excited about the prospect. She had come to love the policeman.

Wyatt used the extra time to pop the steaks in the microwave oven to thaw, changed his clothes and took a shower as well as a clean shave. He chuckled at his own actions. This wasn't the usual Wyatt Earp, cop and bashful date. He was giddy with excitement at what he planned for tonight. His only concern was that Linda may not feel the same way about him. Now he was getting nervous.

It was just 5:30 when he stopped at Linda's front steps. With the grocery bag in one arm he marched up the steps to knock on the door. He stomped the snow off his boots while he waited for her to come to the door. When the door opened he was met by a different Linda. She was wearing a new dress, not jeans, high heel shoes, not boots, and wearing just a little touch of make-up. Wyatt stood at the door looking at the lady standing there.

"Well, come in before we both freeze," said Linda.

"I almost ran away. I thought I was at the wrong house. You look wonderful tonight, not that you don't look nice other times." Wyatt was so nervous he could barely stand.

"Let me help you with the groceries," she said. Taking part of the load, she led the way to the kitchen where the lights were on and the table set. Once he put the bag on the kitchen counter she stepped up in front of him and kissed him passionately.

He held her close and very tightly. He felt his face flush as he stepped back. She took a step closer and kissed him again.

"I was worried about approaching you to ask if you would agree to make our relationship permanent. I guess I didn't need to be so nervous." Wyatt was still reeling from the excitement.

"I was afraid I might scare you off," she admitted.

"Come and sit down, Linda, before I fall down." They each took a chair at the table. "I wanted to ask you how you felt about me and if you felt the same as I do. I wanted to ask you to marry me, to be my wife forever, to have our children, and to name our first son Wyatt Earp VI. I finally realized how much I love you." Wyatt was holding her hand during the conversation.

"Oh, Wyatt, I've never been this happy in my entire life. Of course, I'll marry you. There are things we will have to discuss, but yes, yes, yes, I love you, too."

The two lovers stood and kissed again.

"I guess if we are going to eat tonight I had better get the steaks started," said Wyatt. He took the items out of the grocery bag, handing the DVD to Linda. "I'll need a small pot to boil the cauliflower and a small saucepan to heat the cheese. They worked well together in the kitchen, fixing the dinner and smiling each time they passed in the small area.

After dinner Linda offered to do the dishes while Wyatt was to key up the DVD. They were both too filled with steak to want popcorn with the movie. He wrapped his arm around her as they sat on the couch and she laid her head on his shoulder.

"I'll get you an engagement ring the next time I'm in the city. It will be up to you to set the date, but I hope you will make it at a time my dad can attend. I want your family to be there, too."

"I'll talk with all of them and set a date. I will also let them know our first son will be named Wyatt like his father."

It was late when the movies ended. Wyatt pulled on his boots and coat and stood by the door. Linda circled him with her arms, a chore, since she was so much smaller than her fiancée. There was one final kiss and Wyatt went out into the dark and windy night air. He scarcely noticed the cold.

The next week passed quickly and word of the engagement spread equally as fast. Maggie and Tom were some of the first to congratulate the village police officer on his selection of a potential bride. Saturday afternoon the weather lightened slightly and the commuter plane from King Salmon arrived in Iliamna carrying Wyatt Earp IV. Wyatt V met the plane and took his father and his luggage to the office where they could visit for a short while before he checked into the local hotel. The VPSO quarters had only one bed, one room and one bath. It also had his business telephone and computer. He was required to stay there and put his father in the hotel.

In the office the two men sipped a cup of coffee, supplied by Maggie, and Wyatt V broke the news to his father of his impending marriage. Wyatt IV was ecstatic over the news. "I was beginning to think our line would end with you, son. I'm only sorry your mother isn't here to attend the wedding. Congratulations, my boy."

"Thanks, Dad. We are going to her place for dinner where you will get to see what a good cook she is. Homestead girls are good cooks, you know," Wyatt said with a huge grin.

"I know, son, I married one, too." There was a great love between this father and son, and it was obvious as they teased each other about the family. "I don't know the young lady well, but when I met her she seemed like a wonderful and down to earth person. Have you met her family yet?" he asked.

"No, but if the weather cooperates we can all take the 206 and fly up the lake to visit and break the news to them. I know they will want to meet you, too."

The family meeting continued another half hour when the telephone rang. It was John Douglas from the lodge. "I just wanted to let you know I was back in town and I would like to have a short meeting with you as soon as possible. Will you be in your office this afternoon?"

"I have an errand to run right now, but I'll be back in an hour. I can meet with you then, if it's convenient for you."

"Harry and I will be in your office in an hour."

Hanging up the phone, Wyatt turned to his father, "I have to meet a man here in my office in an hour, Dad. How about I take you to the hotel and get you checked in and you can rest a few minutes before we go to Linda's for dinner."

His father agreed and the two men drove the half mile from the hangar to the hotel. The son helped with the luggage and with checking his father into the hotel. After taking the bags to the room the VPSO returned to his office where he waited for only a few minutes until Douglas and Porter arrived.

"Good to see you again, Mr. Douglas," said Wyatt, shaking his hand and turning to Porter to shake his hand too.

"Nice to see you again, Officer Earp, I won't take much of your time," John Douglas began, "I've been told by Harry that there has been another drug death in the town. That concerns me. You know my policy on drugs at the lodge. I don't allow drugs or drug users on my properties. I want to know: Do you have anyone in mind as a suspected dealer in these deaths?"

"I'm sorry, but I can't give you that information, but rest assured if I had evidence I would make an arrest. I am following every lead available to me. The autopsy and final lab reports haven't come back yet. When they do I'll have a better idea of how to proceed with the investigation. Believe me, this is a very small village and I will find out who is responsible and arrest them." Wyatt hoped he had controlled his anger at the lodge owner pressuring him about the investigation.

"I don't mean for this to be a personal affront, Officer Earp, but I have invested a great deal of money in this community and I can't have a scandal like this affecting the reputation of the lodge or the surrounding community." Douglas was obviously used to being in charge and giving the orders.

Wyatt reached into a drawer in his desk to get a business card. On the back of the card he wrote a telephone number and handed it to Mr. Douglas.

"This is the Fairbanks number of my supervisor, Captain Griffin. If you have a problem with the way I am conducting this investigation I urge you to call the Captain and lodge a complaint. If he doesn't like the way I'm conducting the investigation he a can fire me. If I had evidence I would arrest the man responsible, but there isn't any evidence at this point. Now, if that's all, I have things to do. Please excuse me."

"I'm sorry you have taken this personally, Officer. That was not my intent, but if you aren't capable of solving this problem I will take it upon myself to do so. Good day, sir." Douglas opened the door and stepped out of the office. Porter looked at Wyatt, shook his head and rolled his eyes, but didn't say anything.

Chapter Twenty-Four

Wyatt made a note of the visit by Douglas, just for the record. He checked to see if there were any other messages, there were none. He stepped out of the office to speak to Maggie.

"I will be out of the office for the rest of the day, Maggie. I'll have my cell phone if anything comes up. I'm picking up my dad and we're going to Linda Mason's house for dinner."

"OK, Wyatt, have a good time."

Wyatt drove to the hotel to pick up his father and went to Linda's house for a short lunch. Afterwards, they all went back to the hangar to get the Cessna 206 ready to fly to the upper end of Lake Iliamna to visit Linda's family. He was looking forward to meeting the family and them meeting his father. Wyatt hoped she would have a date picked out for the wedding before they reached the family home.

The flight was scenic and uneventful except for one pack of wolves feeding on a caribou they had chased down and killed on the ice near the shore of the lake. As they approached the small bay near the front of the Mason family home Wyatt saw someone had cleared the ice of snow allowing him to land in front of the house without danger of damaging his landing gear. They had also cleared a path from the lake to the house, making the walk easy for the trio. Linda's father was sitting on his ATV that he had used for snowplowing.

"I saw you land and was coming down to get you." Linda's father was a short, stocky man with a pleasant smile.

"Dad," began Linda, "This is the Iliamna VPSO, Wyatt Earp V." The two men shook hands. "And this is Wyatt's father, his name is also Wyatt but his number is IV." The two fathers now shook hands.

"Pleased to meet you fellas; let's go into the house where it's warm." Al Mason, Linda's father, led the way and opened the front door. Her mother heard them enter and came running from the kitchen to hug her daughter. The little crowd walked to the kitchen and took seats at the table. "Lucy, get these folks some coffee," ordered Al Mason.

It took several minutes for the conversation to get around to what brought the trio this far up the lake.

"I have some news for you, Dad, Mom, and I wanted to tell you in person." Linda was beaming with the news.

"Don't tell me you're pregnant," kidded her father.

"No, Dad, of course not," she attempted to look insulted, but her smile gave her away. "Mom and Dad, Wyatt and I are going to get married."

"Which one you marrying," asked Al, jokingly.

"Oh, Dad, you know which one, the older one of course," she replied returning the joke.

"Oh, my child, that's wonderful news," said Lucy Mason. "When is the wedding?"

Wyatt was anxious to hear the answer to this question.

"I thought I wanted to be a June bride, but Dad will be fishing and Wyatt will be busy with his job, so, if Wyatt agrees, I have chosen February fifteenth."

"I'll agree to any date you choose," said Wyatt. "Let me write it in my notebook so I don't forget."

She scolded him for that remark and everyone laughed. The rest of the next hour was visiting for the men and wedding planning for the ladies. After much talking and a short lunch it was time to get back to the village.

As they put on coats and boots, the elder Earp spoke up. "Before we leave I want to make an offer. I have a business and a house in the Seattle area. If you will allow me to do so, I will fly the entire family to Seattle for the wedding. I'll pay for the hotel for the newlyweds and have Mr. and Mrs. Mason stay with me at my home. You will be my guests for a week. Is that agreeable with all of you?"

"Oh, Mr. Earp, that would be awfully expensive. Are you sure you want to do this?" asked Linda.

"I can afford it, Linda. Consider it my wedding gift to you and my son. I owe him much more than that. He isn't a child any longer, but he'll always be my son and I love him. I think he has made a good choice for a bride."

"Thank you, Mr. Earp," said Linda. "I'll start making arrangements right away."

"We had better head back now. It will be getting dark soon. It's been a pleasure meeting you Al. Lucy, I will be proud to be a part of this family. I hope

I won't disappoint you." Wyatt shook Al Mason's hand and hugged Lucy as he went outside.

It was a short and enjoyable flight back to the village. The senior Earp helped put the Cessna inside the hangar. Before taking his father to the hotel, Wyatt made a stop in his office to check for messages. There were none. "I'll see you in the morning, Dad," he said as he closed the door of the truck.

Now he and Linda were alone as he drove toward her home. "I think your folks liked me," he said as he drove.

"They definitely like you and your father. Come to think of it I like you, too. I hope I didn't cause a problem for you with the date I set. I wasn't sure of the date until I talked with Mom. She really likes you. What I told them was true. I wanted to be a June bride, but it won't work for either of our families. I'll talk with the school administrator and let him know I need a few days off in mid-February. Will that work out for you?"

"Yes, Lonnie Davis will be back by then and he can cover for me a few days. You realize we haven't talked about where we will live after we're married. My little office home isn't big enough for the two of us. I may have to move in with you until we can get a home built on the lot I've been looking at. How do you feel about that?"

"I love the idea, Wyatt. I'm really excited about our future. We haven't talked about children, but I would like several. How about you? How many kids do you think we should have?"

"As many as you like, but the first-born son will have to be named Wyatt Earp VI."

"I thought you might insist on that name for a son, but I get to name the girls." Linda was giggling now.

Wyatt turned into her drive and stopped in front of the house. "I know it's early, but I have to get back to the office and do a little work. I've had a wonderful day."

"So, you aren't staying for dinner?" she asked.

"No, not tonight. I had some messages on my computer I should take care of. I think it's the information from the medical examiner about the last drug death we investigated. I would sure like to get this dealer off the streets. I'm sorry I can't stay. I'll call you later when I get my work done. Good night," he said, kissing her gently.

Linda stepped out of the truck and walked to the house, stopping at the door to wave good bye to her fiancée. Once she was inside he started the truck and drove back to the office.

Wyatt had been correct about the message awaiting him. Bob Dilly had died from a heroin overdose. The powder they had logged as evidence tested to be the same as the batch Linda had found in her parking lot at the school. Wyatt read through all the reports to find they merely confirmed what he already suspected. It was going to be difficult to find evidence against Rick Buntz, or whoever was dealing this heroin in the village. He had printed out all the information and was reading it for the second time when his cell phone rang. It was Carl Lewis.

"I can't talk long," he said. "I'm about to make a buy from Rick. He just left the bar and said he would be back in a few minutes with the stuff. I'll call you later after I make the buy. He wants me to drive toward his place in Newhalen and meet him on the road for the exchange. Gotta go now." Carl Lewis was a savvy cop who had been an undercover narcotics cop for a long time. He knew the chances he faced. "I'll call you in about an hour."

Wyatt was nervous about letting Lewis go out to meet a drug dealer alone and at night in winter, but Carl had said to wait until he called. The time passed slowly and Wyatt used the time to do some domestic chores— a load of laundry, empty the dishwasher and take the garbage to the dumpster outside by the end of the hangar. Two hours had passed and still no call from Carl. Wyatt had become concerned.

Finally, he couldn't control his anxiety any longer and went to his truck to begin to look for the officer. Carl had said he was to meet with Buntz on the road leading to Newhalen. That was the first place he would look. It is about three miles from the office to Newhalen where Buntz lives in a small cabin near the big lake. Two miles down the road, Carl Lewis' SUV was parked on the edge of the road with no one in sight. Wyatt stopped a few yards behind the vehicle and sat in his truck looking at the area before getting out to look at the inside of the SUV. The area was snow covered and there was a set of footprints crossing the road and returning. They were small, perhaps a size six or seven shoe. The VPSO walked carefully to the driver side door of Carl's vehicle and looked inside.

What he saw was shocking. Carl lay on the seat, his eyes open, drool ran from his open mouth and there was a plastic syringe hanging in his neck near the jugular vein. Wyatt nearly panicked as he opened the door to check for a pulse he knew was not there. He closed the door and carefully walked back to his own truck. Inside out of the cold he called Trooper Gene Turner on his cell phone. When the sergeant answered Wyatt told him what had happened. Turner was silent for a long minute before answering.

"You're sure Carl is dead?" asked Gene with a crackling voice.

"Yes, definitely, Gene. He was supposed to meet me an hour ago and never showed. He had said he was going to meet Rick Buntz on the road and make a heroin buy. When he didn't call I drove toward Newhalen and found his SUV on the side of the road. He's inside the truck with a needle sticking out of his neck. I'm going to start documenting the footprints and tire tracks. When I finish, I'll call a wrecker to take the SUV to the hangar and put it inside where I can take fingerprints and get whatever fiber samples I find. That's unless you want to send someone from the crime lab out here to do it."

"Go ahead and get photo documentation and measurements…you know the routine, and I'll call Captain Griffin to see how he wants to handle this. I'll get back to you as soon as I know."

Wyatt hung up the telephone and moved his truck to aim the lights on where the footprints crossed the road. There was no traffic on the road tonight and he was able to gather his evidence without interruption. He was able to get clear tire track photos where the vehicle had parked to meet with Carl. He measured the wheelbase length as well as the width of the axles. He measured the width of the tires and photographed the tread design. These things would tell him what kind of vehicle stopped to meet Carl Lewis. He was entering information in his logbook when his cell phone rang. It was Sergeant Turner.

"Are you able to stand guard on the scene until a team gets there?" he asked.

"Yes, and I can call the local wrecker to come and stand by across the road to prevent traffic from obliterating any tracks. There hasn't been any traffic since I arrived and the weather is cold with no wind. That will help preserve the tracks. How long before the crime team arrives here?"

"I'm guessing a couple of hours. Griff said the crime team will charter a Learjet from Anchorage. He called them while I was on the line with him. There are no shortcuts when we lose one of our own. I'll check the weather and if the Pass is flyable I'll be there at about the same time. Confirm your location for me."

"I'm two miles down the Newhalen road. I'll move my truck to the other side of the scene and call the wrecker to block the road on this side. Call me on this number when you get an ETA." Wyatt ended the call and called a local tow truck to come to the scene, advising him he would probably be here all night.

"I'll bring a thermos of coffee," said the owner of the tow truck.

The two men stood near the tow truck sipping the coffee and talking for nearly three hours until a Chevrolet Suburban with FAA markings and U.S. Government license plates drove to the scene. The leader of the team stepped out of the Chevy and walked, carrying a flashlight, to where the tow truck driver and the VPSO were standing.

"Are you Officer Earp?" he asked.

"Yes, call me Wyatt. You must be from the crime lab."

"From the FBI's major Crimes Investigation Division, actually. My men and I will take possession of the crime scene now. Please make a note of the time. I'm Greg Stein, head of the team. My men will want copies of your notes and we'll take possession of your films. Of course, we will make our own films too."

Huge light bars were set out and connected to the power supply of the government truck. The team was professional in their actions and in gathering the pertinent data and evidence. It was the attitude of the team leader that irritated Wyatt. He walked to his truck parked fifty yards down the road and climbed inside to get warm. Thirty minutes later another government truck arrived. It was Gene Turner.

Gene stopped to speak with Stein before walking to where Wyatt was sitting. "He's a piece of work, isn't he?" asked Gene.

"He'll be gone by morning and I think I can get along without him. I've got measurements of the tire treads, the axle width and the wheel base. I don't have the books to look them up. Will you do it for me when you get to your office?"

"Sure thing, Wyatt, in fact I'll send copies of the photos and the measurements to my office when we get back to your office." There was a sad tone to Gene's voice. "Do you have any idea who could have done this?"

"Yes, but I didn't see anything. Carl called to tell me he was meeting Buntz out here to make a heroin buy and planned to come to my office when he finished. When he was an hour overdue I came looking for him and found him there in his SUV with a needle sticking out of his neck. Whoever did it must have learned he was a narc and wanted to send a message. If the tire prints and measurements match Buntz' old Ford Bronco I am going to take a great deal of pleasure in slapping cuffs on him."

"Don't get too personally involved, Wyatt. Keep your objectivity. We all hate losing someone we work with, but we can't act like vigilantes. We should have the information by morning. I'm going to need to stay with the Crime Team. Just let them do their thing and go away. Do you think the guy from the lodge that Carl was looking into had anything to do with Carl's death?"

"It's possible, but I doubt it. He was out here to make a buy from Buntz and the last time we talked about it he didn't have anything on John Douglas from the lodge or any of his men."

It was near midnight when Stein came to talk with Wyatt. "You can have the tow truck take the SUV away now. We will leave the body inside until we get to the jet where we will put it in a body bag and load it on the plane. We don't have room in the Suburban to make the transfer here."

Wyatt nodded, but didn't say anything. He motioned to the wrecker driver and the hook-up began. Wyatt instructed the driver to be careful going back to town and to drive to the Learjet parked by the flight service station in order for the crime boys to take Carl's body out of the truck. While the wrecker driver hooked up to the SUV the crime team was busy taking down lights and packing their equipment into the back of the Suburban. Once everyone was loaded all the vehicles formed a parade of sorts travelling to the Iliamna Airport. Wyatt never spoke with Stein or his men, but sat in his pickup until they boarded the jet and taxied for takeoff.

Gene left his borrowed Chevy at the FAA station and rode to the Lake Air charter office with Wyatt.

Chapter Twenty-Five

Gene Turner had spent an uncomfortable and very short night on the couch in the small living quarters behind the VPSO office in the hangar. He awakened to the smell of bacon frying. Wyatt heard him stirring.

"I thought you were going to sleep all day. I didn't know whether to fix breakfast or lunch. After all, you've had more than three hours sleep," Wyatt teased the trooper sergeant as he began to awaken.

"I might have slept until lunch if you weren't so noisy in the kitchen," replied Turner. "How does the weather look this morning?"

"It's still too dark to tell, but we can call flight service when you get moving. Do you plan to leave first thing, or do you want to drive out to the lodge and break the news to the owner about losing his new log builder?"

"If you intend to go out there this morning, I'll ride along, but I do need to get back to Soldotna this morning." Turner yawned and stretched his back. "Got any coffee?" he asked.

Wyatt poured him coffee while he stepped into the bathroom. When he returned he sat at the table sipping coffee and waiting for the cook to supply his breakfast. "That Greg Stein is sure a sweet guy, isn't he?"

"Yeah, I'm glad I don't work with him on a regular basis." Wyatt was putting the eggs and bacon on a platter. "He has a good crew, though. They did a great job out there at the scene. I noticed they mostly ignored their leader."

"I've known Greg a long time. He used to be a great guy, but he once made a bad error in an investigation and it cost the state a murder conviction. He's been like this ever since. I think when his calendar says '20 years' he'll hang it up. He doesn't like the job any more. It's sad too; he was a good cop."

Wyatt came back to the table with a plate of whole wheat toast. "Dig in, Gene. We don't get to eat on a regular basis out here in the bush. We eat when we have time. After breakfast I'll put on a clean shirt and we'll drive out to the lodge."

Daylight was beginning to break when the two men climbed into the pickup and drove to the new lodge building at the end of the road. Harry Porter came out to greet the men as they climbed the porch steps.

"Good morning fellas. What brings you out her this time of day?" he asked.

"I'm afraid I have some bad news for you, Harry. Can we come inside a few minutes?" asked Wyatt.

"Sure, Wyatt, come on inside. Mr. Douglas and I were just sitting down to some breakfast. Would you like to join us?"

"No, thanks, Harry. I do need to speak with you and Mr. Douglas, though." The three men walked into the huge log lodge building. This entry was a direct access to the kitchen where John Douglas was seated at the big wood table.

"Good morning, gentlemen," said Douglas as they entered. "I don't believe I've met this officer," he said. "I'm John Douglas, owner of the lodge."

Gene took the offered hand and shook it, "Gene Turner, Trooper Sergeant from Soldotna. I came in last night late."

"It's a pleasure, Sergeant," said Douglas. "What brings you out here?"

Wyatt was the one to give the answer. "We came to deliver some rather bad news, Mr. Douglas. It concerns Carl Lewis, your new logsmith. He was found dead in his SUV last night, a possible drug overdose. We're in the process of notifying his relatives. Since he lived and worked here I thought we should let you know this morning."

"Good grief, what is this world coming to? You and I talked about this. Now I've lost another builder. This is the third death within days. What are you going to do about it?"

"This time we have real evidence and are pursuing an investigation. When we can identify a suspect we'll make an arrest. I don't know how they do it in Houston, but here we try to arrest the correct suspect the first time." Wyatt's resistance to John Douglas' impatience was showing through.

Gene Turner spoke up to cool the tone. "We brought a team out from Anchorage last night and the evidence is now at the crime lab in Anchorage. The investigation is on-going and I can't reveal any other facts, but we're doing our best to find the one responsible for delivering these killer drugs."

"Thank you, Sergeant. Please notify me when you learn something." Douglas sat back down at the table and began to eat his breakfast.

Without saying goodbye the two officers turned to leave ,with Harry following them closely. Outside he spoke to them, "Don't mind Mr. Douglas, he's upset, what with losing his second builder and all. If you need anything just call me."

Wyatt and Gene returned to the truck and drove out of the fenced property. "I think that went pretty well, didn't you?" asked Gene.

The sarcasm brought a smile to Wyatt's face. "Let's go check the weather for you," he said.

Inside the lodge John Douglas finished his breakfast in silence, thinking of what to do about the recent deaths in the village. News of this could impact the reputation of the lodge before it was even open. "I'm going to my office for a while to make some calls. Call me if you hear anything." Douglas picked up his coffee mug to carry it to his office in another part of the lodge building.

Douglas sat at his office desk, thinking for a long while. He finally made up his mind to call Dillon Dixon. "Hello, DD. I want you to come up to Alaska right away. I have a job for you. It's important. I'll e-mail your ticket and arrange a charter from Anchorage to Iliamna. I'll pick you up at the airport here."
Needing no further information or instruction Dillon Dixon went home to his apartment to pack a bag. The following afternoon he arrived in Iliamna on a chartered plane.

Douglas and his associate sat in front of the flight service station, keeping warm by the car heater. "Good to see you, DD. Have you ever been to Alaska before?" asked Douglas.

"No, this is my first trip. The weather is a bit nippy for my taste," commented Dixon.

"I have a problem with a local drug dealer. His products have killed three people in just a few weeks. I don't allow drugs near my business interests, as you know. This dealer has nothing to do with me or my business, but these deaths are making people edgy. I am building a multi-million-dollar lodge at the end of the road behind us. I do not want rumors of drugs in the village to deter high paying clients from booking vacations at the resort. I want this man eliminated. He has killed two of my workers. I didn't know either of them were users or I would never have hired them. Because of your business here I think you should check in at the hotel rather than come to the lodge." Douglas handed Dixon a manila envelope. "This contains everything I have been able to learn about your man. If you need anything at all just give me a call. I'll be at the lodge."

"Sounds good," said Dixon. It was his only comment.

Douglas dropped him off at the hotel and drove away toward the lodge. While driving he used his cell phone to call Harry Porter. "Hello, Harry, John, I'm on the way back to the lodge. I want you to make a list of replacements to interview. We need to get the lodge completed on time for guests by spring. The log work has been completed allowing us to hire a carpenter to do the finish work. I'll be there in a few minutes."

Dixon checked into the hotel without any fanfare, taking a room on the second floor. He went directly to his room to study the material in the envelope Douglas had given him. The information said the dealer was a man named Rick Buntz. He is a small man and lives near the mouth of the Newhalen River, three miles from Iliamna village. The packet contained an old newspaper clipping showing a picture of Buntz. The information sheet said the man was a trapper and pilot. He owned a Piper Super Cub and included the registration numbers. There was little information about the man's personal habits or life. Dixon thought for a long time about how to get close to Buntz. He decided to watch the man for a couple of days before making a plan. He called the lobby to ask the clerk if it was possible to rent a car for a few days. The clerk said there was, but it wouldn't be a new car, but he could have it delivered to the hotel within an hour. The rental agreement and the keys would be delivered to the front desk.

It was only a short distance from the front of the hotel to the front of the hangar where Wyatt's office was located and where he had been at his desk the entire day. His back ached and he was getting tired of sitting. He went to the refrigerator to get a soda and came back to sit at his desk once again when he had an inspiration. Reaching for the telephone he dialed Linda's number.

"It's about time you called me," she teasingly said when she answered.

"Have you missed me?" asked Wyatt.

"Of course I did, silly. I heard about you finding another body. That's why I haven't called you. I thought you were too busy to talk to me."

"Yes, it's been a couple of bad days for me. I don't know if you heard, but the dead man was a man I knew. It's a big investigation. Learjets coming from Anchorage, Cessnas coming from Soldotna and me running around in circles. I didn't even see my dad off when he went home to Naknek."

"You say you knew the dead man Was he a friend of yours?"

"You can't breathe a word of this to anyone, but yes. It was Carl Lewis who worked as a builder at the new lodge out past your place. This is the part you can't tell anyone. He was an undercover trooper."

"Oh my gosh, Wyatt! What happened?"

"Don't tell anyone about any of this, but Carl was murdered."

"Oh my, Wyatt, I knew your job was dangerous, but I didn't realize it could be this dangerous out here in the village."

"I've done this kind of work all my life and I'm still here. I'm not saying it can't happen to me, but I do try to be careful. We just do our job and don't think about how dangerous it can be. It's nothing you need to worry about."

"I can worry if I want to," said Linda, concerned for her man.

"Enough about that. I want to invite you to dinner. I have some nice ham in the fridge and thought I could make ham and eggs and hotcakes for dinner. Want to join me?" asked the VPSO.

"That was the reason I called you to begin with. I was going to fix some pork chops and find a movie to watch this evening if you care to come to my house."

"That sounds wonderful, Love. I need to get out of the office for a while. What's a good time for you?"

"I'll plan on taking the meat out of the oven at six o'clock sharp."

"I'll be there, and don't start without me. Is there anything I can bring?"

As Wyatt climbed into his truck to drive to Linda's place at a quarter of six, Dillon Dixon was walking down the flight of stairs to the lobby of the hotel to sign for the rental car. He signed the papers and the clerk handed him the keys.

"It's the gray Tahoe parked out front, sir," the clerk informed the guest. Please fill the tank when you bring it back and turn it in."

"Is there a map of the local area available?" asked DD.

The clerk reached into a pigeon hole behind the desk, under the room mail boxes to retrieve a sheet of paper. It was a computer copy of the local roads and businesses. Dixon thanked the clerk and asked, "Is there a favorite bar around here?"

"Go out the front door and turn right. It's on the west end of the hotel," replied the clerk.

Dixon zipped up his jacket and walked outside where he found the Tahoe parked in front of the hotel. He turned to his right and found a small bar on the end of the hotel, next to the restaurant. Convenient, he thought. He walked inside the bar where two locals were seated on stools at the bar.

Both men turned to see who had entered and one of them said, "Howdy friend. You stayin' or just passin' through?"

Dixon smiled and took a seat near the man who spoke. "I'm staying in the hotel a few days. Do you live here?"

"Yup, I'm Lenny, and my friend here is Sal. Aircraft mechanics, you know."

The bartender was now looking for an order from the newcomer. "What'll it be Pard?" he asked.

"Give me one of your local beers and buy these two men what they're drinking."

"You like light or dark?" asked the bartender.

"Light," Dixon replied.

A few seconds later the barman came back with three bottles of beer. "Wanna glass?" he asked.

"No, this will be fine."

DD sipped his beer and nodded approval to the bartender. He then turned to the man at the bar who had first spoken to him. "I understand there's a man living around here by the name of Buntz. Do you know him?"

"Yeah, he comes in here almost every evening. He should be coming in soon. Kind of a loner, don't say much and hardly ever says anything to us. He has a Cub and we work on it sometimes. Whatcha want him for?" he asked.

"No reason really, a man in Anchorage asked me to say hello to him if I saw him." Dixon took another taste of his beer.

The conversation died away for a while and Dixon bought another round. He was sipping his second beer when the front door opened and a small man bundled in heavy insulated gear entered the bar. He went to a table against the wall and began to remove his heavy jacket and vest.

The man next to Dixon poked him with an elbow and pointed. "That's him," he said without looking over at Rick Buntz.

"Thanks," said Dixon in a quiet voice.

The bartender called over to the man, "The usual, Rick?"

"Yeah," was his only reply.

The bartender carried a tray with one cold beer on top to the table where the man was seated.

"Run me a tab," said the man.

The bartender returned to the bar and wrote something on a small notepad.

Dixon picked up his beer and walked over to the table. "Are you Rick Buntz?" he asked.

"Yeah, who wants to know?" Buntz replied in a surly tone.

"The name's Dixon, Dillon Dixon. Most folks just call me DD. I met a man in the Anchorage airport who heard I was coming to Iliamna and he asked me to say hello to you if I saw you."

"Who was he?" asked Buntz.

"I don't remember his name. Big guy, maybe six-five, two fifty, wore a coat like yours, had a beard. Said he was a friend of yours. Said you used to work together."

"Must have been Willard; Willard Dunn. Sounds like him."

"Sorry, I just don't remember his name. Anyway, he wanted me to say hello if I saw you." Dixon turned to go back to the bar, but was stopped by Buntz.

"Have a seat for a while. Unless you got some place to be," said Buntz.

"No, I don't need to be anywhere. I'm just here on a little business for a couple of days."

"What brings you to the village?" asked the local man.

"I'm a stock broker. Not like a Wall Street broker, but a stock broker. I deal in mining stocks. They sent me out to look at a huge property near here they are trying to develop. I have maps, but I have to find someone to show me the property."

"I'll take a look at the maps, but if it's the property I think it is, you are going to need to fly around to look at it. The property is over a hundred miles long and fifty miles wide. There isn't any other way to see the property in only a couple of days. Who are the owners?" asked Rick.

"It's a Canadian company. They hooked up with a company from Utah to develop the property. It's supposed to be the largest lead, copper, zinc and gold mine in the world. I've heard those stories before, so I want to see the property before I get involved." Dixon had read about the Pebble Mine and was interested in investing in some of their stock at one point, but this was all nonsense meant for conversation and nothing more.

"I can probably fly you around in my Super Cub if you want to look. I have to know tonight, though if you want to do it, because I have to plug the plane in to heat the engine if I'm going to fly tomorrow."

"How much will you charge?" asked Dixon.

"Hundred an hour," quoted Buntz.

"Sounds fair. I'll meet you in the café in the morning. Nine a.m. good for you?" Buntz nodded. DD went to the bar and bought the three customers each another round and paid Buntz' tab. He zipped his coat and walked outside to get into his Tahoe and familiarize himself with the local road system.

In the meantime, Wyatt drove to Linda's house and parked in front. He knocked on the door at precisely six o'clock. The door opened and Linda pulled him inside where she kissed him hard.

"Welcome home, big boy," she said, smiling.

Chapter Twenty-Six

Dixon was sitting at a table in the hotel restaurant when Buntz arrived, bundled up in his heavy insulated coat and winter boots. He took off his coat and hung it on the back of an empty chair.

"Mornin'," said Buntz.

"Good morning, Rick," replied DD.

"I'm hungry…been getting the plane ready to go. The weather is pretty good, but the ceilings are low. That shouldn't be a problem, since you want to see the countryside anyways."

"I have heard ice is a problem with winter flying here in Alaska. Will that be a problem for our flight today?"

"Not if we stay out of the clouds," commented Buntz. "You ordered yet?"

"No, I haven't. I was waiting for you to get here."

The young waitress arrived at the table with a cup of coffee and placed it in front of Buntz. "You fellas ready to order?" she asked. Both men ordered steak and eggs.

"Exactly how large is this mining property?" asked Dixon while waiting for their order.

"The entire property is more than a hundred miles long. All the land west of here and north are a part of it. Those hills on the other side of the river are included and it runs up the lake past the village, probably 25 or 30 miles. It's all open countryside and we can look at all of if you want, but the only activity right now is out behind Nondalton. I thought we would start up there where they're doing some core drilling and field testing. Did you bring a camera?"

"Only the one on my telephone, but once I get the lay of the land, and if I'm still interested in investing, I'll hire someone to photograph the entire project," saiad Dixon as he sipped his cup of coffee. "What do you think of the project, Rick?"

"I think it will be great for the locals; more business for local merchants, more workers to feed, more fuel to be used, more everything. The Native corporation is against it, claiming it will destroy the fishing industry; the guides are against it, claiming it will ruin the tundra and animal habitat. Personally, I can't make it happen or stop it. I'll have to make a livin' either way."

"The Natives and the fishermen are against it, you say. Are their concerns justified?"

"Probably not, if all the regulations are followed, but people get greedy and try to take shortcuts. If that happens there could be problems. Down in Canada near Trail, British Columbia, I seen a giant settling pond a mile long and a quarter mile or more high. It's been there, I guess, a hundred years and it never gave a problem. I ain't no scientist, but it looks like to me that if they don't use cyanide and mercury and follow the rules it should be OK. The caribou don't care, they move all the time anyway. It will mean digging a huge pit mine that ain't goin' to look pretty, and they will have to put roads where there ain't none now, but that will happen someday anyhow." Buntz' speech seemed fairly objective and fair to Dixon, who didn't have the slightest knowledge about the project. His only information had come from a pamphlet he read at the airport in Anchorage.

Their breakfast arrived and the men ate in silence. When they finished and were drinking a last cup of coffee Buntz said, "You might want to go easy on the coffee. Ain't no bathroom in the Cub."

"I guess we're ready to get started, then," commented Dixon as he waved at the girl to bring the check.

Dixon followed Buntz the three miles from the hotel to where Buntz had his airplane parked behind his cabin. The aircraft was fitted with large, red, plastic skis for operation on the winter tundra. A pair of floats stood on a makeshift platform of logs near the edge of the lake where Buntz had recently taken them off his airplane to replace them with skis.

Buntz assisted the city boy in his acrobatic act of getting into the small plane. He helped Dixon hook up the shoulder restraint and seatbelt. He gave the passenger a quick instruction on keeping his feet off the rudder pedals and on how to use the intercom when talking with the pilot, Buntz, who would sit in the front seat of the two-passenger craft. Buntz fitted the radio headset to Dixon's ears, slapped him on the knee and did an Olympic maneuver to enter the front seat of the plane. He had removed the engine cover and unplugged the electric engine heater before entering. Buntz closed the cabin door and primed the engine with fuel. The starter turned the propeller a few revolutions and the engine caught. He let it idle a few minutes, checking gauges and setting his instruments.

"You ready?" asked Buntz through the headphones.

"Yes," said Dixon into the microphone in front of his mouth.

Dixon had never flown in such a small airplane and was filled with apprehension as Buntz added power and the plane began to move from the shore toward the ice of the lake. Without stopping, Buntz added more power. The tail came up and the Piper left the earth. Buntz banked sharply, only feet above the ice on the lake, while climbing to an altitude of about five hundred feet. As the wings leveled Dixon began to relax as they flew up the Newhalen River toward Nondalton. He now had a view of the surrounding countryside and it was beautiful. Once they reached Lake Clark Buntz began to climb in order to maintain 500 feet above the ground.

"The main camp is only a few miles up this way. Ain't nobody there now, but it's a busy place when the crews are here."

Dixon sat in the rear seat enjoying the flight which lasted nearly three hours. The airplane was slow, cruising at less than 90 miles per hour and slowing to 40 miles per hour when the pilot found a spot he wanted the passenger to see. Near the end of the flight Dixon was beginning to feel the need to rid himself of the coffee he had consumed at breakfast.

Buntz was the first out of the airplane and aided his passenger with his exit. Once DD was out of the airplane Buntz stepped to the front of the craft and relieved himself of the coffee he had consumed at the breakfast table. Dixon took the hint and did the same. Once the engine cover was in place and the heater plugged in the two men walked to the other side of the cabin where the vehicles were parked.

"I want to thank you for a most enjoyable ride, Rick. I may have to get one of these little airplanes. It was fun and informative." Dixon handed Buntz three one hundred dollar bills.

"Glad you enjoyed it. Did you see what you needed to see?" said Buntz, taking the money from Dixon.

"Yes, I did. I will make a positive recommendation to my investors." As Dixon spoke Buntz' telephone rang.

"Excuse me, DD. I have to take this call." Buntz walked a few steps before answering the phone. He spoke quietly into the cell phone and Dixon was unable to hear clearly what was said, but he was able to determine the pilot was about to make a delivery somewhere.

"Meet me at the hotel bar tonight and I'll buy you a drink," said Dixon as he walked toward his Tahoe. As he drove toward the village he pondered the methods available for his use to eliminate the now confirmed drug dealer, Rick Buntz. Dixon thought he should try to follow the pilot to see if he really was delivering drugs to someone. Near the village of Iliamna he pulled into a storage yard filled with idle fishing boats to observe Buntz' passing.

It was a short wait. About two minutes after parking his SUV, Buntz drove by him, looking neither right nor left. Dixon gave him a few seconds and followed. Buntz drove past the hotel and out a road lined with private residences and small businesses, the largest of which appeared to be an aircraft repair business. Buntz' brake lights came on as he approached a camo color ATV parked on the roadway. Dixon knew the dealer would be watching his rear view mirror and pulled into the drive to a very large log home. It was old, but well cared for. Through the leafless trees he could see the man on the ATV pass something to Buntz who in turn passed something out his driver side window to the man now standing on the road. They exchanged a few words Dixon could not hear and the man returned to his ATV and drove away in the opposite direction. Buntz turned around in the roadway and drove back toward the village and his cabin in Newhalen. Dixon returned to his hotel room to call John Douglas.

"He's a cagey guy, John. I saw him make a sale today, but he was very careful about it. I was with him most of the day and he's aware of everything around him at all times. I was out to his cabin today and I saw he heats with oil. I have a plan, but it depends on some things happening over which I have little control. I'll let you know how it works out."

"Be careful, DD. I don't want to lose you in this deal. I depend on you too much for that. Don't take any chances. We can always find another way to take care of him." Douglas was worried about witnesses in this small community.

"I'm going to meet him tonight at the bar for some drinks. I'll give him something to help him get drunk and follow him home. It should be a piece of cake. When is the next plane out of here?"

"Late tomorrow afternoon, weather permitting. Let me know how things go." Douglas was still worried about his friend, Dillon Dixon.

After a much needed nap, Dixon walked down to the restaurant for some dinner. The special today was broasted chicken and steamed veggies. He ordered it along with coffee. The meal was pleasant and the food was very good, far better than he had expected for such an out of the way place. The waitress was the same girl who had served his breakfast. He teased her about the hours she worked and when he finished he left her a very nice tip.

It was now after six and he walked next door to the bar. The same two regulars were sitting on the same stools and the same bartender asked if he wanted the usual. Dixon chuckled at the use of the term usual from his first time visit. Again he bought the two men at the bar a drink.

"Didja go flyin' with Rick?" asked the same talkative patron as last night.

"Sure did. Got me all the way out and all the way back. Never crashed even once," said Dixon.

"He must be a good pilot then," stated the patron.

"Guess so," commented Dixon.

The bartender had just brought Dixon his second beer when Rick Buntz came inside, stomping snow off his boots as he came. Buntz took the same seat he had occupied the night before. "Give him his usual, too," said Dixon as he picked up his bottle and walked to the table where Rick was seated.

"Did you get a nap today?" asked Dixon.

"Nope, had to fuel the plane and change the oil. Out here in the bush we can't just take them to a mechanic to get it done like they do in the city."

"I can see that," said Dixon as the bartender set Rick's beer in front of him.

"Run me a tab," Buntz told the bartender.

"This one is on your friend, but I'll start one later."

"Thanks for the beer, Mr. Dixon. I should buy you one. It's my turn."

"Maybe later, but I want to thank you for the nice ride and the running commentary on what I was looking at. You made my job a lot easier."

"Did you find out what you needed to know for your clients?"

"I have an entire file on what is happening out here, but it was all someone else's version and opinions. I now have first-hand information and made notes on my maps about a lot of the things you explained to me. You were a big help." Dixon was afraid to give specific comments for fear the pilot would suspect he was making this entire thing up as a scam of some kind, which it was.

The two men talked a few more minutes when Dixon got up and walked to the bar for two more beers. The bartender opened the bottles and put them on the bar. Dixon reached in his pocket for cash to put on the bar. At the same time he brought out a small, white pill which he dropped into one of the bottles while the bartender got his change. Back at the table he handed the preferred bottle to Buntz. "I usually don't drink much beer, but this local beer is very good."

"Thanks again for the beer," said Buntz.

The two men made small talk for nearly a half hour when the pill began to take effect. As Buntz became groggy Dixon made a show of helping him put on his coat and walked him to the door. "I'll take him home," he told the bartender.

Dixon loaded the now nearly unconscious Buntz into his Tahoe to drive him to his cabin three miles down the road. At the cabin DD carried the sleeping Buntz inside. It was small, one room with a kitchen and a bed in one corner. He put Buntz on the bed and took off his heavy coat and boots. He covered the pilot with a quilt he had found at the foot of the bed.

Once Buntz was tucked into bed, Dixon went to the oil heater in the living room area. Behind the stove he kicked the oil line until it broke off the fitting and began to spew stove oil onto the wood floor behind the stove. He tore pages from a magazine, wadded them into a ball and laid them on the floor several feet in front of the oil stove, which was now not burning due to a lack of fuel. There was a book of matches on the kitchen table. Dixon struck a match and set fire to the paper on the floor. He watched a moment as the puddle of oil inched its way toward the small fire on the floor. Once he was sure the oil would be ignited he exited the cabin to drive back to the hotel.

Chapter Twenty-Seven

It was three a.m. when Wyatt was awakened by his ringing telephone. The call was from one of the local volunteer firefighters. He had responded to a house fire near Newhalen. Once the fire was controlled and firefighters entered the cabin they found a body, in bed. It was too badly burned to identify, but the size of the body matched the description of the owner of the cabin, Rick Buntz.

Wyatt quickly dressed and drove to the scene. The fire chief, also a volunteer, met him near the tanker truck used to fight the blaze.

"You can go inside if you want, but it isn't pretty. Do you have a body bag with you?" asked the firefighter.

"Yes, I'll get it for you. Have you figured out what happened?"

"We could tell when we arrived that it was a stove oil fire. We could smell it. When we got the flames knocked down we found the body and we found a broken fuel line on the back of the stove. We think the body is Rick Buntz. He owns the cabin. It looks accidental, but who knows. Buntz was a shady character, according to my men."

Wyatt gave the fire chief the body bag and closed the door of his truck. "I'll help you load the body, if you want. Either way I need to photograph the inside of the cabin for my report. Who called it in? Do you know?"

"Yes, a neighbor down the road saw the flames and called us. He said that, at first he thought Buntz' airplane was afire. He drove up here and saw the cabin burning. According to the neighbor no one else was around at the time."

"Yeah, I can see the heat from the fire melted any tracks that may have been in the snow." Wyatt reached inside the truck to get a large flashlight and his camera. "I guess we may as well get to it."

Two men were inside raking embers and dousing them with water. Wyatt began to film the entire interior of the cabin and the burned body on the bed. He took close pictures of the fractured fuel line behind the oil stove. He recovered several samples of the ash on the floor and on the bed. A half hour later he and the fire chief loaded the burned body into the large plastic body bag.

Back in his office Wyatt called Sergeant Turner. "It was time for you to get up anyway, Gene." He gave Turner some sick police humor.

"It must be important for you to call this time of the day," Gene replied.

"I have news that will interest you. Remember the suspected drug dealer Carl was looking at? Rick Buntz was his name."

"Yes, he was the one we thought sold the heroin that killed those two users and Carl Lewis. Did you catch him selling to someone in the village?" asked Turner.

"No, but I had a call around three a.m. to say Buntz' cabin burned down with him in it. I have his body in the back of my truck. Do you want to come and get it this morning or do you want me to keep it on ice?" asked VPSO Earp.

"If the weather is good I'll come out and get it. I'll call you back."

A few minutes later he called to tell Wyatt he was on his way in the Cessna 185. Two hours later he parked his Cessna near the Lake Air hangar and covered the engine. Wyatt met him at the plane and the two men loaded the body inside. It was a chore. Since the cabin space inside the plane doesn't allow for a body to lay flat on the floor, it must be bent slightly to fit.

Inside the office Wyatt gave Turner all the evidence he had gathered at the scene. Each item was bagged and marked for evidence. He had also prepared an investigation report to be sent with the evidence. Turner would take the body and the evidence to the crime lab in Anchorage for analysis.

"Do you want anything else before I take off?" asked Gene Turner.

"Yes, there is. I would like the Colonel to send a letter of commendation to the fire chief and his men for a job well done. These guys are all volunteers, even the chief, but they did an outstanding job of not only putting out the fire, but preserving evidence inside the burned cabin. There was nothing they could do for the victim, but they handled everything else very professionally. I had never met them before tonight, but they have my respect now."

"I'll ask him while I'm in Anchorage this morning."

"OK, Gene, I'll help you get ready to fly out; then I'm coming inside to take a nap. I deserve it." Both men laughed as they walked to the Cessna.

In Houston DEA Agent Greg Hansen called FBI Agent Darren Hatfield. "My sources say Dillon Dixon has vanished. We had a man watching him and his office. One morning he never showed. We have no idea where he went.

You remember he's the right hand enforcer for Amerimex Trucking. We were watching him because of his connection to two recent deaths. They were made to look accidental, but I don't buy it.

"When Stan Andrews died we knew it was murder, but there was no evidence to back it up. I'm at my wits end on this one. We know they are bringing drugs into the U.S. in their trucks but can't find them. We know Stan was murdered, but we can't prove it. And I just got word that the truck driver, who brought the first load of cactuses to the new Nevada plant where Stan was killed had died mysteriously in Mexico. There are too many people dying out there and we can't prove anything. I think we either give up or expand our investigation." Hansen was venting on his FBI counterpart.

"Come over to my office and we'll try to make sense of what's going on. I think the big boss is John Douglas. I think he's the one wanting to take over the U.S. sector of the Escobar Cartel. Bring your file and I'll get ours. We can compare notes and mobilize a real task force to investigate every unanswered question. How soon can you be here?" Hatfield would never admit it, but he was as frustrated as Greg Hansen.

Two hours later the two men, with two assistants each, sat in a conference room comparing notes and making plans. "One thing the border people tell me is that there are cactus plants coming into the United States via Amerimex Trucking. A border patrolman noticed that they bring extra clay pots in each load. The pretext is that the plants must be transplanted, thus the reason for the Nevada warehouse.

"The thing the Border Patrolman noticed was the color of the pots. They are transported in red, yellow and black pots with white accents. They say, at the Nevada warehouse that the transported plants will be transferred to new pots that are red, yellow, black and blue with white accents. I have checked with the U.S. Department of Agriculture and they don't know why they need to change the pots. They only need to sanitize the soil in the pots. I would like to get some samples of the discarded pots but they seem to disappear." DEA man Greg Hansen was taking notes and laying out one of the inconsistencies which needed to be followed up.

"How do you want to go about getting samples of the pots? Do you want to go to the warehouse with a warrant and seize them? Or do you think we can pull some samples off the trucks at the border?" This bit of random brainstorming came from Darren Hatfield. "Why do you think the color of the pots is significant, anyway, Greg?"

"Escobar had an entire research and development department. He did things we didn't know were possible. You remember he built those big speedboats from fiberglass impregnated with cocaine, ran the boats across the Gulf, and melted the fiberglass down to recover the cocaine once they reached U.S. soil. I have a hunch they are doing the same thing with the pots and the reason for the different patterns in the paint scheme is so to never throw the wrong pot away or send the wrong pot to a garden center for sale. I know this sounds like science fiction, but look at what Escobar did with those hundred-thousand-dollar boats."

"OK. Greg, we find a way to confiscate, steal or otherwise get some samples of the pots from the trucks coming across the border." Hatfield pointed at one of his assistants: "Make a note. Now, Greg, what about Dillon Dixon? Where do you think he is right now?"

"His boss is building a big lodge somewhere in the bush of Alaska. He's there now and I suspect Dixon is up there for some reason. Dixon is Douglas' enforcer. If he had dirty work to be done he would send for Dixon."

"I have some connections in Alaska and I can have one of our agents go to wherever this lodge is located and check it out." Again, he turned to his assistant, "Make a note."

"Finally," said Greg Hansen, "I would appreciate it if you could have the FBI Crime Lab review all the evidence from the scene where Stan Andrews was killed. I talked with him just a short time before he died and he said there was a truck arriving and he was in charge of the loading dock at the warehouse in Nevada where the transplanting was to take place. Stan was a careful man and I don't believe his death was an accidental gas explosion. I think there must be something in the evidence we sent to the crime lab to verify that."

Darren Hatfield turned again to his assistant. "Make a note and make the call personally. I want some action on this."

"Thanks, Darren. I don't mean to throw all this in your lap, but most of what I've asked for is out of my hands. Your scope of authority in these areas is much broader than mine. And, of course, I can't help but blame myself for not preventing Stan's death. I made a huge mistake."

"We have a plan of action now. Let's keep it rolling. I'm going to let you make a plan with the Border Patrol for getting those samples off an Amerimex truck. You work with them all the time as it is. I'll let you know what my office in Anchorage has to say. Is there anything else now?" There were no comments. "OK, let's go to work," said Hatfield.

Late that same afternoon Dillon Dixon returned to his office. He checked his mail and his computer for messages. Next he called the Amerimex Trucking Company dispatcher to come to his office for a conference.

"Welcome back, Mr. Dixon," said the dispatcher.

"Thanks, Fred. Any problems while I was gone?"

"No, sir, I sent a driver to pick up the truck left by the dead driver. He'll be back on this side of the border in two days. I was going to fly him down there to get the truck, but we had another truck going that direction, so I put him in the passenger seat. I talked with the manager of the plant down there and he said the cactuses would survive the extra days with no problem."

"Good. Let me know when Ray's truck is back in the yard." Dixon made a note in his computer before asking the next question. "Have you found a replacement driver yet?"

"We have three good applicants and I'm checking out their credentials as we speak. His truck should be back in the regular rotation on the next round."

Thirty-six hours later Ray Thiel's truck was checking into the Border Patrol Station with the new driver at the wheel. The officer on duty checked the manifest and found the driver was not the one scheduled on the paperwork. The Border Patrolman stepped up to the driver side of the truck and asked the driver to step down.

Steve Buick, the new driver, climbed down with all his log books in hand to follow the officer into the office.

"It says here the driver of this truck is Ray Thiel," remarked the policeman.

"Yes sir, it was, but he died suddenly and the company sent me down to Puebla to bring the truck home. There are live cactus plants in the van and they need care. We don't want to lose the load for lack of care. We have an agricultural warehouse in Nevada. That's where I'm supposed to deliver the trailer." The driver presented his credentials and his dispatch notice to the border guard.

"Wait here and I'll check with my supervisor to be sure everything is in order." The Border Patrolman went to another office to speak with his supervisor.

"Sir, I have one of those Amerimex trucks out front. It has a different driver than on the manifest, but the driver says the original trucker died and he was sent to bring the truck back to the U.S. It's one of those trucks we got the notice about. The DEA wants samples of the cargo. This might give us a good opportunity without arousing suspicion."

"Good thinking, Ned. I'll send Will out with you and open the van." The supervisor reviewed the text of the notice and added, "They want samples of the cargo, mostly they're interested in the pots the plants are in. There are two kinds with different color combinations. Take a couple of each for testing and I'll call the DEA number while you have the driver busy."

Ned met with Will at the desk in the front office where the driver was waiting. "Because of the delay en route, my boss wants us to look at the cargo and to take a couple of samples. Do you have a problem with that?" asked Ned the border guard.

"No, not at all. I've been instructed to do whatever you guys want. I'll open the van for you. It's dark inside; you should take a light with you."

The three men walked to the back of the truck where the driver opened the locks securing the rear doors. Will climbed into the long trailer with an LED light in his hand while Ned stood with the driver behind the open doors.

"Just grab a couple of the potted cactus plants and a couple of the empty clay pots, Will," instructed Ned. "Hand them down here and I'll put them in a box and give the driver a receipt."

Will lifted two potted plants, one from two different packages, and did the same with the empty pots. He handed the goods to Ned and climbed down from the van. The driver secured the doors and followed them inside the office once again. Ned wrote a receipt for the items taken and signed the manifest allowing the man to cross the border with his truck and cargo.

Chapter Twenty-Eight

Two hours later DEA Agent Greg Hansen had a call from a Border Patrol Officer in El Paso, Texas. The report was that an Amerimex truck had just crossed the border carrying potted cactus plants. The driver was different than the one listed on the manifest, giving the border guards cause to sample the cargo in accordance with the memo sent by the DEA office. Hansen immediately called Darren Hatfield at the FBI.

"We have our samples, Darren. Customs officers just took them off a truck crossing the border in El Paso, Texas. Can you have someone from your office pick them up and get them to the crime lab?"

"That was quick," stated Hatfield. "Not even two days and we have the samples in hand. I love it when a plan comes together. Yeah, I'll call the El Paso office and give them instructions. Good work, Greg. It will still take some time to get the results, though."

"I know, man, but it's a step in the right direction. Thanks."

"While I have you on the phone, I had a call about a suspicious death in a place called Iliamna, Alaska. The reason the Anchorage office called me was the notices we had sent out regarding John Douglas and Dillon Dixon. It seems Dixon was in Iliamna at the time, as well as Douglas. Dixon stayed at the hotel. The Anchorage office sent a man over there and learned Dixon had been drinking with buddies of the fire victim. He left town the day after the fire. And get this. The house fire was fueled by a broken fuel oil line feeding an oil stove in the cabin. Does that sound suspiciously like the explosive fire that killed your man Stan Andrews in Nevada?"

"Wait a minute!" exclaimed Greg. "One of the items found at the scene in Nevada was a burned Piezo crystal igniter from a bar-b-que grill. We thought it was just something from the motorhome, but the broken LP gas line let propane fill the living area. If somehow the igniter was tripped it could have set off the explosion."

"Good thinking, Greg. That could be step two in the right direction. And since Dixon is Douglas's enforcer, and he was in Alaska as well, and close enough to be at the Nevada incident when it happened, I think we finally have a logical direction for this investigation. How do you want to go about this now?"

"I don't have any idea where the town of Iliamna, Alaska is located, but find out if there is a police force there."

"Good Idea, Greg. I'll get back to you."

Dillon Dixon was in his office when he received a phone call from Tony Bucco, the warehouse manager in Nevada.

"Mr. Dixon, this is Tony Bucco. I was told to call you if there was anything unusual with a shipment."

"Yes, Tony, has something happened?" asked Dixon.

"I'm not sure, sir. You remember Ray Thiel? A driver just came in with his truck. The load is OK and Customs signed off on the manifest, but the driver said because he wasn't the driver assigned to the load they would have to look at it. He opened the van and one of the cops got inside and took two plants and two extra pots. They gave him a receipt for the items and sent him on his way. He said it looked like a routine search, but I thought I should report it to you."

"You did the right thing, Tony. Keep your eyes open and call me if anyone comes nosing around."

"Sure thing, Mr. Dixon," replied Tony Bucco.

Being a cautious man, Dillon Dixon didn't believe in coincidence. It was entirely possible the customs officials were just following up a detail, but if so, why did they take samples of the cargo? Were they stopping the truck because of the destination? Was the stop in connection with the death of the guy at the warehouse in Nevada? Things were running smoothly at the new warehouse and it would cost a great deal of money to move the location and he didn't want to do that at this time. This was a question he should talk over with Douglas.

"Hello, John, can you talk?" asked Dixon.

"Yes, I'm in my office with the door closed. What's the matter? Is there a problem?"

"I'm not sure, John, that's why I called you. We had a driver bring Ray Thiel's truck back to the warehouse in Nevada. When he crossed the border the Customs agents said they needed to check the load because there was a different driver than listed on the manifest. The driver let them check and the agents took two plants and two new pots from the load and sent him on his way. I would like to think this was just a routine check, but I have never had Customs take a sample of the load in the past. I've seen them use sniffer dogs and all kinds of meters, but they never take samples of the load. This new wrinkle worries me."

"It does sound fishy, DD. Has there been any suspicious snooping around the Nevada warehouse?"

"None we know of. Tony said he hadn't seen anyone strange around the yard. I'm just worried that the two recent deaths connected with the trucking company may have started some kind of investigation. I don't like this at all." Dixon's paranoia was showing.

"Don't panic just yet, DD. Let me call Carlos. He has more connections in that area than we do. Perhaps he has heard something. I really don't want to tell him we're having a problem, since I'm trying to expand our presence in this business. But, if there is an investigation involving us, he will know about it. We can make a change in the shipping process, but it will be expensive. I would rather not do that. I'll get back to you with what I learn from Carlos."

"Sorry to bother you, Boss, but I thought you should know."

"My job is to take care of problems like these. You did the right thing, DD. I'll call you after I talk to Carlos. It will probably be tomorrow before I have an answer."

In Anchorage, FBI Agent Phil Bishop called the commander of the Alaska Air National Guard to ask if it was possible to get a ride to Iliamna, as a training mission, of course. The commander was happy to oblige the FBI man and arranged for an ANG plane to transport Bishop to the flight service station in Iliamna. The federal government would buy the fuel for the trip.

Bishop called Captain Griffin in Fairbanks to ask about the VPSO in the village. Griff assured the FBI agent the man, Wyatt Earp V was more than competent and qualified to assist in any investigation he had in mind. Griffin gave him a short version of Wyatt's resume.

When the Air National Guard plane landed at Iliamna Wyatt was waiting for the FBI agent. Captain Griffin had advised the VPSO of the arrival of the fed. Bishop climbed into the old pickup, tossing his small bag into the back seat. He put out his hand and said, "Hello, I'm Phil Bishop. You must be Wyatt Earp. Are you related to the original?"

"Yes, I'm, fifth generation. Pleased to meet you."

"Can we go to your office to talk a while? I've never been to Iliamna before and I'll need some guidance."

"Sure, not a problem." Grabbing his thermos, Wyatt asked, "Want some coffee?"

"Later, maybe, but first I have a few things to check out, if it's OK with you?"

The two men walked through the front door of the Lake Air charter office, said hello to Maggie and continued on to Wyatt's little office down the hall. Inside Wyatt closed the door for privacy prior to asking any questions.

"OK, Phil, exactly why are you here?" asked Wyatt.

"What I'm about to tell you can't leave this office. Understand?" asked Bishop.

"Of course, but I want you to understand I've been a cop a long time. I don't need instruction on behavior. This is a small community and I chose to be a VPSO here, but I did my twenty years and retired as a street cop in Fairbanks. Now, do you want to start again?" Wyatt had just scolded the FBI agent.

Bishop grinned and put out his hand, "I'm sorry, you're right; the town is small, the problems are the same. In fact the root of the question, 'why I'm here,' is an international problem. I sometimes forget you and I do the same job. I didn't mean to offend you."

"I just want you to know I do understand the English language. I've been to two county fairs and a dog show. You can talk straight to me and I'll understand." Wyatt had finished scolding the fed. "Now, what is the real reason you're here?"

"It has to do with a man building a lodge here. He's very wealthy and owns several trucking companies as well as other interests. My information says you have had several deaths in this community recently which were drug related. My information says one was a heroin user, one was an undercover policeman, and one was a drug dealer. I'm told two of the victims were employed by John Douglas, the owner of the new lodge. Is all this correct?" asked Bishop.

"Yes, it is, but there was another death, a trapper, who died using the same heroin. What you may not know is that a sizable amount of heroin was found near the local school some time back. It matched the heroin found at the first and second overdose death scene. The undercover officer killed was Carl Lewis, an experienced officer and a good cop. He was attempting to make a buy from a suspected local drug dealer who must have learned he was a cop and stuck a needle full of heroin in his jugular vein. The third death you mentioned was the suspected dealer, I think, who killed Carl. The dealer, Rick Buntz, died in a suspicious house fire. All the evidence from the last two deaths is still at the Anchorage crime lab." Wyatt gave Bishop a thumbnail description of the recent deaths. "Three drug related deaths in a short period of time in a village of 120 people is an extremely high percentage."

"I agree with you, and I think I can help in your investigation, too," began Bishop. "We suspect John Douglas, more specifically one of his trucking companies, is bringing heroin, cocaine, meth and other drugs, into the United States from Mexico. We believe he is affiliated with the head of the former Escobar Cartel, Carlos Mendoza. This cartel is one of the largest in the world. Nothing comes from South America without going through Carlos Mendoza. It is our belief John Douglas is attempting to become the agent for all the business done by Mendoza in the U.S.A. Douglas has an enforcer by the name of Dillon Dixon. Dixon was in Iliamna at the time of the death of the drug dealer, Rick Buntz. It is our belief that Douglas wanted Buntz killed to keep attention away from his new enterprise here in Iliamna. We have only circumstantial evidence connecting all these items together. That's why I'm here…to learn whether Dixon was involved in the killing of Buntz."

"It sounds like a big deal, Phil. What can I do to help you?"

"Specifically, I'm here to learn if we can tie Dixon to Buntz. I'm going to need your help with that, since I have no connections here. Do you think you can help me?" asked Bishop.

"Buntz used to come to town in the evening and drink a few beers at the bar in the hotel. We can go over there and ask the bartender if Dixon had been there or had a beer with Rick. Buntz was never a social person, but perhaps one of the regulars saw them there."

"Thanks, Wyatt. I want to apologize for my attitude earlier. Do you think we can have that coffee now?"

After finishing coffee the two men drove the short distance to the bar entry in the hotel. It was early afternoon, but the bartender was busy mopping the floor. There were two patrons sitting on the last two stools, sipping on beers. Inside the bar Wyatt stopped to speak with the bartender, "Hello, Fred, how you doing?" he asked in a friendly tone.

"Good, Wyatt, how about yourself?" he replied.

"This is Phil Bishop, Fred," said Wyatt, introducing the FBI agent.

Fred nodded.

"Listen, Fred, you knew Rick Buntz pretty well, didn't you?" he asked.

"As well as anyone, I guess."

"Did he seem to be associating with a new person in his last few days?"

"As a matter of fact, he did, Wyatt. There was a guy in town for a few days. He came in and asked for Rick…."

The statement was interrupted by one of the men at the bar. "Hey," he said, "We seen him, too, and he bought us a beer."

"Hold on a minute. We'll come talk with you in a minute," said Wyatt politely. "Now Fred, go on with your story."

"This guy came in and asked if Rick came in here to drink. I told him yes and that he usually came in in the early evening. The guy said he would come back and left until later. Rick came in right after that and the stranger bought the house a round. The guy said he wanted to hire someone to take him out to see the new mining properties. He hired Rick and the next day they went flying. That evening they were in here and Rick got really drunk. The stranger had to drive Rick home. The guy left the next day, but Rick's cabin burned down that night after the stranger took him home. That's about all I know," said Fred the bartender.

Phil Bishop took a photo from his jacket pocket. "Is this the man, the stranger who asked for Buntz?"

Fred looked at the picture, "Yup, that' him. I don't know what his name was."

"Thanks Fred you have been very helpful," said Phil as he turned to show the picture to the men at the bar.

"Yeah, said the first man. He bought us a beer." The second man only nodded.

Wyatt turned to Fred. "I would like you to come by the office and make a statement for me when you have a few minutes. It's important, Fred, so I hope you can stop by today or tomorrow."

"I have a girl coming in at four in order for me to go to the store and get a few things for the bar. I'll stop then, if that works for you."

"I'll make it a point to be there. Thanks, Fred."

"You want us to come sign a paper, too?" asked the man at the bar.

"No, but thanks anyway. Fred's statement will be enough." Wyatt didn't think the bar patrons would make credible witnesses.

Wyatt and Phil left the bar and once outside Phil said, "I think I had better get a room for the night. I'd like to be there when the bartender makes his statement and I think we need to drive out to the lodge property and speak with John Douglas." The two men walked to the hotel lobby to register the agent as a guest.

Chapter Twenty-Nine

"Officer Earp, good to see you again," Harry Porter greeted them from the front porch. A sensor at the gate had alerted the foreman to an approaching vehicle.

"Good to see you, too, Harry. My friend here is FBI Agent Phil Bishop. Would it be alright for us to come in and speak with Mr. Douglas for a few minutes?"

"Come on in. I'll ask him if he has time to talk with you."

Bishop and the VPSO climbed the porch steps. "How is the construction coming along?" asked Wyatt.

"Pretty slow since we lost Carl Lewis. He was a true wonder at log work. We have been trying to finish the trim and interior work. Supply is a big problem out here. We can't just go to the local hardware or lumber yard when we need something. We had three conex containers full of material and parts, but we are down to just one now. We make nearly all the trim boards as well as the door and window casings and trim. It's a slow process," explained Harry. "Have a seat at the table. I'll get you some coffee and go speak with our boss."

When Harry had gone to find John Douglas, Phil Bishop commented on the construction, "Wow, this is some place. It must have cost millions to build this lodge."

"I haven't seen it all, but what I have seen is first class. Douglas told me this was going to be a wilderness retreat and getaway for high dollar executives. I'm guessing the fee will be somewhere between three and five thousand dollars a day. I know it's out of my price range."

"Mine, too. I wonder where he got the money to build it?" asked Phil, without expecting an answer.

It was then that Harry Porter returned. "Mr. Douglas will be with you in a minute. He's on the telephone right now. Can I get more coffee or some breakfast for you boys?"

"No thanks, Harry," said Wyatt. "We appreciate the offer, but we have to get back to the office for a meeting in a short while. We just came out here to check some details with Mr. Douglas."

"Is it true? Someone burned up in the house fire the other night?" asked Harry.

"Yes, tragic thing. An oil line broke and the cabin burned from the stove oil leak. Did you know the victim, Rick Buntz?"

"No, I didn't know him, but I have heard of him. They say he was a loner. I don't get to town much, so I never met him."

At that moment John Douglas entered the kitchen. "Good day, gentlemen, good to see you."

"Good to see you again, too, sir," greeted Wyatt as he stood to shake hands with the lodge owner. "Mr. Douglas, I would like you to meet Phil Bishop of the FBI. He came out from Anchorage to assist in the fire investigation, the one over at Newhalen."

"Yes, I heard about that. Pleased to meet you Mr. Bishop. Have you been to Iliamna before?"

Bishop, too, shook the owners hand, "No, sir, it's my first trip. It's kind of an out-of-the-way place. What made you decide to build this huge lodge out here?"

"I came here on a fishing trip and fell in love with the place. I knew other company executives would feel the same way and bought the property from an old homesteader. It's been an expensive and sometimes exasperating task, but I think it will be worth the trouble." Douglas seemed to be relaxed and cooperative. Not at all concerned that Phil was a FBI agent. "I'm very busy today, Agent Bishop. What can I do to help you?"

"I had a call from our office in Houston asking me to check on travel by one of your Houston employees, a Dillon Dixon. He does work for you, doesn't he?"

"Yes, he manages my trucking businesses while I'm away. What travel are you concerned about?"

"He recently made a trip to Alaska and his absence came up in connection with another case in Texas. He isn't a suspect in any wrongdoing in Texas we're just following up on details. Can you tell me the reason he came to Iliamna this week?"

"Certainly; he brought me some papers to sign. We recently lost a contract in Texas and moved one of our oil field trucking companies to North Dakota. There were contracts which needed to be signed. The usual business contracts, you understand. It was more productive for him to come here than for me to make a trip to Houston."

"We noted Mr. Dixon stayed at the hotel while he was here. Was there a reason for that?" asked the agent.

"Yes, there was. We were doing interior construction and the dust in here was horrific. We thought it best for him to stay at the hotel because of his asthma. The dust would have been devastating for him."

"I see," said Bishop. "By the way, do you know a local man by the name of Rick Buntz?"

"No, but I've heard of him. The rumor was that he was a drug dealer. I don't know if Officer Earp has told you, but I have a zero tolerance policy on this property when it comes to drugs. That policy is in place with my trucking companies as well."

"I admire your strict policies on drugs, sir, but I wonder, is it true that one, no, two, of your employees died of drug overdoses?"

"Yes, it's true and it shocked me. I had no idea either of those men were users. Had I known I would never have hired either of them, and if I found out later I would have fired them instantly. I say again, I don't allow drugs of any type on this or any of my other properties." Douglas was emphatic in his tone.

"I admire you for that, Mr. Douglas, but I'm just following up details on another case. I thank you for your candor. My main concern was to determine the reason for your assistant's travel to Alaska. I don't know the details of the case it refers to, only that it was up to me to interview you about Mr. Dillon Dixon and his trip to Alaska. Thank you for your time, sir."

"Yes, thank you Mr. Douglas," said Wyatt. "We must be getting back to the office for our next meeting."

"Good to see you again, Officer Earp. Please come again."

Harry Porter escorted the two policemen to the edge of the big veranda and watched them as they drove out the front gate.

"Well Phil, how did you like Mr. Douglas?" asked Wyatt, with a smile.

"He's one of the best liars I've ever met. "I'll bet he's on the phone right now giving Dixon the details. Do you think I can use your computer to send this information to Darren Hatfield in Houston?"

"Yes, we still have a little time before Fred the bartender comes to the office."

The two men entered the front office where Maggie stopped them. "Here, Wyatt," she said, handing him a plate of cinnamon rolls—big, fresh, hot buttery cinnamon rolls.

"Does everyone in town feed you?" asked Bishop.

"Only the young, good looking ones," said Wyatt as they walked to his office.

Inside the office Bishop sat at the computer to forward his report while Wyatt went into the small kitchen to make coffee to go with the juicy rolls. Fred was a half hour late arriving to make his statement about Rick Buntz. The time was well used eating rolls and washing the sticky sugar glaze from their hands. Both officers were sugar sated by the time he arrived.

It was late when Bishop went to his hotel for the night. Wyatt was finishing his daily reports when the telephone rang. It was Linda.

"Do you remember me?" she asked. "I'm the woman you promised to marry."

"What was your name again?" he teased.

"Wyatt Earp, you're terrible. I don't know why I put up with you."

"I guess I am, at that. I'm sorry I haven't spent much time with you lately, but I've been a little busy. How are things at the school?"

"Good, the kids are getting bored with class. I'll have to find something for them to do for a change of pace. Got any ideas?"

"Maybe; most of the kids have snow machines, don't they?" he asked.

"Yes."

"Would it be permissible for you and me to escort the class, on snow machines, up the lake ice to one of the little streams and catch a mess of grayling and bring them back to the school for a fish fry for the parents and kids?"

"Oh, Wyatt, that's a wonderful idea. The kids will love it, the school board will love it, and the parents will love it. You are so clever. I'll ask the principal for permission and arrange a date. We will need an ice auger and some fishing poles, but the kids and their parents can furnish them. This is such an exciting idea. Thank you, Mr. Earp."

"You're welcome, ma'am. Let me know when and I'll be there."

"I'll call you tomorrow morning after I talk with the administrator. Good night, Lover."

"Language like that could get you in trouble with the school board," said Wyatt.

"If I get fired you will have to support me."

"It might be worth it. Now, go to bed. I have more work to do. Call me when you have a date and time. Bye."

The following morning Wyatt returned the empty plate to Maggie. "I haven't heard from the FBI agent. Can you die from cinnamon roll poisoning?" he asked her.

"Only if you eat too many," she replied.

"Then he's a gonner," joked Wyatt.

Wyatt drove to the hotel to find Bishop in the restaurant eating steak and eggs for breakfast. Wyatt ordered coffee.

"Want some breakfast?" asked Bishop.

"No thanks, I ate the last of the cinnamon buns for breakfast. What's on your agenda today?" he asked.

"I called the Guard and they are sending a plane for me in a little while. I would appreciate a ride to the flight service station after I eat. The Air Guard plane will pick me up there. I also want to thank you for your help. You made a crappy assignment into an interesting investigation. I think we found good answers and gave the folks in Houston ammunition against Dixon. In the end we may be able to prove he killed Rick Buntz. Thanks again."

"I've enjoyed working with you, Phil. Come out here again in the summer when you can spend some time fishing and swatting mosquitoes."

"I'd like that," replied Bishop.

When Bishop had finished his steak and Wyatt had downed this second cup of coffee the two men drove to the flight service station to await the airplane. This would, once again, be used as a training mission for the Alaska Air National Guard pilots.

Chapter Thirty

Two days later Wyatt loaded his snow machine and Akio with fuel, food, large thermos bottles of hot cocoa, first aid supplies, and extra blankets in case someone was hurt or suffered from the cold. Linda led the nine snow machines into the village and Wyatt's office where he took over as leader of the pack. They were to motor down the road to Newhalen where the group would move onto the lake ice for the ten mile trip up the lake to Eagle Bay where a small stream emptied into the big lake. A local had told Wyatt that the grayling fishing was good there this time of the year.

It was a fun trip for Wyatt and Linda as well as for the children who raced each other and zigged and zagged across the ice. When they arrived at the mouth of the little stream Wyatt unloaded the power-driven ice auger and began to bore holes in the thick ice. The VPSO had brought one canvas shelter which he erected and placed a small propane heater inside in the event any of the children became too cold. Fishing was brisk from the outset and limits were caught before anyone suffered frostbite. Wyatt served the students hot chocolate and sandwiches while they watched him clean the fish and place them in a plastic cooler. The plan was to return to the school where parents were to be waiting to fry the fish and give prizes for the largest catch.

The entire outing took roughly three hours from the start until the snow machines were all parked back at the school. Wyatt carried the cooler full of cleaned fish into the lunch room to be cooked and the awards made. School officials joined in the festivities and parents laughed with the children.

When the fish was served Wyatt sat at a table next to Linda. "This is the way life is meant to be lived. Having fun with the children, laughing with your neighbors, and enjoying food you caught yourself."

"Yes, I know, but sometimes life gets in the way of living. It's sad, but that seems to be the way things go. That's why I love being with you. Things are simple with you in my life. No complications, nothing painful, only happiness and joy. I hope you will always be there for me." Linda leaned her head over onto Wyatt's shoulder.

"Teacher's got a boyfriend, teacher's got a boyfriend," students began to taunt, embarrassing both Linda and Wyatt.

"I guess we've been found out," whispered Wyatt.

"Yes, but I'll bet they don't know how many children we plan to have," she giggled.

It was very dark outside when they finished with the little celebration. This time of year there would only be about five hours of daylight, but the reflective snow cover and moonlight made it a twilight time all night long. Each of the students was instructed to follow their parent's vehicle home, driving slowly and carefully. Linda rode her machine to her cabin while Wyatt rode his to the maintenance garage where it had been stored and where his pickup was parked inside. It was late when he returned at his office to see if there were any messages for him.

There was one from Phil Bishop. "Call me." was all it said.

Checking the time he decided the FBI agent would not be in his office, but would probably be available on his cell phone. He dialed the number and Bishop answered on the first ring.

"What's up?" asked Wyatt.

"It didn't take Douglas long to call Dixon. My office in Houston says a private jet with Columbian registration numbers landed in Houston, and an Amerimex Trucking Company car met the plane. It refueled and took off again. The pilot didn't notify FAA he had a passenger, but Dillon Dixon hasn't been seen since the plane took off. I'm betting Douglas called him and told him to get out of the country. We checked the registration and found the plane registered to a company operated by the Escobar Cartel. Our office called Amerimex Trucking and asked for Dixon, but they said he was out of town and the man in charge was Lloyd Turpin. It seems we're always one step behind."

"There isn't much point pressing him until the crime lab comes back with solid evidence of a crime. You might as well sit back and relax until there is something to arrest him for. And even then, you may not be able to connect John Douglas to the crimes. He stays insulated from the actual commission of any crimes. He probably orders them, but he never commits them. I've been out of the office all day and don't know if he's still at the lodge, but I'll check tomorrow."

Wyatt had been a cop a long time and learned a case seldom progresses in a straight line. It usually takes all kinds of twists before it comes to an end.

It had been a wonderful day with Linda and her students and Wyatt had enjoyed the entire outing. It had been a long time since he spent a day ice fishing and riding the snowmobile. He found, to his own astonishment, that he loved being with the children, baiting hooks and taking fish off lines. The kids had been a lot of fun for him today. He chuckled to himself about Linda mentioning their proposed family. Another thought crossed his busy mind at that moment. He would have to stop at a jewelry shop the next time he went to either Anchorage or Soldotna in order to buy an engagement ring. He made a note to learn Linda's ring size. He had planned to use his mother's wedding ring when they married.

It was late and Wyatt was exhausted. It was time to quit for the day. His last act while at his desk was to make a note to check on John Douglas tomorrow. He may have decided to leave the country, too.

His morning was started with a visit from Tom Dempsey. Wyatt was at his desk when the pilot entered.

"Light snow and warm temperatures with visibility good and no runs on the books. Life is like cocoa and toast, they never come out even." It was unusual for Tom to have enough time to stop by the office and joke around.

"Good morning to you, too, Tom," replied Wyatt.

"Maggie has some errands for me to run in Anchorage today, Wyatt. I wondered if you would like to ride along to keep me company?"

"I have one thing to do this morning, Tom, but I can be ready to go by ten o'clock. Is that good enough for you?"

"Perfect. She's making a list for me right now, and Pearson, the mechanic up the road is ordering some parts from Stoddard. The parts order hasn't been called in yet, so if we can get out of here by ten we'll be right on schedule. See you then."

Not waiting for an answer he turned to go back to his own office out front. Wyatt checked the time and decided he should go to the lodge now if he was to see Douglas today. He slipped into his heavy coat and walked to his truck. It was snowing lightly, a dry snow with small flakes. Colder weather was surely on the way thought Wyatt.

Harry Porter opened the door when Wyatt arrived at the lodge. "Is Mr. Douglas in?" asked the VPSO.

"Yes, he is, come on inside. Looks like we may get some snow today," commented Porter as they walked to the kitchen.

"I think we will see colder weather, too."

"Do you want coffee?" asked Harry.

"No, thanks, I just need to speak with Mr. Douglas a moment. I'm supposed to go to Anchorage with Tom Dempsey today, so I had better keep moving."

Harry nodded and walked out of the room to get Douglas. He returned moments later, following his boss.

"Ah, Officer Earp, to what do I owe this pleasure?" he asked. "You seem to be a regular around here lately."

"I'm sorry to bother you, sir, but I had a call from FBI Agent Bishop and he wanted me to ask you where we could contact Dillon Dixon. He seems to have left Houston and his company people can't seem to locate him."

Douglas gave a small chuckle, "Yes, DD does that sometimes. It's infuriating to say the least. Just when I need him he vanishes without telling me where he's going. He is seldom gone more than two or three days. Is this something I can help you with, Officer Earp?"

"I don't think so, sir. Bishop just asked me to inquire as to his whereabouts. The FBI doesn't let me in on what they do. I'll call Bishop and let him know you were unable to help him."

"Sorry you made the trip out here for nothing. I wish I could help you."

"It's OK, sir. I see you're coming right along with the lodge. Do you think you will be able to take clients this summer?"

"I hope so. Losing our log man set us back a little, but Harry and Don are getting things done quite well. I've had a number of inquiries about bookings for this summer and I have told them all to check back in May. Which reminds me, could you give me the name of some good, reputable fishing guides who would be interested in working for us? We will pay good wages and the tips from our clients should be very generous."

"I think you should have no trouble at all finding guides to work for you. I'll make a list for you and bring it out in a day or two." Wyatt stood to zip his coat, "Do you have any questions for me, Mr. Douglas?"

"No, you are always very courteous and helpful and I thank you for that."

Wyatt returned to his office and called Phil Bishop with the information he had not learned on his trip to the lodge. Bishop was amused and thanked the VPSO.

At ten o'clock Wyatt climbed onto the right seat of the Lake Air company twin engine plane for the ride to Anchorage. While waiting for Tom to finish his pre-flight Wyatt dialed Linda to tell her he was about to take off for Anchorage for the day and asked her ring size. It was a 6.

It was dark at 7:15 when the two men put the twin engine plane back inside the hangar. Wyatt walked to his office to check for messages and call Linda. He went to the front of the hangar to start his truck and drive to Linda's house. He rapped on the door. She opened it wearing a bathrobe and slippers.

"I didn't expect you this evening, Wyatt. Come in, please."

"I just returned from the big city and I have something for you. I was so excited about it I couldn't wait until tomorrow." Wyatt was beaming as he pulled off his heavy winter coat.

"It must be important to get you this excited," she teased,

"Actually, it is. I want to make it official and ask you to marry me in a proper way." He dropped to one knee. "Linda Mason, I am in love with you and I am asking you to be my wife. Will you marry me?"

"Of course I will, silly. I have already set the date and made the plans for the wedding with your father's help." She was now holding his hands in hers.

Wyatt slipped one hand free and reached into his pocket. "That being the case, will you accept this ring as a symbol of our engagement?" He opened the small box to display a white gold ring with five large diamonds set perfectly on top.

"Oh, Wyatt, it's beautiful, but you shouldn't have bought such an expensive ring."

He slipped it onto the third finger of her left hand. "If you don't like it I can take it back."

"You wouldn't dare," she said as she wrapped her arms around his neck and kissed him hard while nearly choking him with her hug.

"Then, you like the ring?"

The two sat on the couch for a long while, just holding each other. Finally, Wyatt said, "I guess I have to get back to the office before people start to talk. I love you Linda Mason."

Chapter Thirty-One

Greg Hansen and Darren Hatfield were deep in a strategy meeting when the call came from Phil Bishop, FBI Agent from Anchorage, Alaska. The agents in Houston put the call on conference call, a device in the center of the table, "Hello, Agent Bishop, this is Special Agent Hatfield and DEA Agent Hansen. Did you get the information we requested?"

"Sorry, sir, but Douglas was close-mouthed about the whereabouts of Dixon. The local Village Public Safety Officer, a very capable cop, by the way, went back out to the lodge Douglas is building and asked again about Dixon. He called me later to tell me Douglas gave him the cock and bull story about how he takes off from time to time without notice and never tells him, Douglas, where he's going. Douglas seems comfortable with wherever Dixon is headed and didn't show any clue of leaving his lodge. I wish I had better news for you."

Hatfield was the first to answer, "When you go fishing, sometimes you get a bite and sometimes you don't. I have some good news for you, though. You can pass it on to the VPSO when you get it. The crime lab called and said they were sending the reports from all the cases I had listed on the rush report. One thing they said they found was the burned bar-b-que igniter was taped to the victim in Nevada, making it the cause of ignition in that fire and the death a murder. It also said the residue checked out in the fire in a place called Newhalen, Alaska was intentional and traced the fire source to some burned papers recovered from the fire. I give your Public Safety Officer credit for being thorough on that one. The lab said the fires were likely the work of the same individual. You say Dixon was seen in the area prior to the fire, and a worker in the warehouse in Nevada had seen a truck parked outside the fence with a license plate owned by a rental company. The vehicle was rented by Dixon. We, Hansen and I, are going to the judge to get felony arson warrants and murder warrants for Dillon Dixon."

"That's good news, but is there anything to tie Douglas to the crimes?" asked Bishop.

"Not at this point, but we are obtaining wiretap warrants for Douglas' phones, both home and office here in Houston. I'll see if we can include the phones at the lodge and his cell phone. If Dixon calls we'll learn where he is located and possibly get them to admit complicity in the arsons and murders," stated Hatfield.

"Good luck with that one, sir. Douglas is a cagey one and I doubt Dixon will contact him directly. But I'll pass the good news on to Wyatt in Iliamna."

"Thanks again, Bishop. We'll be in touch."

After the call Bishop thought about the information a few minutes before calling Wyatt. "Hello, Wyatt, how are things in the village?"

"Everyone is happy without you in town stirring things up, other than that only the snow. And with Christmas upon us I hope it stays quiet. Uh, you don't have bad news for me, do you?"

Phil Bishop chuckled, "No, but I have some good news."

"You got me a promotion and a pay raise?" Wyatt said jokingly.

Bishop snickered with him, "Not that good, but good. I just got off the phone with the agents in Houston and they're expecting the written reports on the evidence in these cases. We asked to have it all rechecked and rushed. They found evidence of murder in the Agent Andrew's death in Nevada and a connection to your fire victim. That fire, too, was arson. You can now call that one murder. The Houston agents are attempting to find Dillon Dixon for both cases."

"There isn't much I can do about all that unless Dixon decides to come back here. This is an out-of-the-way spot if he does decide to come back into the country. Douglas could hide him at his lodge without too much trouble unless someone spots a newcomer."

"Well, good luck to you and Merry Christmas, if I don't talk to you before then."

"You, too, Phil. Thanks for the call."

Wyatt put the phone back in its cradle and leaned back in his office chair. He had been grateful for the lull in serious activity in the past few days. Now he must forward the information he had just received to his boss in Fairbanks, though there wasn't much either of them could do about it unless Dixon returned.

Two days later DEA Agent Greg Hansen and FBI Agent Darren Hatfield were in Hatfield's Houston office attempting to devise a plan to get Dillon Dixon to return to the U.S. Nothing seemed to be a viable plan as long as he was hiding in Columbia. It would take some major catastrophe in the Amerimex Trucking Company to get him back. The brainstorming was coming to a fruitless conclusion when Hatfield's secretary came into his office with a handful of documents from the National Crime Lab. She laid the pile on the conference table and was about to leave the room when Hatfield asked her to wait until he could give her a number of the documents to forward to Phil Bishop in Alaska.

He was thumbing through the stack when one of the documents made him sit up and stop to read the paper.

"Greg, take a look at this," he said excitedly, handing the document to his DEA counterpart.

Hansen read the document while Hatfield sorted the rest of the stack of documents for his secretary to send out. He gave them to her and she left to continue her chores.

"Wow, Darren, now I know there is a God. We sat here all morning trying to figure out how to get Dixon to come to us and it falls in our laps."

"OK, now that we have probable cause to arrest John Douglas. We need to organize a small arrest task force to take him down." Hatfield was making notes as he spoke. "Call Bishop and let him know. Tell him he can enlist that village cop, Wyatt what's his name. In the meantime, I'll put a team together from here and make arrangements for a plane to take us to Alaska for the arrest. I want to have a team from this office stand by until we get to Alaska before taking down the Amerimex Trucking Company officers. When word of the raid and the arrest of Douglas gets out, I think Dixon will catch the first plane home."

Hansen rubbed his chin, "I think you're right, but I also think our friend Carlos Mendoza is going to be upset. He's a powerful man and this could start world war three here in the western hemisphere. This man has billions of dollars and has never hesitated to use it to fight DEA or any other agency attacking his cartel. This will start a war that will cost lives in South America and here in the United States."

Hatfield was writing another note, "You're right. I'll call my boss in Washington D.C. and let him know the plan. He can coordinate with your director there also. I think we need to go ahead with our plan as quickly as possible and arrest Douglas before he moves to Columbia with his right-hand man."

Hansen stood to leave, "I'm going back to my office and get the ball rolling. Call me if there are any changes and let me know the timetable."

It was nearly five in the afternoon when Hatfield called Hansen. "It took all day, but things are set to go for tomorrow. Be at our hangar at 4:00 a.m. It will be nearly five hours flying time and I want to arrive as early as we can. It will be you, me and five FBI agents. Have your man Bishop and the local officer, as well as two Alaska State troopers, meet us at the local airport. The local policeman can, most likely, coordinate all that as well as arrange transportation for the team. I have a team set to go here in Houston when we notify them we have Douglas in custody. Any questions?"

"Only one: I'll need an ETA for us in Iliamna, Alaska in order for the rest of the team to arrange travel. I'm told the village is quite remote."

"You will have it in ten minutes," replied Hatfield.

Chapter Thirty-Two

It was twenty-five degrees below zero at seven thirty the following morning when Wyatt entered the flight service station to check on the two suburbans the federal officers had requested. He heard the state Beechcraft King Air reporting in as he entered the office. Bishop, along with Sergeant Gene Turner and two other troopers, were on board. Wyatt obtained the keys to the big Chevys and went back outside to start the cars in order to warm the engines as well as the interior of the vehicles. His own pickup was also running outside the front door of the FAA building.

Upon landing, the pilot taxied to the Flight Service building and shut down one engine to allow the passengers to exit the plane. Bishop and three troopers stepped off the plane. Once off, the pilot taxied to the Lake Air hangar to plug in the engines and cover them with insulated covers. Wyatt sat in his truck waiting for Gene Turner and Phil Bishop. They climbed into the truck with Wyatt for a meeting to coordinate the raid on the lodge.

"Have you heard from Hansen and Hatfield?" asked Bishop.

"Not directly, but I heard their plane checking in a few minutes ago. They should be arriving right about now. Which one of them is in charge of this party?" asked Wyatt, wanting to know who he was going to be taking orders from.

"The plan, as I understand it is for you to get us to the lodge and to stand by. Hatfield and Hansen will do the knock and enter. I will be with them to identify Douglas. It will be up to you to see to it no one sneaks out the back way. I don't expect gunfire, but you know how these things go, always expect the unexpected. These warrants are federal jurisdiction, so Hatfield will be the lead officer and in charge." Bishop recited the plan as he knew it, hoping the advantage of surprise would make this warrant service quick and without incident.

"I'm not clear on the details, Phil. Is John Douglas implicated in the murders here in Iliamna?" asked Wyatt.

"No, but we hope to make him complicit. The Houston office was given a report about some cargo on a truck they inspected. It was a load of cactus plants. They were to take the plants to a warehouse in Nevada and disinfect the potting soil and repot the plants in new pottery, destroying the old pots. The report from DEA confirmed that once the pots were broken up and the enamel discarded the clay could be dissolved in water and then the slurry could be chemically treated. By using different densities of the same chemical they could extract heroin and cocaine from the clay. We always suspected Amerimex Trucking of importing drugs, but until now we couldn't figure out how it was done. It seems the baked enamel glaze hid all traces of the drugs mixed in the pottery clay. It was a clever scheme, and it took us a long time to catch on to it."

"I guess that explains how John Douglas can afford to build that multi-million dollar log cabin down by the lake." Wyatt stopped talking to roll down his window a slight bit to listen. "It sounds like the other plane in arriving."

"I hear it now. I'm going to have to go out there for a meeting with Hatfield and Greg Hansen, my boss," said Bishop.

"I'll wait here, Phil. Just let me know what you want me to do. Gene will be riding with me."

"Thanks, Wyatt, I'll get back to you as soon as the plan is set." Bishop climbed out of the truck to walk to the ramp where the Gulf Stream jet was stopping.

There is a gigantic difference in the meaning of the word cold in Texas as opposed to the same term as used in Alaska. Hatfield and Hansen stepped off the airplane wearing stylish Texas cold weather attire. By the time they reached the bottom of the air stair they knew their mistake. "Let's go inside the Flight Service Station to talk," said Hatfield, pulling his collar up against the minus 25 degrees temperature.

Wyatt instantly recognized the problem and jumped from the truck to speak with Bishop and Hatfield.

"How many people need coats?" asked Wyatt.

"Five," replied Hatfield, without additional comment.

"Wait inside. I'll be back in five minutes." He climbed back into his truck to drive to the Lake Air hangar where heavy parkas were hanging to be used by such guests. He loaded the coats into the cab of his truck and drove back to the Flight Service Station. Bishop helped carry the parkas into the warm building for the Texas agents. The meeting was short and when it finished Hatfield instructed Wyatt to lead the way to the lodge.

All the agents put on the parkas, most of them over their other jacket before leaving the building to get into the waiting, warm, suburbans. Gene Turner chuckled as Wyatt re-entered the pickup.

"Chechakos," muttered Turner.

Wyatt turned his truck around and waited for the other vehicles to fall in behind him. It was only three miles to the lodge, but these city folks could get lost, he thought. Wyatt led the small parade through the gate at the lodge and stopped at the front porch, as always. Bishop was the first out of the Chevy and climbed the stairs to the porch with the other FBI and DEA agents following.

Just as Bishop reached the front door it was opened by Harry Porter. "What can I do for you men?" he asked.

"Yes, Mr. Porter," said Bishop displaying his badge. "We are here to see Mr. John Douglas. We have a warrant. Please step aside."

Porter stammered a little, but stepped out of the way for the party to enter. "Where is he?" asked Bishop.

"In his office, follow me." Porter had never had contact with police in his life and thought it better to cooperate than to object.

The group, led by Porter, walked through the kitchen area into a large dark room and on to a hallway with many doors and good lighting. Porter stopped at the second door on the left and was about to knock when Bishop grabbed his wrist and held it. Bishop motioned for the foreman to step back. He turned the knob and quickly pressed the door open. Hatfield stepped to Bishop's side, Glock in hand.

"Mr. Douglas, we are federal officers with a warrant for your arrest. Please step out from behind the desk." It was Hatfield speaking firmly but politely.

Douglas nodded and began to comply. "For what are you arresting me?" asked Douglas.

"Transporting and marketing dangerous drugs. We will read the entire warrant as soon as we make sure you are unarmed." It was Hatfield again, explaining the process.

"I will want to call my lawyer," stated Douglas.

"We will allow you to do that once you are remanded to official custody." Hatfield was doing all the talking.

Douglas stepped out from behind the desk and raised his hands. One of Hatfield's men pat searched the prisoner and found nothing but a small pocket knife which he placed on the desk top. "We're good, sir," said the junior agent.

"Do you have a heavy coat, sir?" asked Hatfield.

"Yes, on the rack near the back door. Where are you taking me?" he asked.

"To the airport and on to Houston, sir." Hatfield spoke as the officer who had searched him placed handcuffs on the wrists of the prisoner.

Douglas turned to see Porter. "Harry, call the office in Houston and tell them what happened. Have my lawyer find out where, exactly they are taking me and to meet me there."

"Yes, sir, Mr. Douglas," Harry paused a moment, thinking. "Do you want us to continue construction, sir?"

"Yes, Harry, someone will have to keep the place secure and the heat running. I'll be in contact with you as soon as I can. If DD calls, let him know about this and have him call the office. I'll have the lawyers make certain the office is open until he can return."

"All right, Mr. Douglas, let's go to the car. And Mr. Porter, I am leaving the property in your care as Mr. Douglas has instructed." Hatfield took Douglas by the arm for safety and led him down the steps and to the car, stopping at the back door to put a large fur lined parka around the prisoner.

The entire party returned to their vehicles and, with Wyatt again leading the way, returned to the Flight Service Station where the federal agents, with their prisoner, boarded the airplane to return to Houston with one stop in Anchorage for fuel.

Bishop, Turner and Wyatt stood in the cold to watch the jet taxi to the runway and take off. Turner used his hand-held radio to summon the King Air to fly Bishop and the troopers back to Anchorage and on to Soldotna. Wyatt returned to his office with a full day of reports to write.

Late in the afternoon the VPSO stood to stretch his aching muscles. He hadn't noticed before, but his office was very cool. He found a sweatshirt and slipped it on over his uniform shirt before going to the front office to ask Maggie for a cup of coffee.

He was back in his own office when the telephone rang. It was Linda.

"Hi, handsome. How is your day?" she asked.

"It's fine. I've been in the office most of the day. The feds and some troopers came this morning and we all went out to the new lodge to arrest John Douglas on a federal warrant. We all came back to the airport and they loaded up in their little jets and flew away. I've been doing reports since they left town."

"Good Lord, why did they arrest Mr. Douglas?" asked a shocked Linda.

"The FBI and DEA have proof he and his trucking company are involved in transporting drugs out of Mexico. They said they have evidence that Rick Buntz was murdered, too. The murderer skipped the country to South America, but he also killed someone in Nevada. The feds are just waiting for him to come back into the country. The killer worked for Douglas and his trucking company."

"It sounds as though you have had a busy day. Would you like me to cook some dinner for you tonight?"

"That would really be nice," answered Wyatt. "What can I contribute?"

"Just bring you. I'll do the rest." She giggled and added, "I might even have a glass of wine with dinner."

"OK, I'll finish up here and be out there around six." Wyatt felt his body and mind relax knowing he would be spending the evening with her.

As he hung up the phone he remembered a call he needed to make. It was to his father in Naknek.

"Hello, Dad, how are you?"

"Good, son, how about you?" asked Wyatt Earp IV.

"I've been busy recently, but it should slow down until after the first of the year."

"How is your lady friend?"

"She's great, Dad. I'm going out to her place for dinner tonight, which reminds me, I have a big question for you."

"Shoot," said the elder Earp.

"I've been thinking and I wondered if you would allow me to give Linda Mom's wedding ring for our marriage ceremony?"

There was a short pause on the other end of the line. "I think it would be wonderful, son, and I know your mother would be proud. I'll have it cleaned and the stones checked. You can pick it up the next time you're in Naknek."

"Thank you, Dad. I bought an engagement ring, but I really wanted to use Mom's wedding ring."

"I'm happy you asked. Will you and Linda be coming here for Christmas dinner?"

"If that's an invitation I'll ask her tonight when we have dinner."

"It's an invitation. Oops, I have another call. I'll talk to you tomorrow. Good night, Son."

"Good night, Dad. I love you."

Wyatt turned off the light on his desk and went to his living quarters to change clothes and shower before driving to Linda's for dinner. He mustn't forget to ask her about having Christmas dinner with his father.

He was about to leave when his telephone rang again. It was Harry Porter at the lodge. "Officer Earp, glad I caught you. I just had a strange phone call. It was from Mr. Douglas's right hand man, Dillon Dixon. He didn't say where he was calling from, but he wanted to know all about you guys arresting Mr. Douglas. I told him all I knew about it, but he kept asking questions about where he was taken and all kinds of stuff. He said he might come up and run the lodge for a while. I don't know if Mr. Douglas wants him to do that, and I don't know how to get in touch with him. What do you think I should do, Mr. Earp?" There was a stressful tone to his question.

"It's late in Houston now, but I'll call first thing in the morning and see what I can find out and get back to you then."

Chapter Thirty-Three

The following morning, early, a sleek, silver Learjet landed and taxied to the small parking apron near the Flight Service Station. The door opened and one passenger disembarked. The door closed and the jet taxied back to the runway for takeoff, leaving the passenger standing in the cold. A pickup turned on its headlights and drove slowly to where the man was standing. He opened the passenger door of the truck and climbed inside. The truck turned around in the spacious parking apron and drove away, down the road toward the new lodge.

"You must be Harry," commented the passenger.

"Yes, sir, I am. I work for Mr. Douglas and manage his property here on Lake Iliamna. You must be Dillon Dixon."

"That's me. I work for Mr. Douglas, too. I manage his trucking companies down in the lower 48. I've been away on a business trip and just now returned. I understand Mr. Douglas has been arrested by the FBI."

Harry Porter noted a coldness in the man's voice, "Yes, sir, they came to the lodge and arrested him. They said they had a warrant and showed him a piece of paper. They came in and went to his office, just shoved me out of the way and walked right on in. Mr. Douglas didn't argue. He just let them talk and waited for them to take him away. He said he wanted to call his lawyer, but they said he had to wait until he was remanded, whatever that means. They loaded him up and took him to the airport and loaded him on a big jet and flew away. I ain't never dealt with the FBI, but they didn't waste any time. They just took him away."

"Is there a local police force here?" asked Dixon.

"We have a VPSO. That means Village Public Safety Officer. He's sort of an Alaska State Trooper, but he works like a local policeman. The one we have is named Wyatt Earp. Everyone thought it was a joke, but he really is a relative of the old-time marshal. Mr. Douglas liked him. He comes out here sometimes to have coffee. You know how Mr. Douglas was about drugs. We had an employee who died of an overdose of heroin and Mr. Douglas was really mad about it. He gave the VPSO heck and told him he had to stop any and all drug business in Iliamna."

"Did they catch the person who sold the heroin?" asked Dixon.

"I don't know, but I don't think so. We hired another logsmith to replace the one who died and he died the same way. Mr. Douglas really got mad at the village cop then. Mr. Douglas wants this place to have a good reputation and hated it when DEA, state troopers and the VPSO all started coming around. It made the lodge look bad."

"Well, Harry, you can relax. I didn't come to stop you from working. I'm sort of like John. I'll manage the business end here and you continue to manage the construction. John wanted to have this place ready by spring and attaining that goal will be your responsibility. I know John watched the pennies, but I want this project completed. If you need something, just get it. I want to know about any extraordinary purchases, but I'll approve almost anything to get the place up and running by the spring season. Any questions for me?" asked Dillon Dixon.

"No sir, Mr. Dixon, I have one man working with me and I'll have to hire another carpenter, but the log work is finished and only the interior finish work needs to be done. We can work inside all winter without any problem. Getting material is sometimes a problem, but if you will allow me to order and ship stuff by air carrier I'll have the place ready to open by mid-May."

They stopped at the front steps and Dixon went inside the lodge while Harry plugged the truck into the outlet on the bull rail. Inside Harry showed Dixon to a room that was two doors down the hall from the office. Harry fixed breakfast for Don Zapo, Dillon Dixon, and himself. It was early, but since everyone was up and moving Harry decided to cook up some ham and eggs with hash browns potatoes and toast for a get-acquainted breakfast.

Harry introduced Zapo to Dixon and poured coffee and orange juice.

"I'm not here to manage the construction, you still work for Harry," Dixon was explaining to Zapo as Harry sat at the table. "I still manage the trucking companies down south, so I'll be on the phone a lot."

"I think we'll start on hanging the doors and begin trim work on the two executive rooms in the loft," said Harry to Zapo. "If all goes well we should have them finished in two weeks. When we finish those office/rooms upstairs I'm going to give you a week off while I have more material sent in. If you want to go home or anything, I'll see you get a plane ticket."

"Gee, thanks, Harry. I ain't been out to home in a long time. I wanna go see my mom in Medford, Oregon. I been sending her money 'cause she's sick and can't work no more. I'd like to go there for a week."

"OK, Don, as soon as we know when the upstairs rooms will be done I'll get you a ticket to Medford. You have to promise to come back, though."

"Oh, I'm coming back, Harry. You pay good and I like it here in the summer. Winter ain't so good, but summer is great." It was true, Don was making better than average wages and had his room and board furnished for him. He helped with the construction and did the menial chores like cutting wood and sweeping the lodge floors, keeping the sawdust to a minimum.

Dixon was finishing his breakfast and wiping the egg yolk from his plate with a piece of toast. "Is there a store in town where I can buy a heavier coat?" he asked

"No, but give me your size and I'll have one sent from Cabela's in Anchorage. It will be tomorrow if I order it this morning." Harry Porter knew it would take a while for the new boss to become accustomed to living conditions in the bush.

"Just a regular, large will do," said Dixon as he picked up his coffee cup and walked away toward the office.

Harry glanced at the time. It was now eight a.m. His office was a small room with a view of the lake off to the side of the kitchen area. He thought it was handy because of the proximity to the coffee pot. "Take care of the clean-up for me, Don. I'm going to my office for a while."

Dixon was in Douglas' office making a series of phone calls. The first was to the Amerimex offices in Houston.

"Amerimex Trucking, Shirley speaking," the voice was friendly and pleasant.

"Shirley, this is Dillon Dixon. I need to know where they're holding Mr. Douglas. Do you have that information handy?"

"Hello, Mr. Dixon. Are you back home now?" she asked.

"Sort of. I'm at the lodge in Alaska. I don't want that information to get out, but you can call me here. Do you know where they are holding Mr. Douglas?" he asked again.

"Mr. Costello is representing Mr. Douglas in this matter. He is a criminal lawyer with the company law firm. He said to refer all calls about Mr. Douglas to him, but for you I think I can tell you what you want to know. He is being held in the federal jail facility here in Houston. He has a bail hearing tomorrow in federal court. This is just awful, Mr. Dixon. We, the office staff, we don't know what to believe and are worried about the office closing."

"Don't worry, Shirley, the office isn't going to close. I'll be running things from here for now and I want you to keep me informed of any developments, any developments whatsoever." Dixon wanted to impress her with his authority. "I'll need the number for the federal jail and for the lawyer, Costello."

She quoted the numbers and thanked him for being there to reassure the staff.

The next call for Dixon was to Carlos Mendoza. "Carlos, my friend, how are you this morning? I'll wager your temperature is warmer than mine."

"Senior Dixon, you must have reached Alaska without incident. Have you learned the whereabouts of Mr. Douglas?"

"Yes, I have. They're holding him in the federal jail in Houston. He has a bail hearing tomorrow. I'll give you the name of the law firm and the name of the lawyer for this case. John should be out on bail by tomorrow afternoon."

"My informant at the Border Patrol office says there is a raid planned at the Nevada warehouse. He didn't know why, but said it was to be a big deal. See if you can find out what this is about. I've ordered Bucco to clean the place up before they arrive. There is a lot of pottery there and I want you to have a truck pick up the pottery and chemicals as quickly as possible. Bucco will have it loaded on one of the empty trailers. Just park it somewhere until we can relocate the lab."

Dixon made a note, "All right, Carlos, and I'll let you know as soon as I can find out anything about John."

His next call was again to Amerimex Trucking Company. "Me again, Shirley. Let me speak with the dispatcher." She put him through to the dispatch center for the trucking company. He talked at great length with the chief dispatcher, making arrangements to have, not one but two, trailers picked up at the Nevada warehouse. After hanging up the telephone he leaned back in the office chair to think. Suddenly he had a thought.

"Carlos, sorry to bother you, but I just had a thought. I may need a little help here. Can you send me two men, good men, you know the ones I mean?"

"Yes, I can send them. Are you expecting trouble?" asked Carlos Mendoza.

"I hope not, but just in case I do, I want help nearby."

"Do you want them in Alaska or Texas?"

"Texas," replied Dixon. Things are getting out of hand in Houston. I think I should send five men and a new manager for the company there, thought Carlos.

It had been quiet in Iliamna in the days leading up to Christmas. Many of the locals take this time of year to visit relatives or vacation in Hawaii. Wyatt had more time on his hands and was able to spend evenings with Linda. He found it comforting to watch TV and have dinner with someone. He had been alone all his life but found he enjoyed the family life. Linda was nearly ten years younger than Wyatt, but it didn't seem to matter to either of them.

Harry and Don finished the rooms in the lodge loft and cleaned away all the construction mess. Harry handed Don a round trip ticket to Medford, Oregon and an envelope with a nice bonus inside. He drove the hired man to the Iliamna airport where he was to catch a plane for Anchorage. "See you in a couple of weeks when you get back. Have a good Christmas and New Year, Don."

"Thanks, Harry. I'll be at that number I gave you if you need me, Merry Christmas."

Harry sat in his truck to watch the plane Don had boarded take off toward Anchorage. With nothing in particular to do he drove to the front door of the Lake Air charter office and paid a visit on VPSO Wyatt Earp.

"Come on in, Harry. Want some coffee?" said Wyatt when he answered the knock on his door.

"No thanks, Wyatt. I just put Don on an airplane to go visit his family for Christmas and thought I should stop and wish you a Merry Christmas, too."

"I'm glad you did, Harry. It gives me a chance to thank you for being so helpful during my first months here. Are you staying here over the holidays?"

"Yes, I have one guest and he pays me."

"Is Mr. Douglas back?" asked Wyatt.

"No, but Mr. Dixon, he's sort of Mr. Douglas' assistant, has been here for a while. He hasn't said when he plans to leave. He spends all his time on the telephone. I can't imagine who he talks to all the time."

"What do you hear from John Douglas?"

"Not a word, but the last I heard he is still in jail. I was told he has a court date the first week of January."

"How is the construction coming along?" asked the VPSO.

"We're nearly finished on the inside of the lodge building. My helper just left to go home for two weeks for Christmas, but it's too cold to work outside and the outbuildings don't have heat in them yet."

"You can come by my office any time, Harry."

"I may do that while I have this free time. You can stop out for coffee at the lodge, too, Merry Christmas." Harry turned to leave.

"Hey, Harry, is the man staying at the lodge named Dillon Dixon?"

"Yes, that's him, really quiet, stays to himself. I seldom ever see him except for meal times. Want me to have him come see you?" asked Harry.

"No, I was just curious. See you later, Harry."

By the time Harry had reached the front door Wyatt was on the telephone with Captain Griffin. "Hello, Cap, have you missed me?"

"Well, as I live and breathe, Wyatt Earp. You really do exist." The captain welcomed the call from his VPSO.

"Sure do, Cap. I have a request for you."

"What can I do for you, my man?"

"Get into your computer and see if there is a warrant for the arrest of Dillon Dixon. I think there is a federal warrant for him for murder and arson—one for killing a DEA agent in Nevada and one for killing a drug dealer here in Iliamna."

"Hold on, let me check it out." There was a long pause with elevator music playing. "There sure is, Wyatt. Do you have a lead on him?"

"He's here, staying at the lodge by the lake. I think I should have some backup before I go out there to arrest this one. He's a dangerous man."

"Good idea, Wyatt, I'll call you back as soon as I know when it will be there." A half hour later Captain Griffin called back, "Turner is on his way and a plane with three troopers is on the way from Anchorage. They should all be in your office in two hours. Are you going to be OK until then?"

"Yes, he's been here a few days, but I only found about it a few minutes ago. He doesn't know I know he's here. I'll have the Flight Service folks let us use their suburban again. I'll call you when it's over."

Sergeant Turner was the first to arrive. An hour later the King Air arrived with the three state troopers. Turner and Wyatt met the plane and made a plan of attack.

Chapter Thirty-Four

The state-owned King Air arrived two hours later. Gene Turner and Wyatt had spent the time in Wyatt's office. When Flight Service called to inform Gene and Wyatt of the impending arrival of the state aircraft the two men jumped into Wyatt's truck and drove to the other end of the field to meet the plane. Three troopers got off the plane. The ranking trooper, a captain, asked where their vehicle was waiting. Turner pointed to the black suburban parked and running in front of the Flight Service Station. The three troopers carried their gear to the vehicle and climbed inside. Gene and Wyatt sat in their pickup, waiting for the team to load up. Once everyone was loaded into vehicles Wyatt led the way to the lodge. The three troopers jumped out of the suburban and raced up the front steps. The captain knocked loudly on the heavy wooden door. Gene and Wyatt waited at the foot of the steps.

Harry Porter answered the knocking on the door. "Hi fellas, what can I do for you?"

"Please step aside," ordered the captain. "We have information Dillon Dixon is on the premises and we have a warrant for his arrest."

Harry had a puzzled look on his face. "He ain't here. He caught a plane about an hour or so ago. He went back to Houston."

The captain turned to the trooper on his right, "Call Anchorage and have a couple of troopers go to the airport and stop him."

Harry was shaking his head, "Ain't gonna do no good, fellas."

"And why not?" asked the captain.

"He chartered a Learjet to meet him when he got off the PenAir plane. He's left by now."

The captain was shaking his head, he turned to the trooper to his left, "Go inside and check it out."

Harry escorted the trooper inside. Once the trooper and Harry returned to the front deck the captain stormed away, climbing into the suburban and slamming the door. Wyatt and Gene turned to get into the pickup. Both men grinned and waved to Harry as they drove away.

"Tell me, Gene," said Wyatt, "is that how they teach warrant service at the trooper academy these days?"

Gene chuckled, "I don't know. It's been a long time since I went to the academy."

Back at the Flight Service Station the captain used his radio to summon the King Air. When it arrived at the front of the station the three troopers loaded their gear and climbed the stair to depart. None of them spoke with Wyatt or Gene.

Wyatt looked at Gene. "Was it something I said?" he asked.

"I don't think so. I would guess he is worried about how he's going to justify the cost of this sight-seeing trip." Both men were laughing as they drove back to the hangar to get the trooper Cessna 185 ready to fly back to Soldotna.

"Next week is Christmas and I plan to take the week off. I haven't had a day off in a long time. I'm going to see my dad before he goes outside for the winter and I want to spend some time with my future bride. I'll be in Iliamna most of the time, in case there's an emergency."

"I almost forgot, I have some good news for you," said Gene.

"What would that be?"

"Lonnie Davis will be back right after New Year's Day. He told me he was looking forward to working with you again."

"That is good news."

The trooper removed the insulated cover from the cowling and climbed into the pilot seat.

"Merry Christmas, Gene," said Wyatt as he closed the door.

Wyatt decided to go to his office and file the report on this fiasco before taking the afternoon off to visit Linda and help her trim the Christmas spruce tree he had cut for her.

Dillon Dixon had chartered a small business jet from a firm in Anchorage. The plane was small, but could travel at nearly 500 miles per hour at an altitude over 30,000 feet, making it a very comfortable trip. There would be one stop in Seattle for fuel. The trip, including the stop for fuel was just over seven hours. As he neared Houston he called the office to have dispatch send a car to pick him up and gave directions to the private hangar he had rented for the pilots and plane for the night. Dixon owned a very nice home on the outskirts of Houston where the company car dropped him off.

After a much needed night of sleep Dixon began the task of catching up on his boss's legal matter. His first call was to Mr. Costello, the criminal lawyer handling the legal affairs for John Douglas.

"Ah, Mr. Dixon, Mr. Douglas said you might call and that I was to give you any information you needed."

"Thank you, Mr. Costello. John and I have worked together for many years. It has been my chore to keep him out of trouble, but I let him down this time. Is he going to have a bail hearing soon?"

"Yes," said Costello, "it's set for December 27th two days after Christmas. The federal lawyers are going to argue he is a flight risk, which I will counter with his being a property owner and a business man with three companies in addition to Amerimex Trucking operating through his offices in Houston. I think the judge will allow bail, but I also think it will be very high and cash only."

"Do you think they will allow me to visit him down at the federal jail facility?"

"Possibly, but I can't guarantee it. I see John this morning and I'll ask him to put you on his visitor list. It might get you inside if he requests it. Since you are an officer in his corporation they may see it your way."

Dixon gave the lawyer his cell phone number, "See what you can do and call me at this number. I will need to go to the office and check on things this morning."

"I'll call as soon as I have an answer for you."

Dixon's next stop would be his office at Amerimex Trucking. He hoped the men he asked Carlos Mendoza to supply were here by now. His pickup was parked inside his garage with a full tank of fuel. He climbed the stairs to the second floor of the Amerimex offices where his office was located in a southwest corner. He greeted the receptionist and asked her to call the head dispatcher to his office.

"There have been two men checking every day to see if you had returned, Mr. Dixon. I think they are Spanish or Mexican. I haven't given them any information until I talked with you."

"Thank you, Shirley. I'm expecting them. If they come back, please let me know and allow them to come to my office. Are there any urgent messages, other than those concerning Mr. Douglas?"

"No, sir, dispatch has been able to take care of everything up to now. There have been hundreds of phone calls for Mr. Douglas, but I declined to answer any questions."

"I'll try to sort some of this out today, Shirley. I'm going to my office now. Have the dispatcher come in when he arrives." Dixon took the handful of notes from the receptionist and walked to his office.

The chief dispatcher, Ryan Gilfoyle, came in a few minutes later. "Welcome back, Mr. Dixon, we can use you around here right now. We found out Mr. Douglas had been arrested when a lawyer came in here and started asking questions about the trucking company. At first we didn't want to tell him anything, but it turned out it was the lawyer the boss had hired. If it's OK with you I'm going to let you handle all the calls relating to that mess. I just want to run the trucks."

"It looks like you've done a great job of it, too, Ryan. Are the trucks still running to and from Puebla?"

"The Border Patrol and Customs revoked our import license. We had to shut our trucks down on that run, but there's a Mexican company bringing the cactus plants to the Nevada warehouse. I was able to subcontract the haul and keep the product moving. I guess you heard about the fire at the Nevada warehouse. A dock hand was killed in the fire. I heard he was a DEA agent. I think the cops are still looking into that one."

"Yes, I heard about it. Now, what about the other contracts with Amerimex Trucking? Are we still running all the cross country freight hauls?"

"Yes, sir, everything is normal except the trips to Puebla in Mexico. I can't understand how a bunch of cactus plants can cause such disruption. I hope you can find out and get us moving again."

"You're a good man Ryan. I don't know what I would do without you right now. Just keep us running and making money until it all gets sorted out."

The telephone on his desk rang. It was Shirley. "Those men are back and want to see you, sir."

"Send them in as soon as Ryan leaves," instructed Dixon.

Minutes later two well-dressed men entered the office. "I'm Pablo and my friend is Marco. Mr. Mendoza sent us to assist you with whatever you need."

"I have only just returned myself and I haven't been able to see Mr. Douglas. He's still in jail and waiting to have a bail hearing. I'm going to attempt to get in to see him this afternoon. Give me your telephone number and address and I'll call you as soon as I'm able to see Mr. Douglas."

"I think you should expedite that visit, Mr. Dixon. Carlos is becoming impatient with this situation. You are generating too much attention." The two men stood and Marco handed a business card to Dixon. "Call me this afternoon," Marco said, as they left the office.

Dixon didn't like the tone used by Marco, but didn't challenge him. He was about to dial Lawyer Costello when his desk phone rang, again. It was Shirley.

"Mr. Dixon, there are some federal police officers here wanting to speak with you."

Dixon's heart skipped a beat. "Send them in," he said as he reached into his desk for a hidden semi-automatic handgun which he placed in the top drawer of his desk after jacking a round into the chamber. He remained seated as the two officers entered. The second officer closed the office door behind him.

"What can I do for you men?" asked Dixon.

The taller of the men displayed his badge and credentials. "I'm Darren Hatfield with the FBI, and my friend here is Greg Hansen with the DEA. I want you to stand up, sir. I have a warrant for your arrest on the charge of murder of a DEA agent and murder of a suspected drug dealer in Alaska. Please step out from behind the desk."

Dixon rolled his desk chair back a few inches and pulled open the center desk drawer. He reached inside quickly to retrieve his handgun. Hansen took one sideways step from behind Hatfield and drew his weapon as Dixon thumbed the safety on his 9MM, pointing the weapon at Hatfield. Hansen beat him to the trigger striking Dixon twice an inch left of center on his chest. The sound of gunfire inside the closed office was deafening and was heard throughout the building. Dixon was thrown backward, the shots spinning him to the left as he fell. Almost instantly the door burst open and a crowd of office workers filled the room.

Shirley, the receptionist was at the front of the group. Hatfield was holding his badge out in front of him. "Young lady, go to your desk and call 911. We need an ambulance here. The rest of you back out of the office. We will need statements from each of you, but first we need to get this man to a hospital."

Hansen was on his radio calling for assistance from his team of agents who were nearby. Within minutes the office was full of EMTs, Houston police, and DEA agents.

The EMTs loaded the wounded man on a stretcher and carried him away with two DEA agents and two Houston police officers following. Hansen's team did the interview with each of the people who witnessed the scene while Hansen and Hatfield followed the ambulance to the hospital. As in any officer involved shooting there would be an investigation and both Hansen's weapon and the handgun used by Dixon were taken as evidence by the Houston police.

Dillon Dixon was pronounced dead upon arrival at the hospital.

Pablo and Marco were in their hotel room watching the evening news when the announcement was made of the death in a shooting at Amerimex Trucking Company. The victim was the company manager, Dillon Dixon.

"It looks like the DEA saved us the trouble," remarked Pablo. Marco only nodded agreement.

Chapter Thirty-Five

Wyatt enjoyed Christmas Day with Linda and her family who had come down the lake by snow machine to have the Christmas celebration as a family with the daughter in Iliamna. Wyatt's father had flown in from Naknek to be with the family on this joyous day. When all the guests had arrived and the first eggnog toddies consumed, Linda called all the guests to the living room where presents were to be offered. Most of the gifts were handmade from skins trapped along the lake.

One gift however was different. That gift was from Wyatt Earp IV to Wyatt Earp V. It was the wedding ring, worn for so many years by Wyatt Earp's loving wife and his son's mother. There were tears forming in the eyes of both the younger Earp and his bride-to-be.

Dinner was a mix of cultures. Sandhill crane, shot by Linda's father, was the main course. Baked potatoes, green beans with ham, sweet potatoes baked with marshmallows on top and finally, pumpkin pie with whipped cream.

While the guests lounged in the living room Linda and Wyatt washed the dinner dishes and cleaned the kitchen. Out of sight of the family and guests, Wyatt hugged Linda tightly and kissed her passionately. "I haven't felt this good at Christmas time since my mother passed away. I love this family time. I love you, Linda."

She pressed her head against his chest and squeezed him, "I love you, too, Wyatt. This is the way Christmas should be."

Linda's family sort of camped on any flat spot in her small house for the night while Wyatt's dad took a room at the hotel. It was late when he received a message on his E-mail from Greg Hansen, the DEA agent in Houston, Texas.

It was a long message detailing the attempted arrest and the shooting of Dillon Dixon at the Amerimex Trucking Company offices. Hansen informed Wyatt that John Douglas was still in federal custody, but would have a bail hearing soon. At the end of the message Hansen wished Wyatt a Merry Christmas and thanked him for his help in the case.

Wyatt read the electronic letter twice before printing it to paper. He checked the time and decided it was too late tonight to call Harry Porter at the lodge and deliver the message. He would take care of that duty in the morning.

He turned off the lights in his office to go into his living quarters. He had purchased a five-pound box of good chocolates for Maggie and bought a huge red bow for the top. He wrote a short card and took the gift to her desk in the front of the hangar. It was small thanks for all she and Tom had done for him since his arrival in Iliamna. The office was dark and quiet and Wyatt stood for a while looking out the front window, across the valley toward Roadhouse Mountain. His entire world was snow covered with a huge moon illuminating the landscape. "There truly is peace on earth, but sometimes you have to look past the ugly to see the beauty of it all."

The following morning Wyatt drove to the lodge to deliver the news about Dillon Dixon. Harry opened the door and welcomed him. "It seems quiet with all the big bosses gone," said Harry. "Want some coffee?"

"Sure, Harry, Merry Christmas," Wyatt began. "I have some bad news for you and I don't know any other way to say it except that Dillon Dixon was killed when he pulled a handgun on one of the federal agents who came to the Amerimex office to serve an arrest warrant on him. Dixon pulled the handgun and tried to shoot the agent, but a DEA agent with him was ready for it and shot first. Dixon died on the way to the hospital."

Porter was quiet for a moment before speaking, "I'm sorry about that, but I really didn't like him. There was something dark inside him. I know I should feel sorry for him, but I don't."

Wyatt stood silently.

"What about Mr. Douglas?" asked Harry quietly, "Is he OK?"

"As far as I know. I was told he has a bail hearing soon, but the word is that it could go either way. The Feds will say he's a flight risk and the defense attorney will argue he is just a business man with local responsibilities. I guess we will have to wait and see."

"I don't know what to do, but I guess I'll keep working until the supplies run out and hope I have an answer by then. I have an account at the bank in Anchorage to buy material and pay the bills, so I'm set until spring. The lodge will be ready to open by May. I will have to have sheets and towels and a lot of other items shipped here for the opening, but the lodge building and the outbuildings will be finished. We finished the dock this fall and Mr. Douglas hired a couple of guides to take the clients fishing and hunting. I hope he can come back and run the business side of the lodge."

"I don't think anyone can answer that question right now, Harry. We'll have to wait and see. Thanks for the coffee. Stop by the office when you get to town. I'm always glad to see you." Wyatt stood, zipped up his coat and turned to leave, but turned back to speak again. "For what it's worth, Harry, I want to thank you for everything you have done for me up until now. You have been a good friend and I appreciate it."

"Thanks, Officer Earp. I was just trying to return what you gave me."

Wyatt waved and continued to the door. "You can call me Wyatt, Harry."

Wyatt stopped at Linda's house to visit with the family while on his way back to the village. Linda's parents were seated at the kitchen table drinking coffee and eating breakfast when he arrived. "We're leaving to drive back home, soon. We want to get home before dark. Sometimes the ice on the lake cracks and leaves big gaps of open water. I don't want to drive into one of them in the dark. Tell your father thanks for a good day. I like him. We will have fun together in the future. Mamma is already getting ready for the trip to Seattle and the wedding."

"I am looking forward to that myself, sir. I hope we will see you before then, though."

"You two can come up to the homestead any time, young man. Call me if you need some caribou. I can shoot one for you and bring it down here." That's just the way it is in the bush.

Life in the village of Iliamna had nearly come to a stop after Christmas. The temperatures dipped, and stayed, to near minus 45 degrees. There had been little wind, which made it bearable. The ice on the lake shifted and made loud cracking noises as the mercury in the thermometer dipped. Moose, caribou, wolves and other tundra wildlife grew heavy coats of fur to withstand the cold and were seen browsing on the winter scape near the village. Man, however, could only put on more clothing and thicker gloves when working out of doors. Most residents chose to stay inside except to find food or firewood. Without wind the heavy spruce and birch wood smoke hung like a fog over the village. For Wyatt, patrol was reduced to distress calls and welfare checks.

Tom and Maggie had closed the office and stayed at home due to the extreme low temperature. They were, of course, on call in case of an emergency. Aviation, for conventional small aircraft came to a near standstill when the temperatures passed minus 20 degrees. Their engines are air cooled and the oil temperature is controlled by a radiator type device which cools the oil. At extreme temperatures the oil coolers tend to congeal with the thick oil causing lubrication difficulties. Some of this can be avoided by stopping the air flow through the oil coolers, but it was best not to fly at these temperatures unless absolutely necessary. Jet engines function differently and can fly in these low temperatures, but most turbine engine airplanes are unable to land at remote sites and on snowy airstrips. Since there are no real highways or cross-country roads out in the Iliamna area ttravel is mostly restricted to snow machines.

Wyatt did make one patrol each afternoon when school was letting out, but that didn't start until after New Year Day when school was back in session. Each afternoon he tried to make sure all the children arrived at home safely. Once he had finished with that chore he made a stop at the school teacher's home to be sure she, too, had arrived safely. He was always thanked with a kiss.

In early January the federal court system resumed its normal schedule and a bail hearing was set for John Douglas. His plea of not guilty had been heard at an earlier hearing, but his bail hearing was, once again set back. With it now back on the docket, attorney Costello was at the jail complex to confer with his client.

"I submitted our version of your involvement on the transportation and sales of dangerous drugs. I wrote it as you instructed, placing the blame on your assistant whom, without your knowledge, directed all the drug activity conducted at your company." Mr. Costello went on to itemize the charges and the lack of guilt or involvement by John Douglas. "I think we stand a pretty good chance of having this judge grant bail in spite of the prosecutors' objections."

"I don't care what it costs, get me out of here! Sitting in here is costing me a great deal of money. It isn't just the Amerimex Trucking Company, it's the other four companies as well. I have payrolls and expenses and obligations to meet. I must get back to my businesses." John Douglas was seething.

"You have to calm down, John. We can't afford to insult the judge. Keep quiet and keep a straight face. Let me do all the talking," Costello cautioned him again.

Lawyer Costello was waiting at the defendant's table when a U.S. Marshal led John Douglas to the courtroom. The officer removed the handcuffs before leading him into the court to stand behind the defendant while court was in session.

Douglas took the seat next to Costello, but said nothing, only looked straight ahead with a blank stare.

The judge, a man in his mid-sixty's, sat on the bench reading the defendant's file. The prosecution made its statement, recommending Douglas be held in federal detention until trial as he was considered a flight risk. The man had a great deal of cash and holdings, was tied to a South American drug cartel, and if found guilty of the current charges he could spend the rest of his life in jail. The prosecution also stressed the fact that several murders had been committed in connection with this case and it was likely John Douglas had a hand in these deaths.

When it came Costello's turn to speak he rose slowly. "Your Honor, the prosecutor has painted a dire picture of my client while forgetting the fact all this is speculation and that my client is presumed innocent until proven guilty. At this point my client has been proven guilty of nothing. My client is a business man, a property owner and a contributor to this community. The charges the prosecutor refers to may well have taken place, but by an associate of Mr. Douglas and without his knowledge. Mr. Douglas has been held for an extended period of time during which he has been unable to direct his business. In fact, his assistant was shot and killed in the offices of one of Mr. Douglas' trucking companies while Mr. Douglas was being held in federal jail. This in itself testifies to Mr. Douglas' innocence. I recommend Mr. Douglas be released on his own recognizance and allowed to return to directing the operations of his companies."

The judge tapped the pencil he was holding on the file in front of him, thinking about the arguments presented. "Having heard and considered the motions before me I make the final decision. First, Mr. Costello makes a valid point; Mr. Douglas, so far, has been found guilty of nothing. However, the prosecutor also makes a point that Mr. Douglas has the means to abscond from this jurisdiction. I have decided to release Mr. Douglas from federal custody upon deposit of one million dollars, cash only bail. This amount should ensure Mr. Douglas' appearance in court on the given date. Mr. Costello, you can make arrangements for bail with the bailiff of the court." With that he stood, picked up the file from his desk and walked from the courtroom.

The federal prosecutor stood at his table shaking his head and mumbling something unintelligible.

Costello turned to his client, "The marshals will take you back to the jail where you will be allowed to arrange for payment. I'll set a time with the bailiff to transfer the money to the court. How soon can you make the transfer?"

"Give me a time and I'll have it there. Will they accept a bank check or does it really have to be cash?"

"I'll confirm it with the bailiff, but usually a bank check will suffice."

"Get it done, I want out of here," growled Douglas.

Costello nodded to the Marshal standing behind his client and the officer took the prisoner, sans handcuffs, to the waiting police van for the trip back to the jail complex.

An hour later, with the bank draft delivered to the court bailiff, Costello waited in the outer waiting room for John Douglas to be released by the guards. Neither the lawyer nor the client spoke as they exited the facility.

Once inside Costello's Cadillac Douglas said, "Get me to my office. I have to see what's going on there. Thank you for getting me out. I'll see you are properly compensated. How long before the trial?" he asked.

"The date hasn't been set yet, but it should be on the docket by the end of the month. We, you and I, will have to meet and discuss our strategy for the trial. It will be a week before the prosecution submits their arguments, and I'll need to meet with you before we submit ours."

"OK, call me and let me know when you want to meet. In the meantime I have a great deal of catching up to do. With DD out of the picture I'll have to make some changes. I have some investors I must notify and of course learn what DD had been doing." Douglas didn't know how he was going to replace Dillon Dixon, but he would have to do it soon.

Chapter Thirty-Six

John Douglas instructed Costello to drop him at the office. He climbed the stairs to the second floor where his office staff and his personal office was located. A ripple of surprise went through the staff as he entered.

"Hello, Mr. Douglas," greeted the receptionist, Shirley.

"Hello, Shirley. I'll need to have a meeting with you in a few minutes. I want to know exactly what happened here the day when DD was killed."

"Oh! Mr. Douglas! It was awful."

"I know, Shirley, but we'll talk about it in my office. Give me a minute to get settled and come into my office and we'll talk."

"Yes, Mr. Douglas. Call me when you're ready."

John Douglas went to his office and inspected every corner to see if it had been searched or if the police had planted an electronic device of some kind there. He looked in wastebaskets, under the phone, behind pictures and every other space he could imagine something could be hidden. He checked his file cabinet and desk drawers as well as the secret phone list hidden under his pull-out writing shelf in his desk. He found nothing. After fifteen minutes of searching he called Shirley. She entered carrying a note pad.

"Are you all right, Mr. Douglas?" she asked after sitting down.

"I'm fine Shirley, but I need to know exactly what took place the day Dillon was shot. I know it must be painful for you to recall, but I need a first-hand account of the incident."

Shirley delivered an accurate account of the events of that day. Her eyes were filled with tears as she spoke. When she finished telling the long tale she dried her eyes. "It was horrible, Mr. Douglas."

"Yes, it must have been. Please, Shirley, was there anything else that day that you remember, anything out of the ordinary?" Douglas spoke softly, calming her somewhat.

She dried her eyes with a hankie she carried. "You know," she said with surprise, "There was something. Early in the day, before Mr. Dillon arrived, there were two men in the office looking for you or him. I didn't think much about it until just now, but they were strangers, Mexican, I think."

"Thank you, Shirley. You have been most helpful. I'll see to it there is a bonus in your next check for the stress you have endured."

She stood to leave, "Thank you, Mr. Douglas, for being so kind."

"You earned it, Shirley. Oh, one other thing. Did the visitors leave a business card with you?"

"No sir, but if they return, I'll remember them." Wiping her eyes again she left the office.

"One more thing, Shirley, wait about fifteen minutes and call Lloyd Turpin and Ryan Gilfoyle to my office for a meeting."

Once Shirley was out of the office Douglas dialed Carlos Mendoza on his private phone. "Hola," he answered.

"Hola, Carlos, John Douglas here."

"Senior Douglas, you are out!" he said, astonished.

"Just now released, and I wanted to speak with you about replacing Dillon Dixon. I have men who can replace his management skills, but I need someone to do other things from time to time, you know what I mean."

"Of course, John, I know exactly. DD had called me and I sent two men to your office, but they were unable to see Mr. Dixon. Those men are still in Houston and have kept me abreast of the events in your office, a tragic loss, John, tragic."

"Yes, it is, but it would have been avoided if I hadn't been in jail at the time."

"Are you out for good?" asked Carlos.

"No, out on bail, but my lawyer says we will likely beat the charges by laying all the blame on DD. I have been out of the office too long and need to reorganize immediately. I'll start that process today. I only called to reassure you things are nearly back to normal now. I'll have to contact the trucking company from Mexico City that took over the delivery of the cactus plants."

"Don't worry yourself about that, John. We will find another way to get our product into the U.S. We have shut down the ceramics plant in Puebla. We will have another arrangement soon. I'm just glad you are out of jail and back in the office. Stay well, my friend."

Worry instantly consumed him when he hung up the telephone. Carlos wasn't his usual chatty self. He feared some of the changes about to be made in his trucking business.

His intercom jingled and Shirley spoke, "Mr. Turpin and Mr. Gilfoyle are here, sir."

"Send them in, Shirley."

Still concerned about his future, Douglas greeted the two men. "Lloyd, Ryan, have a seat. I am making some adjustments since the incident with Dillon and I want to include each of you in the new arrangement."

"Thank you, sir," said Turpin. Gilfoyle just nodded.

"Lloyd, I want you to take over as general manager of the company. You will head all the companies and do your best to keep all our trucks working. I expect you to generate new business and keep the costs at a minimum. Do you think you can do the job?"

"Yes, of course, Mr. Douglas. I thank you for having confidence in me."

"I'll have a new contract for you to sign by the end of the week." Douglas made a note on the pad on his desk. "And now to you, Ryan, I want you to manage all the daily business and schedules. You will be in charge of all the dispatchers as well as the drivers and mechanics. Lloyd will have charge of the office staff, so you won't have to deal with all that. And like I told Lloyd, your job is to keep the costs down and the trucks moving. You two will be in charge of the day to day business. I have great confidence in each of you. I am still dealing with court issues and will be preoccupied for some time. It will be your jobs to keep us solvent."

"We both thank you, Mr. Douglas."

"There will be a substantial pay increase with the increase in responsibility for each of you. I expect you to earn it. I wouldn't have selected you if I didn't think you were capable of handling the responsibility. Now, take the rest of the day off and come back tomorrow to organize your departments."

Once the two men were out of the office Douglas called his business attorney to have new contracts drawn for each of the new managers. He had nearly finished reading recent correspondence that had come in since the last time he was in the office when his intercom jingled again. Again, it was Shirley.

"Mr. Douglas, those two men you asked about are in the office asking to see you."

"Send them in, Shirley, and please see that we're not disturbed."

Douglas recognized the men immediately. They were two enforcers working for Carlos Mendoza. "Have a seat, gentlemen," said Douglas when they entered.

"We won't be here long, Mr. Douglas. We have been sent to you by Mr. Mendoza. Mr. Dixon asked him to send us, but he was shot before we could meet with him. We assume you have an on-going problem and we came to solve it for you. We would rather not discuss it in this office and invite you to a private meeting in our hotel."

The men hadn't given their names, but Douglas knew who they were. "I would be happy to meet with you. What hotel are you staying in? And what time would you like to meet?"

"That information won't be necessary, Mr. Douglas. We would rather you come with us right now. We understand the urgency of the situation and are here to help."

Douglas' heart was pounding, but agreed to go. "I'll have my receptionist take all my calls and tell them I'll be back in the office in the morning."

"Very good, Mister Douglas. We will wait for you in the outer office."

Chapter Thirty-Seven

Half the month was gone in this the new year when Harry Porter called to speak with Wyatt. The deep cold spell was beginning to moderate and Wyatt had been able to patrol the village with ease. He told Harry he would be out to the lodge within the hour.

"I'll have the coffee on the stove," replied Harry.

Harry was waiting when Wyatt arrived. "Take off your coat, Wyatt. I have some pie and coffee for you. I'm worried and need your advice about some things. I hope you have time to talk."

"Thanks, Harry, I always have time to talk with you," said Wyatt as he took off his heavy winter coat. "Do you have a problem out here?"

"That's what I want to talk about, Wyatt. I don't know if I have a problem." Harry poured the coffee and set a large piece of fresh apple pie in front of him before sitting at the table across from the VPSO.

"The pie looks delicious, Harry. Did you bake it?"

"Yes, but don't tell anyone. I like to bake."

Wyatt finished the pie before sipping his coffee. He leaned back in the huge wood chair to relax. "Good stuff, Harry. Now, what was it you wanted to talk about?"

"You remember Mr. Douglas. He left here and went to Houston to tend his businesses. He got arrested for a bunch of stuff and put in the federal jail. Several days ago he got out on bail and went to work in his office. His new manager said he made some changes because Dillon Dixon was shot and killed by the FBI and DEA. The receptionist, Shirley, told Turpin, the new manager, that two men came to the office and Mr. Douglas left with them and hasn't been seen since.

His lawyer is looking for him, the DEA and FBI are looking for him, and the marshals from the court are looking for him. They called me to see if he came back here, but I haven't heard from him."

"I don't have any information about his disappearance, Harry, sorry."

"The part I want to ask you about is that I had a call from some guy named Pablo who says he is the new head of all of Mr. Douglas' trucking businesses and will be the new owner of the lodge. He wanted to know how soon we can open and what we needed. He told me to stick to the schedule and finish the project. Yesterday I got a letter from an attorney in Texas saying the new owner of the lodge is Pablo Marquez. I called Amerimex Trucking Company and the receptionist, Shirley, told me Mr. Douglas hasn't been seen since he left that day with the two men, Pablo and Marco. She said they came back with legal papers that said they were the new owners of the businesses. She sounded scared when she talked to me."

Wyatt tried to assimilate this new information. "Exactly what is it you want from me, Harry?"

"Is there any way you can check and find out what happened to Mr. Douglas and if this letter I got is real?"

"May I see the letter?" asked Wyatt.
"Sure, I'll get it for you. You can take it with you, but I need it back." He left the kitchen to get the letter, returning in about a minute. "I don't have any way to find out if all this is real or fake. I don't want Mr. Douglas to come back and find out I gave away his lodge."

Wyatt scanned the legal papers. "They look legitimate, Harry, but I'll have them checked out. You say the girl at the office there said John Douglas has vanished?"

"That's what she said," reported Harry.

"It may take a couple of days to check it out, but I'll try to get some answers for you."

"I appreciate it, Wyatt, I just didn't know who else to turn to."

"I'll make some calls as soon as I get back to the office and I'll let you know as soon as I learn anything." Wyatt stood to put on his coat. "Thanks for the coffee and pie. You're a good cook."

Back in his little office he called Captain Griffin to relay what he had learned from Harry. The captain showed concern and told Wyatt he would see what he could learn, that he would call the FBI and DEA in Houston. "It could take a few days to get an answer from them, so don't get impatient. I'll get back to you when I have news."

Midafternoon three days later there was a knock on his office door. It was FBI Agent Hatfield and DEA Agent Hansen. "Come in, Gentlemen. How can I help you fellas?"

Once inside the office with the door closed the two federal officers began, "You made an inquiry about a man we arrested in Texas. The man, John Douglas, was released on bail and was not supposed to leave Houston. The information I am about to give you is confidential and cannot be repeated. I'm telling you this, because you were a great help in the initial arrest and your captain tells us you're a good cop. We would like your help in getting us inside the lodge to search the offices of John Douglas and Dillon Dixon. Do you think you can arrange it?"

"I think so, but what makes this so important?" asked Wyatt.

"John Douglas was released from federal jail on one million dollars bail. He went to his office, making changes in the management to compensate for the loss of his right-hand-man, Dillon Dixon. While he was working in the office two men, identified as Mexican or Spanish decent, came to the office and Douglas left with them. He hasn't been seen since. The two men he left the office with are now running the business. There was a big shakeup and the men Douglas promoted were sent back to their old jobs. Tensions in that office are extremely high." This bit of information came from Darren Hatfield.

"What do you think has happened to Douglas? Was he kidnapped or killed?" asked Wyatt.

"Probably," it was Greg Hansen speaking now, "Douglas and his trucking company were doing business with the Columbian drug cartel. We were able to get evidence from one of their trucks entering the U.S. which started a chain reaction leading to the arrest of Douglas and the subsequent attempted arrest of Dillon Dixon. Dixon pulled a handgun on Darren and I shot him, killing him and costing us a key witness against the cartel. Douglas and his lawyer used Dixon's death to shift the blame to the dead man and away from Douglas. The judge released him on bail and he went back to his office. Two men came to the office and led him away, and like Darren said, he hasn't been seen again.

"FAA ran the numbers of business jets departing Houston at or around that time and found one Learjet, registered to a Columbian company with ties to the cartel. We think the two goons put Douglas on the plane and sent him to Columbia. The head of the cartel, Carlos Mendoza, has been calling Douglas on a regular basis for months. We think he was taken to South America for a conference with Mendoza. We doubt he will ever be seen again. I realize all this is a lot of intrigue and not much proof, but Carlos Mendoza is the benefactor of our arresting Pablo Escobar and putting him in prison. Mendoza now controls the largest drug cartel in the world. Escobar's money has never been found. It is nearly all cash and totals in the billions of dollars. Now you know the reason for secrecy and the urgency of finding any evidence we can retrieve."

"So, a lodge in remote Alaska, in a village of 120 people, has become the center of a world-wide investigation." Wyatt chuckled. "My, aren't we important?"

"You may find this humorous, but there are more than a thousand officers worldwide, working on this case. Some of those officers have died in the process. We don't find it amusing." DEA agent Hansen was glum and without humor.

"Lighten up, Greg," said Hatfield, turning to Wyatt. "It is very frustrating to have the case take a turn for conclusion and then have the witnesses killed or vanished. All we want to do is follow up on any possible leads in the case. The cartel has us out funded and outmanned. It would help us out and save us a lot of time and money if you can help us get into that office."

"Let me make a call," said Wyatt, turning to his desk. He dialed the number given him by Harry Porter who answered on the first ring.

"Hello, Harry, how are things?"

"Fine, I guess. Did you find out anything for me?"

"Possibly. I have a couple of men here connected with the case. They would like to come out and take a look in Mr. Douglas' office, if you'll let them."

"I guess it will be OK. Bring them out if you want."

"Thanks, Harry, we'll be right there."

Wyatt hung up the phone and turned to Hatfield. "He said OK and to come right out."

Hatfield smiled, "I wish things were that simple in our world," he said.

"Me too," chimed Hansen. "Officer Earp, I apologize for my short temper. I'm not used to dealing with honesty and straight-forwardness. Thank you."

"Forget it, I understand. I was a city cop for twenty years. Believe me, I do understand. Let's go out to the lodge and see Harry. Maybe he will part with another piece of his famous apple pie."

Harry met the three law enforcement men at the kitchen door and invited them inside. He poured coffee for each of them. "What is it you're looking for here at the lodge?" he asked.

"We want to be honest with you, Harry. We don't have a warrant and you don't have to let us look in Mr. Douglas' office, but it would be a great help. You are welcome to watch us while we search, if you like, and we will leave you an inventory of any items we take from the premises." It was Hatfield giving the explanation.

"Finish your coffee and I'll show you to the office. I ain't got nothing to hide. I really don't think Mr. Douglas did either," remarked Harry.

Once inside the office Hatfield and Hansen did a thorough search, reading files, scanning billing statements for the lodge, searching for hidden spaces and safes. Nothing was found in the search except a phone bill with a huge number of long distance numbers listed. "I see you have a copy machine. If we leave you a copy of this billing sheet, may we have the original?" asked Hansen.

"Sure. The bill has been paid anyway," offered Harry.

After nearly two hours of searching, the phone bill was the only document taken from the office. "Thank you for being so cooperative, Harry. We appreciate it and the wonderful coffee." It was Hatfield giving him thanks and making a receipt for the single item taken.

"I don't know if Wyatt told you, but I got a letter from some lawyer saying there are new owners of the lodge. I haven't heard from Mr. Douglas and I don't know what to do." Harry was looking for the answer he had never gotten from anyone.

"We can't advise you on that, Mr. Porter, but if you'll show me the letter I'll try to see if it's genuine." It was agent Hatfield giving the statement.

Harry showed the letter to Darren who studied it and wrote the names of the law firm on a pad. "I'll check it out and get back to you as soon as possible."

Wyatt drove the two agents back to the airport and his office.

"I've heard you're getting married soon," said Hatfield.

"Yes, the middle of next month," replied Wyatt.

"There goes your carefree lifestyle," teased Hansen.

"I'm marrying a school teacher. Perhaps she can teach me some manners."

"You do very well for a backwoods marshal," said Hansen. "I'm impressed. I wasn't expecting to meet a real lawman in 'end of the world Alaska.' You do well. If you ever decide to move to civilization come see me and I'll hire you in my unit. Thanks again for your help."

"That goes for me, too, Wyatt. I've been on this case for a very long time and your name keeps popping up at every turn. You have done more from your hangar/office than the FBI and DEA have accomplished in years of investigation. You're a good cop."

Because of the cold weather Wyatt drove the two agents to the PenAir hangar to wait for the afternoon flight to Anchorage. Once they had boarded he returned to his office to do the reports and to call Captain Griffin.

Two days later he received a message from the FBI office in Houston. It was a copy of a news report stating; "A body has been recovered near a beach in the small country of Belize, an apparent victim of shark attack. Identification on the body indicated he was an American tourist from Houston, Texas. Fingerprint analysis confirmed the identification. The name given is John Douglas, owner of Amerimex Trucking Company as well as other businesses in the Houston area. Police have been unable to locate relatives of the deceased."

After reading the news report Wyatt drove to the lodge with a printed copy in his hand. Harry greeted him at the door where the VPSO gave him the copy.

"Come inside, Wyatt. Have some coffee while I read this."

"It isn't good news, but I think it's what you expected. Sorry you had to learn the answer this way."

"I suspected this kind of thing, but it's sad. He did bad things, but for me he was a good boss and treated me well." The sadness was etched on Harry's face.

"What do you hear from the new owner?"

"He's been busy. He's coming here on the fifteenth of May to inspect the lodge. He's sending some wood carver here next month to start building a sign for over the gate. We will be known as 'Mother of the Wind Lodge.' I don't like it, but at least it will be spelled right. He says I will be the new manager, but he is sending some guy to manage the lodging business and do the bookings, things like that. The new guy will be here next month to get the rooms ready and hire staff. His name is James Kasper. I've never heard of him, but he used to work for Hilton Hotels and is said to be good at his job. I hope so, because I don't know anything about that business. I'm getting too old for the construction business anyway."

"Are you keeping Don Zapo on with you?"

"I would, but Don wants to move to the city to spend his money on women and whiskey. He's not much of a thinker, but he's been a good worker. I'll be sorry to see him leave."

"Well, Harry, I'm glad you're going to stay. I like your coffee and pie. I'm going to be out of town for about three weeks starting the middle of February. I'm getting married, you know."

Harry laughed aloud. "Everyone in town knows. Congratulations, she's a nice girl."

"Thanks, Harry, good luck with the new owner. Call me if you have any problems. I'll be the VPSO in Iliamna for a long time, I hope. Lonnie Davis is back now and he'll be covering for me while I'm gone. You know Lonnie, he'll keep the peace. See ya later, Harry."

He returned to his office in the Lake Air hangar to be handed a plate full of fresh cinnamon rolls, baked by Maggie.

Chapter Thirty-Eight

The time passed quickly as the wedding date approached. Wyatt's father flew up to Iliamna for a day with the bride and groom prior to his flying out to the Seattle area, where he had already made many of the arrangements for the wedding. Parents and family of the bride were to stay in the house with Wyatt Earp IV. He had rented the bridal suite in a large hotel near downtown Seattle where the honeymoon would begin. Wyatt's father had rented an entire lodge on Lake Union where the wedding was to be held.

The bride and some of her friends had been busy making her wedding gown. Wyatt told the bride he was wearing Carhartt jeans and jacket to the wedding, bringing moans and loud objections from the bride and her friends. In reality Wyatt's father had arranged a tuxedo rental for the occasion. The school had made arrangements for a substitute teacher during the two weeks she was to be gone from her duties.

Wyatt was amazed at the number of gifts arriving by mail each day. The contents of some, from former partners and coworkers in the Fairbanks Police Department, made him suspicious due to the number of pranks he had perpetrated on them during his career there. Confessing his trepidation to his bride-to-be she agreed to open those gifts in private after returning to Iliamna.

PenAir arranged to have a turbo-prop airplane pick up the entire wedding party at the Iliamna Airport on the given date. They flew the party to Anchorage where they boarded an Alaska Airlines jet bound for Seattle. Two limousines were waiting to take the entourage to the north side of Seattle where Wyatt Earp IV resided.

Everyone in the party was excited and joyful as they became more acquainted. Wyatt stayed in a bedroom with his father while the others filled the other rooms. Linda and her mother shared a bedroom where they checked and rechecked her wardrobe and things a bride takes to her wedding and would treasure for the rest of her life. The next, and final, day before the wedding was spent with last minute shopping, and for some, sightseeing. It was a real treat for Linda's family to come to the lower 48, even for a short visit like this.

The day before the wedding Wyatt and Linda spent a great deal of time sitting close and holding each other. Everyone who saw them knew the love they shared. Once they took his father's car and drove into town for a couple of hours to escape the family hubbub. That evening there was a large dinner party at a local restaurant where two of the guests consumed too much wine and had to be assisted to the car at the end of the evening, but most were sober and visited with each other and took turns giving blessings to the couple of honor.

The morning of the wedding there was a huge breakfast at the house. The wedding was scheduled for one in the afternoon, but the bride, the mother and other lady guests needed time to prepare for the ceremony. Wyatt and his father spent most of the time in his study/office speaking about the past and the future. The guests would be leaving tomorrow to return to Alaska, but Wyatt and Linda were flying to Hawaii on a honeymoon, compliments of his father.

Wyatt's father had hired a limo to transport Linda, her mother and father and family to the wedding. Linda insisted Wyatt not see her in her wedding gown prior to the ceremony. Wyatt's father drove his own car, with Wyatt V by his side, to the lodge where the wedding was to take place. When the men arrived, there were two men standing on the front walk of the lodge. It was Darren Hatfield and Greg Hansen.

"What are you two doing here?" asked Wyatt.

"We were invited," replied Hatfield.

"By whom?" asked the groom.

"By your Captain Griffin and his Sergeant," said Hatfield, pointing a thumb down the sidewalk toward two men standing near the corner of the lodge.

Wyatt looked to his father, puzzled. "Yes, I invited them," he said. "I didn't think you would mind."

"Thanks, Dad," said Wyatt, slapping his father on the back and walking to where Griffin and Turner stood.

"Good to see you, Cap, and you too, Gene."

"You know us, Wyatt, we'll go anywhere for free food" said Turner.

Now the two federal agents joined the group. "I know you have a schedule to keep, Wyatt, but we all wanted to be here for the wedding. I've known you for over twenty years and I hope to be your friend for many more," said Captain Griffin. "Gene and I and the two feds have talked it over and can't figure out what this school teacher sees in you, even in a small place like Iliamna."

"You just go ahead and wonder, Cap." Wyatt chuckled aloud. "Thank you all for coming. I didn't expect it. This was supposed to be a small private wedding, but my dad couldn't stand it, I guess. I have to go inside now, but there is a reception scheduled for later. I'll be able to talk with you then."

"Don't you worry about us, Wyatt. We only came for the food. Congratulations, man." There was a full round of handshaking and back slapping by all the officers. His guests filed inside to find seats. Wyatt and his father waited inside the outer reception area several minutes until an usher came to escort them into the main dining room where the ceremony was to take place. The usher asked them to wait until the music started before entering the main room.

A moment later an organ began to play and the usher returned to motion them inside. Chairs were placed in rows facing the front with an aisle between. As they entered the room Wyatt could see his bride, dressed in her wedding finery, standing to one side in the front of the onlookers. The usher motioned for Wyatt and his father to follow him down the aisle and the three began a slow march to the front of the hall. Near the front Wyatt's father stepped aside as a maid of honor escorted the bride to his side. The usher motioned for the pair to take the last few steps to the small podium together. The organ music stopped and the hall became quiet.

Wyatt and Linda waited while a pastor in white robes made his way to the podium. Once there he placed a Bible on the stand and stood quietly in front of the crowd. Finally, he spoke.

"Welcome, ladies and gentlemen. Before I recite the vows with this couple the father of the groom would like to say a few words. He stepped aside and motioned for Wyatt Earp IV to come to the front.
The elder Earp stepped to the podium with several note cards in his hand. He stood looking at the guests several seconds before speaking.

"Ladies and gentlemen, for those who don't know me, I am Wyatt Earp IV, father of the groom. I asked to speak here today in order to explain why I am so very proud of my son, Wyatt Earp V. First, I would like to explain that we are direct descendants of the famous lawman. The original Wyatt Earp arrived in Rampart, Alaska in the late fall of 1898 and spent the winter there selling cigars and beer to the locals. In the spring in 1899 he made his way to Nome where he intended to be a gold miner, but fate changed his plan. He partnered with another man and bought a hotel and saloon where the partners mined gold from the pockets of the miners.

"Wyatt Earp, the original, was an amazing man. He was a lawman, businessman, a saint and a scoundrel. He lived 48 years with his common law wife, though they never married. For two years he lived in Nome where he was known as a drunk and a fighter. He was unfaithful to his partner/wife during the last year, meeting a nineteen-year old Native lady who worked in the hotel as one of his ladies of the evening. His health deteriorated badly and his wife, Josey, convinced him to leave Nome in the year of 1901. Wyatt Earp never knew his Native lover was pregnant with a son and never saw his offspring. She named her son Wyatt Earp Junior. She died when Wyatt Earp II was young and he was raised by a caring person in Nome. His first born son was named Wyatt Earp III. He was my father. And I was named Wyatt Earp IV. When I married my wonderful wife agreed we would name our first son Wyatt Earp V.

"I give you this short family history in order for you to understand that we carry the famous name, not to honor the original Wyatt Earp, but to honor the nineteen-year-old Native girl who loved him and produced all the new generations of Earps. In closing I am asking Linda Mason, before she becomes Mrs. Wyatt Earp V, do you agree to name your first born son Wyatt Earp VI?"

He gazed, sadly, from the stage directly into the eyes of Linda whose family was seated behind her. She stared at him a few moments, tears forming in her eyes.

"Yes, Mr. Earp, Wyatt and I have already agreed to that stipulation. His only regret to me is that his mother didn't live to attend this wedding."

"Thank you, Linda," said Wyatt Earp IV. "You can proceed with the wedding now, Pastor."

He stepped down from the stage to seat himself next to Darren Hatfield. "I hope my son isn't the last lawman in history carrying the name of Wyatt Earp. It's in his blood."

96724855R00121

Made in the USA
Middletown, DE
02 November 2018